P9-DEY-639

I've travelled the world twice over,
Met the famous: saints and sinners,
Poets and artists, kings and queens,
Old stars and hopeful beginners,
I've been where no-one's been before,
Learned secrets from writers and cooks
All with one library ticket
To the wonderful world of books.

THE SURGEON'S KNOT

Neil Aitken was a brilliant, tough, abrasive Scottish surgeon. America beckoned with its promise of high pay, superb research facilities, and above all, escape from the thankless grind of a National Health Service Hospital in the slums of Glasgow. Then he found himself fighting for the life of a would-be suicide, daughter of one of the grandest of Glasgow's shipping magnates. The family took him up with embarrassing enthusiasm. Aitken was not to be seduced by gracious living. He still aimed for new horizons, but for all its violence and squalor, Glasgow was in his blood . . .

ARTHUR YOUNG

THE SURGEON'S KNOT

Complete and Unabridged

ULVERSCROFT
Leicester

First published 1982 by
William Collins Sons and Co. Ltd.
London

First Large Print Edition
published October 1983
by arrangement with
Collins, London & Glasgow
and
St. Martin's Press, Inc., New York

British Library CIP Data

Young, Arthur *1925*—
The surgeon's knot.—Large print ed.
(Ulverscroft large print series: general
fiction)
823'.914[F]   PR6075-0/

ISBN 0-7089-1037-8

This book is for May,
with all my love.
A.Y.

Published by
F. A. Thorpe (Publishing) Ltd.
Anstey, Leicestershire
Printed and Bound in Great Britain by
T. J. Press (Padstow) Ltd., Padstow, Cornwall

1

ON Fridays, come six o'clock, the city lads put up the shutters. Not for bribe nor blandishment would a GP be winkled out before Monday.

All over the place texts of the Hippocratic oath got turned to the wall, the asps on the rod slithered off, and medical fists became tumbler shaped. Strong doses of Crawfords Five Star would give back the aura of godhead for a few hours and refuel the fires of vocation before Monday came round again.

The contract said seven days: no let-up. If I say emergency I mean what I want it to mean. So, telephones by the hundred were switched to one of the emergency treatment services.

That's where George and I came in. That's where we had been most Fridays for the past few years. That's where we were that particular Friday.

Benny McIndoe ran such a service.

Benny had been in the same year as me. After a spell in house jobs he had tried

1

general practice. What he found there appalled him. He said to me after:

"I'll do anything, *anything*, but that."

And Benny never again put his name to a Health Service contract.

From then on his aim in life was to find a situation where he did the organising, but other people did the work.

It was at that time the Emergency Treatment Service—E.T.S. for short—came good. Benny got in on the ground floor.

These schemes had been operating in a small way since the sixties, but in their early days the political climate was unfavourable. The Minister and the Executive Councils blew cold air on them, so they were slow to flourish: but the big row of 1966 changed all that.

After the fuss, enough money was fudged in allowances to pay for deputies. The city GPs piled on the charabanc and the emergency services never looked back.

A big organisation called Air Call sewed up most of the action in the major towns, but Benny stretched a point here and undercut a pound there. He soon had his own clientele, and took holidays in the Bahamas.

He ran his service from a flat in Renfrew

Street. It had telephones and radios and sector maps of the city all over the wall. It was just like the telly—if you didn't look too hard.

He had a fleet of Ford Escorts. They looked very antennial. One stuck out of the front wing: that was for football results and chat shows. Six-hour stints in the bucket seats produced unbelievable tedium. One stuck out of the roof: that was for the R.T. system.

Apart from the aerials, anonymity was everything. There were no blue flashers: no red crosses. You wanted to keep it all very quiet indeed or you would get flagged down for an aspirin and I kid you not.

That night George and I had been in the deep South. For six hours we had dodged in and out of those dusty concrete cubes. My squawk box had played a constant tune, and by God I knew who was paying the piper!

You're on a string, boy, and if it's pulled you better skedaddle.

By eleven-fifteen it had settled, though. There was only one call left on the slate:

"Where is it, George?"

"Govan, doc. Govan."

Govan lay east of us: on the way home. We were due to finish at midnight.

3

"We could make it the last, Geordie. Then food and bed?"

That plan suited him:

"Great idea, doc. The wife's got an ashet pie in the oven for me."

He got us on to Paisley Road West. That would lead us home. We would stop at Govan on the way.

When George had a mind, he could drive cars up closes, almost to the bedside. But even with his best efforts I had done a lot of hiking that winter night. I had been frozen and thawed out umpteen times—all except my feet that is. They stayed refrigerated. My shoes had become ice-boxes in which my feet were glaciated misery. I had been pounding around on two stumps that began somewhere above my ankles.

As we went townwards I held my feet up to the blast of the heater, but it didn't help.

George's job was to peer for street names and numbers. When he found them, it was my job to practise for the stair-climbing Olympics:

"Four up, left, doc," he would say.

This particular time, George's homing apparatus latched on to a row of demolition specials.

4

By some quirk of planning, there were left here and there isolated blocks of tenements. You saw them all over the city. The contractors had sliced away the buildings on either side leaving fluttering wallpaper and fireplaces sixty feet up, ready to warm the winter night.

One by one the houses in these blocks fell vacant: but not for long. The winos got in: or the squatters: or the yobboes with the fire-lighters and cans of paraffin.

So the corporation joiners bolted corrugated iron sheets over doors and windows until the buildings looked like Fort Apache ready to stand off the Indians. Except that all the self-respecting Redskins for miles around had lit out for the reservation long since in case they met the Cummlie boys on a bad night on the Lanliq.

As it was a few poor souls were left in isolation. The odd light shone here and there: and at night you could still hear a stairwell closet clank and flush.

If you didn't get moved out in time your chances of a visit from the yahoos were quite good. You got some choice though. You could get your house set on fire, or your head broken, or your granny raped, or your life's blood let out through a hole in your liver. Variety was everything.

George stopped at one of these gutted shells. I clambered out. I nearly fell, for my frozen feet had given up the ghost. I stamped on my stilt-stiff legs and surveyed the close. Usually I negotiated these canyons with Swan Vestas and a kind of bat-sonar I had developed, but that night there was a light to see by: a two-watt special, untouched by vandal hands. Thanks to the Labour council I could see it all. If the rotten Tories had been in, I would have missed its glory in the darkness.

There was beautiful spray calligraphy: "Tongs ya bass! Jess & Dick the Cummlie boys! Cummlie Rule!"

I wondered what had happened to the Pope. The number of people who used to want him stuffed was something terrible, but he had gone out of fashion.

There was a lake to negotiate. It was covered with the fronds of early ice. I waded through the egg shells and lager cans and chip papers that lay awash. Then I climbed the worn steps, admiring the flurry of snow as it blew in the empty window frame on the stairwell.

6

I banged on the door. For my pains I got a lady on her high-horse. Bug-eyed she was with imagined outrage:

"You the doctor, then? No' before time. I thought you were never coming, so I didny. I was just away to Yorkhill Hospital so I was, if you hadny have come—"

The participles, both past and present, were precarious, but there was no doubt about the venom. It came over in a threatening whine. The doctor was bought and paid for. He came with the insurance stamps. Some of them would have had him living in a tepee on the bloody landing.

Two youngsters peered at me from behind her skirt: a boy and a girl. Not that they were holding on to it: not that pair. They were looking out for themselves already.

She carried another child in a shawl. She shoved this bundle at me for instant diagnosis:

"It's the wee wean. She's right no' well."

I chewed the inside of my cheek a bit. It hurt and minded me to keep my mouth shut. I did that a lot on these capers. It saved wear and tear.

I got her quietened and chivvied them all back inside. I took two steps after them: then

7

three back. The room was being stewed into a frowst you could have cut up and sold in half-pound bars. I was dripping sweat in fifteen seconds. Any sensible pit canary would have stuck its legs in the air and cheeped unconditional surrender.

The heat source was a three-kilowatt electric fire. Two cores of the flex were stuck in a wall socket with match-sticks. The earth wire waved in the air looking for a home. The fire sat on a kitchen chair in a faint, blue haze as the wood charred quietly to itself.

I was shocked:

"You don't go out and leave this on?"

"Why not? It's fair freezing, so it is. I just leave it on. Besides I'm feart to touch those matches."

No wonder burnt weans were all the rage. I let her be. It was her fire: and her weans. So at last I got to the business with her: sad Sadie.

"Sit down then. Let's see the wee lass."

She sat down on a chair. It was the only seat in the room.

As she fiddled with buttons and pins, she told me the story.

At six o'clock the wee wean had brought up its tea: Heinz beans, a poke of crisps and a bit

8

of Mars bar. You think I have you on? Listen kid, I was there. I counted the beans and the crisps. Served in a sauce of chocolate vomit they were still there on the floor. Well! There must be something wrong. No one gets sick these days no matter what they eat. The government doesn't allow it.

As she went on I looked about the room. There was a patina of dirt that had taken generations to achieve. It was greasy with ten thousand fry-up meals and the window painted shut forever. It was sooty with fires blowing back from wind swirls since last century: filthy with decades of river fog.

There was a small table with a pack of margarine, a jar of Golliwog jam, half a sliced loaf in its wrapper: and a mixture of cups and plates and cutlery, layered with tea dregs and cold fat and egg.

There was a Baby Belling cooker. It was rusted and stained and ran with brown goo. There were two cots in the shadows of the bed recess. Grit crackled on the floor. A tap skiddled into the sink at the window.

No wonder it showed in her face. Sad Sadie all right; but could you blame her?

By this time she had opened the shawl two fingers' worth. I shook my head:

9

"No! I'll need more than that. Take the clothes all off, please."

The woollens had a well-washed look: charity hand-downs.

I thought about where I would put my bag. The floor seemed sticky.

I looked at the boy.

"What do they call you?"

"Johnny."

"Want to hold my bag?"

"Aye."

But his voice had raised a tone. We were pals now all right.

"Here then."

My working uniform on such nights was an old trench-coat. It had big pockets. They took bottles of pills, and phials for injections, and thermometers, and scissors, and a stethoscope.

That coat had been vomited over, bled on and sprayed with pus, but I still tucked the tails in behind my knees so it didn't sweep that particular floor.

I squatted in front of her. I pulled out the stethoscope and hung it round my neck, but I knew I wouldn't be using it to hear anything with. The real tools were a listening ear, a pen and a scrip pad. A memory that had heard a million histories didn't come amiss either.

By this time the infant had emerged from the wrappings. She was blonde and blue-eyed and glistening and bright and active. There wasn't a thing wrong with her.

Nature's own purging had already done the job.

I felt her tummy and thought about all of this. I thought particularly about sad Sadie. Oh, there was cause for her upset all right: but was this enough? You could tell she wanted to burst.

At such times it helped if you had seen *Dr. Finlay's Casebook* on the telly. I was lucky. I was raised on that guy.

But if you had been to medical school, you wanted to forget it.

I put on my Tannochbrae act, all father and friend to the working classes.

"What else is wrong? What's the matter?"

She went to answer. But under her coat, which had been pastel blue at one time and which was fastened with a pin, something heaved. The wee wean bounced up and down.

I didn't believe it.

"For the love of God! What's in there?"

11

"I'm expecting."

"When are you due?"

"Next week."

"Busy girl!"

"It wasn't me. It was him."

There's only one kind of him in a voice like that.

"Where is he then?"

It was like putting a knife in a ripe boil. There was the real problem. The poison burst out, green and putrid.

"He's away with his fancy woman, so he is. Up in Barmulloch."

"Is that right? That's a shame!"

Tears started. There must have been so many. I left her for a moment to wipe her face: compose herself. I swivelled left, still kneeling. A pair of eyes levelled with my own.

"What's *your* name?"

"Elizabeth."

"You're pretty."

So she was. Her eyes were green, her face oval.

Johnny chipped in from the other side:

"See what I got."

What was a ten-bob piece. He moved the bag to his other hand and delved in a raggy pocket for it. He held it out in his palm. It was new and shiny. I could make out no trace of flesh through the dirt.

"I got one too."

The green eyes were happy, even in that cheerless mess.

"Did you? Who from?"

"My dad."

Their mother burst in:

"He had to take the three of them, so he did. For a few days. Him and his fancy woman. They just had to. I had to go into the Maternity Hospital. I've got funny blood. I've to go back in next week to have the baby brought on early."

More tears ran:

"It isn't fair. He shouldn't get off with it!"

By God and he shouldn't. But I wasn't there as justice. I was there as the instrument of a caring society.

Mind, I would have liked to care for that bastard for five minutes.

What she had needed was someone to let out at; someone to blame for the fire and the filth; someone to hurt for her broken marriage. It might as well be me.

I did my ten-minute listening act. Then it was midnight and I had started before nine that morning and I thought she had had her money's worth.

You have to return it if it's to be of any use. Empathy, it's called: but I hadn't enough left to go round.

Besides I wasn't going to solve one damn thing for her.

"I'll give you some good medicine for your baby. She'll be as right as rain."

I gave her some sugar pills from a phial in my left hand coat pocket. "Crush them up in milk."

I got back to my feet and fished in my right hand pocket. That's where I kept the liquorice allsorts.

I fished some out for Johnny and Elizabeth. Not for nothing was I known the length and breadth of Glasgow South for my compassion and understanding. Comfits will cure all.

But for her, for sad Sadie, the real patient, the true victim, what had I?

Someone had wound up the clockwork in a social worker. There was food, clothing, even hellish heat to prove it. There was a white bed to have the baby in, special blood, and visits from the hospital chaplain.

But she knew and I knew, that these were

the coupons on the soap powder pack: the plastic toys in the corn flakes.

At night, with the light out, and that terrible fire still on, when she got into bed and closed her eyes, then she knew the enormity of her true illness.

She was human and alive in the real world.

No system invented, nor yet to come in her lifetime, was going to sort that lot out.

Shame and gall and hurt and humiliation were going to be her constant fare.

Pills would be a platitude. Liquorice allsorts had their limitations.

I stood up to go. She stood up with me. She put the babe on the couch.

"Put her clothes back on!" she told the other two. "I'll let the doctor out."

The pair of youngsters fell on the baby with shouts and tickling fingers. They were proud of their sister. She gurgled and chuckled at them.

Me? I was transfixed. She was going to usher me out. It was a shit house: no more. But it was her place and she would do me an old honour she had learned in a day when she still had pride.

Humble? I nearly went on my knees to her. But, there, why should I have been surprised? It's one thing about this game: ten thousand times a year you get speared through with dignities and courage when you least expect them.

Dr. Finlay, what did I do then?

I fished out a hanky. I carried a hanky in that coat too! I reached out and cupped the back of her head in my hand. I pulled her nearer:

"Here. Blow."

I wiped her nose and dried her eyes. I got her to spit on it and scrubbed the smudges from her face:

"I'll bet she's an old bag, that fancy woman. I'll bet he'll be back."

You wonder why they ever want them back, but they do. It's all they think about.

"Do you think so?"

"Sure! I see this a dozen times a week. He'll be back to see this trio and his new baby."

There in that awful face, like a pound of mince gone bad, was a ghost of hope.

The comics must leave them laughing. The docs must leave them hoping.

Ever told anyone he's going to be dead in six months? Don't! Not the folks in my parade.

Fudge. Blind them with science. Tell great roaring lies.

But leave some hope.

Then it was time to go. Besides, if I didn't I would go blue for want of oxygen, or die of heat stroke in the inferno generated by that awful bloody fire.

At the entrance I stopped and looked at the moon plain that lay around.

No wonder sad Sadie wanted love. You needed something more than welfare hand-outs to survive that atmosphere.

Every building, every landmark, every point of recognition for a mile in all directions had been razed to a streetscape of stupendous nothingness. There was no meaning, no reason for the whole bleak area. The roadways of cobble-stones, lined with pavement kerbs and set with regular iron drains wound around in aimless quadrangles.

The feet that had once walked there had been force-marched away: and the way of their going was none the less violent because the order to move had been wrapped up in planning jargon.

Ah well! From scenes like these I was about to scarper, thanks to a slice of luck I had had a few months before.

I went over to the car. George had the engine going.

"A good night's work, George. Midnight. Let's trundle home."

"That's for me, doc. That pie's putting the 'fluence on me."

I eased myself into the passenger seat and put my bag between my knees. I shut the door and my eyes as George let in the clutch.

"Oh God." I vowed as a million times before. "Not long now. Not long."

Then I would leave that degraded sister behind in her battered but and ben: then I would desert this brave, hard-hammered brother in his exhaust-stale cell: then I would leave this demolished city of my birthright and sail for the greenback stakes.

What I had to sell they wanted in big expensive slabs.

You see I had this felicity, this dollar-bill commodity. At the sharp end of medicine, at the cutting edge, I had it made.

It had taken a long time to forge and sharpen and hone fine, but I was almost there.

I'll come back to all of this later, but you can believe that on the open market I knew I could make my pile. And I was heading for the biggest, openest market on earth, the good old US of A.

I was just settling to dream of my Stateside life-style to come, when the squawk box crackled:

"Medic A.Q.! Medic A.Q.! Come in!"

We had code letters. That was us.

"Medic A.Q. receiving. Over."

The telly had nothing on this patter. Real life drama and that.

"State your position and status, please."

"Finished all calls. Proceeding to base eastwards along Paisley Road West."

"Listen, doc! Do me a favour."

Now to the nub of things:

"Anything for you, Cathy my love."

Grub from the coffee stall, no doubt. But no—it wasn't so simple.

"Well, look. There's a real hurry call from a place up in the 'Shields. You're nearest. Would you like to scoot up and do it on your way home?"

I looked at George:

"What about your pie?"

"Och, t'hell, doc! We'll rate an after midnight call—and it'll only take five minutes."

After midnight the rate went up.

19

"Fine! I'm all for money."

So I accepted the call and we swanned up the 'Shields.

In the days of the tobacco lords, millionaires were not all that hard to come by around this Clyde-spawned city. These well-heeled citizens spilled out into the country to live: to Kilmacolm, out by the Trossachs, to watering places like Helensburgh. Their big mansions still dot the countryside for miles around.

Later shipping became more important than tobacco and the dredging of the shallow river brought yards and docks to the city. A lot of owners wanted to stay close to the action, so they built their big stone palaces out west of the city, or in the green fields to the south of the river where they could watch the ships as they arrived with the cargoes and profits. In its day this latter area was real plummy, so the term South Side came to have an expensive ring to the local ear.

At least it used to. It had all got a bit frayed at the edges by my time. Pakistanis and dropouts and just plain poor Glasgow folk lined the south river bank then. Each year they lipped a little further up the hill as the big old houses were sold for death duties and then split into flats.

But at the top of the hill there was still a select section of real estate with its *amour propre* intact.

Any time in the past calls for Pollokshields had been confined to the lower reaches: the rat nibbled bits at the edges. The word was that a few practitioners with smart suits and smooth bedside manners had a strangle hold on the hill-top area. Practice there was kept exclusive and private. The docs did their own night work. The E.T.S. was for the lower orders.

That time George drove on up to the big houses.

"My! My! Going to see how the rich people live, are we?"

"That's it, doc! One of the toffs."

We turned into a winding drive ninety miles long. It was lined by rhododendrons the height of a telephone pole. The city sounds were muffled as I clambered from the car and did my funny act without feet again.

There was a Mercedes coupé at the door. It was all hood down and sporty despite the winter. I raised my hat to eight grand worth of machinery. Not long now, I promised myself.

The front door would have taken a coal lorry. The bottom half was panelled with a whole mahogany tree: the top half let in light through plate glass cut and etched with enough fruit and flowers to do the Lord Provost's banquet at Christmas.

A white button said: Ring.

I pressed it. In the depths of the house it said: boing! boing!

That cheered me up. A paradox to end the day. That was a cue for a song if I ever heard one.

"A paradox! A paradox! A most ingenious paradox!"

I was singing the laughing bit that comes next when the door opened on a little blonde bint. She had straight wheat-straw hair and white eyelashes. They contrasted in a startling way with big blue eyes which were shaded to navy by spots of deeper pigment, splashed like ink in her irises. She had a face the shape of a birthday dumpling split by a big, white grin. Black glacé boots came to her knees. The last of the mini-skirts showed her thighs chubby with puppy fat and made my touch-up finger twitch.

But to business I told myself.

Introductions at midnight on such occasions had been superfluous in my experience until then. I waved my black bag at her and said:

"Where's the problem?"

A brisk march to the body was then indicated, but she halted me with a straight and unblinking look. It was a different approach anyhow, so I looked right back and waited for the next bit.

I liked what I saw. Not one of your dolly birds: but nothing frumpish either. I decided it was the character about to emerge from her teenage splodge in a couple of wide high cheekbones and a chin that was used to being kept up, that made her different.

Yet that wasn't enough to account for all of the attraction. What trumped the trick was her eyes. So help me, they twinkled despite her worried face.

You could bet your books of green shield stamps you would never have a dull moment with her.

"Are you the doctor?"

The question came through very strong. I thought about the mackintosh and the song. Perhaps there was room for doubt?

I waved my bag in her face and nodded. Time was fast adying.

It made no difference.

"Where is Dr. Armour?"

Enough was enough: especially after a six-hour stint on the disaster bus.

"Aw, c'mon, love! You're not expecting the plumber, are you? And how am I supposed to know where Dr. Armour is? His phone is through to the emergency service and I've got the call from there, and here I am, and if we could just get on with it . . . "

I wasn't really cross: but I wasn't being arch either.

"Oh! I am sorry! But we're so anxious. And we're so used to him. We're private patients you see."

I saw all right. I had what was left of my red Clydeside flag ready to run up the flag-pole. Private patients were going to be my staple diet in a few months' time: but that would be far from home, and on my own terms, and if I liked their faces and their wallets.

That would be a whole different pot of porridge. Right here and now, on my patch, in this sad, smashed city with its lost people, private patients was fighting talk. Still, she

24

was too young to know what it meant: just a lassie. And she was too nice.

I stuffed the red flag up my jumper again.

The bright eyes were fixed on me without a blink.

"Maybe he's ill," I suggested.

She seemed awed at the idea.

Dr. Armour must be quite a guy, I thought.

"I'll do my best. Where do we go?"

To save time I started the run-up as we crossed the hall. It was about the size of the centre court at Wimbledon.

"What's your problem?"

"It's Mummy."

"Uh-huh?" I encouraged.

We were centre court by then.

"She's collapsed."

"Aw, not again!"

It was out before I could stop it: but as it was in quiet disgust, she couldn't quite make it out.

"What did you say?"

I had a smile for such occasions. It was supposed to cover my inner feelings. It was a bit overworked. I suspected that the wear and tear showed through and I looked like a Gorgon.

I put on the grin for her. She didn't turn to stone, but she was taken aback.

Seventeen collapses are guaranteed every Friday night. No bastard ever—but ever—faints, falls down, swoons, or even gets plain, paralytic drunk. They all collapse. And, by God, the doctor better come quick.

A bit slower she went on:

"We were coming for her—Johnnie and me—"

Despite the collapse, I liked the bird. I liked her even better with her grammar showing. I bet myself she licked the jam spoon and lined her peas up to eat at the end.

"We couldn't get in. There was a light on upstairs. Johnnie broke a window. We found her."

By this time we had reached the staircase at the far end. It would have held the chorus of *Aida*, elephants and all.

"Ah-hah?"

My face was easing back to normal. Then she said:

"She was lying in a puddle of blood!"

It came with a rush at the end.

I was twenty-two stairs up in the air and my love affair died on the spot. I could have survived the collapse—but a puddle of blood? I ask you!

I asked her.

I stopped and looked at her.

"A *puddle* of blood?"

"Yes!" Her voice squeaked in agitation and her eyes shone brighter.

I didn't want her crying, but collapses and puddles of blood are hard to take at any time. At that time of the morning they were too, too much.

"I haven't seen a puddle of blood all night. I'm quite encouraged. Let's go and look at it."

Those eyes looked at me straight. She blinked hard. She wasn't going to shed a single tear for a rotten bastard like me.

We finished the steps and crossed a corridor where six greyhounds and an electric hare could have performed. A door opened on to a narrower, wooden stair going up to the attic. There was a smell of dampness and disuse about it. There was a chill, too, that penetrated my string underwear.

We hiked up to another corridor, this time narrow. It ran the length of the roof space. Many doors led off it. I supposed this would be where the servants lived at one time.

"Along here," she said.

Here was a room that had been a nursery. I was amazed at the size of the old toys. There was a rocking horse as big as Black Beauty and a doll's house that would have done for Snow White and the dwarfs. There was a draught screen covered in old scraps and then varnished.

It must have been used as a schoolroom too, for there were some desks and chairs with sparred backs: a blackboard on an easel.

Mummy lay under a quilt. A young guy was sitting by her head. He was chittering with cold as he consoled the form under the cover, with little useless pats.

It helped to do something, I supposed.

Blondie explained who I was as we approached. Then:

"We found these."

These were a couple of pill bottles. One was for Boots aspirin and had held a hundred tablets. The other had held 25 milligram amitryptiline tablets: sixty of them. Both bottles were new. Both bottles were empty.

Things were looking up. There might even be some pathology under the blanket.

"Are they a help?"

She had blinked away her tears.

"Yes. Yes. Good thinking."

I knelt down and twitched the quilt away. Then I said:

"*Cheesus*-christ!" with feeling. My love rekindled on the spot.

Mummy was collapsed, all right. She was ivory white, with air hunger and a pressure in her boots. As for puddles of blood, she had damn near exsanguinated herself in a lake of bloody vomit, which lay congealed beside her like six pounds of liver.

I noticed that an electric fire was sitting near her feet. A dental plate was nestled into a hanky beside her head. Her feet had been raised. A hot water bottle nestled at her back. It had been carefully wrapped in a towel.

I looked at blue eyes. They were grey in that light. The spots in them looked black.

"You've been in the Brownies!" I accused her.

It was like petting a puppy. A smile appeared. We communicated at all kinds of levels.

"I bet you were the Pixie Sixer."

"Did I do right?"

"Honey! You'll get the magic mushroom all to yourself for a whole week."

She giggled. Giggled! I hadn't heard such a

wholesome sound for years. Oh, but I liked this kid.

But I needed some fast action then. I looked at Johnnie for help.

He had tight black curls barbered to a close cap over his skull. They ran into curly side chops and well down his neck.

The stylish, manly effect was being spoiled by a pale tint coming to his skin and a crop of sweat beads on his forehead:

"I feel funny."

It was the sight and smell of the blood. At least he didn't say he was going to collapse: but he was no use to me.

I looked back at the Pixie Sixer:

"Want to improve your shining hour?"

She nodded.

"Go down to the car. In it will be George. I want him to do two things. One! He's to get the ambulance and the police for an escort. Two! I want him up here with some intravenous fluid and a giving-set. In a hurry."

She held up two fingers:

"Ambulance and escort. Intravenous fluid."

"Right!"

I heard her clatter on the bare boards in the

30

corridor and down the stair. Johnnie said: "Uuuuuuh!" and keeled over. He lay making a moaning sound.

I didn't have too much time for his problem. I got him by the feet and lugged him out of the road, pulled down his tie, crooked my finger under his top shirt button and yanked. The button ripped off and spun in the air. At that he would live.

I went back to Mummy and knelt down to get at her. She was looking a very blue do indeed. It wasn't surprising. She had lost one hell of a lot of blood and the room, outside the range of the fire, was utterly chilling. It hadn't been heated since God knew when. I was beginning to shiver myself. I wondered how long she had lain there before bright eyes got to her.

She had on a skirt and a blouse. I undid the skirt band and zip. I pulled out a fistful of undervest to get at her belly: that was where the monkey lay. I tucked the loose clothes up and put my hand on her.

She was rock-rib skinny and palpation was easy. There were no lumps and she wasn't rigid. So, she had a big internal bleed, not obviously due to tumour and not apparently complicated by peritonitis.

"Now how in hell do we know how many pills she took and what time was it at? And did she have an ulcer?"

There was a sound from the floor behind me. Johnnie said:

"Both bottles were full this morning. I picked them up for her from the chemist's."

I looked round. Johnnie had propped himself up on an elbow.

"What time did you last see her?"

"About mid-morning, I suppose."

I nodded. I wondered about the amitryptiline. That was an anti-depressant drug.

"Has she been depressed?"

"I'm not sure. She had been seeing Dr. Armour lately—about her nerves. But I never heard her use that particular word."

He thought a bit and then went on:

"She's always been close. She doesn't let on much about what she's thinking. But she had been very quiet lately. Not her usual self."

It sounded like depression. The picture was getting clearer.

I said:

"Has she ever tried this sort of thing before?"

"Not so far as I know."

"Any idea what caused her upset?"

32

"No. At least—she hasn't had much fun in the marriage stakes, and Murdie—that's her second husband—he's been difficult to take lately."

Well, no-one was going to operate on her hysteria or depression or whatever it was, but sure as hell someone was going to have to do something about this huge bleed: and fast. The practical problems were immense.

I had begun to scheme in my head.

"D'you happen to know if she ever had any ulcer trouble? Recurrent indigestion? That sort of thing?"

The sweat shone on his brow. His colour was awful. It all became too much for him again. He lay back down on the floor.

"No. No. I'm sure she hadn't."

He put his hands over his face.

I kneeled at Mummy's side. I poked a finger in her eye. It was dry, glazed and showed not a blink.

I shook my head. Mummy was going out under my very eyes.

"C'mon, Geordie! Chop! Chop!" I muttered to keep my spirits up.

I opened my bag and rummaged about.

Doctors are worse than women when it comes to bags. Since two or three doctors swapped about in shifts every night, you can imagine what they got like.

Under the paediatric penicillin packs and the bottles of pills I found some hydrocortisone and some Aramine.

I thought they might help—although what she needed was blood: oodles and oodles of it.

She had thin arms with fine bones. Her veins were small and fragile. With the fall in circulation volume they had become collapsed. However, with a bit of tongue biting I got a fine cannula in and taped it into place. I needed to keep it open. I might not get another one so easily. I put the two injections in slowly.

George thumped up the wooden stairs and into the room. He had a giving set, bottles of intravenous fluid and a drip stand stuck under his arms and poking from his pockets.

He was not a trained first aid man, but he had been at this sort of thing many times.

Even he was startled. He looked at Mummy with a knowing eye.

"For God's sake, doc! D'you think she's going to make it?"

The Pixie Sixer was at his heels. Until that moment it had all been exciting, I think, but as I looked at her and watched his words sink in, she reacted. After all it was her mother.

The sparkle left her. She looked small and cold. The nearness of death menaced her own small humanity.

I said: "It's miserable up here. You can't do any good now. It's better that you go downstairs—both of you."

Johnnie got on his feet and went to her.

They went out. He still looked terrible. She looked as if she needed to be picked up and cuddled.

George gave me a couple of specimen bottles. From the cannula in the vein I sucked out two samples of blood. I gave them to him to label. They would be wanted for grouping and cross-matching.

"What d'you want?" asked George.

"Well, she wants her volume up very fast, and she must have an electrolyte imbalance by now. She would be the better for a bucket of bicarb, but I don't have any with me. Let's give her a bottle of Ringer lactate first, then some Dextran. That might hold her."

I hoped my rule of thumb biochemistry would do.

I got the drip going:

"Let that in fairly fast, George. Change the

bottle when it's ready. I'll need to fix her admission."

From that address it should have been the Vic or the Southern General, but as I headed for the Carntyne race track on the first floor my mind was on devious matters: and I can be very twisted if I put my mind to it.

A double door at the end of the corridor was open. There was light and talk. I went along and pushed the door wide.

"Can I talk to you for a moment?"

"Surely. Come in. Would you like a drink?"

Now, I like a drink. I like three drinks in fact. And when I saw Johnnie stick his nose in a glass of wholesome amber fluid I felt real jealous.

But I never drink when I'm working. It's a simple rule. I keep it strictly. I'll tell you why later.

"No thanks. Not just now. I want to tell you the score as briefly as I can."

I gave them the professional jazz:

"She is acutely ill and she has more than one problem. The main one is this huge loss of blood. She has ruptured a big vessel inside somewhere. Then she has all this aspirin and amitryptiline in her stomach. They are being

36

absorbed slowly. By now her system must be full of drugs. So, she's poisoned and in severe shock from loss of blood. She's also suffering from exposure from lying in that room so long."

The Pixie Sixer had gone black under the eyes as the gravity of the illness struck home. The tears that she wouldn't let slip for me, she let fall freely for her mother. She nuzzled into her man and made his shirt wet.

"Johnnie! Johnnie! I do wish we could find Daddy."

Johnnie hugged her back in a way that meant only one thing.

At a time like that I was jealous?

Well, yes. For the briefest moment. They each had someone to care about.

All protective and managing like he stuck in his oar again:

"You'll get her into a nursing home, then?"

Not so much a rhetorical question; more you'll do what I tell you. He had the kind of voice that went with Old Boy ties, arse-flap blazers and the car in the drive.

I could feel my red Clydeside drawers show through the hole in my breeks.

"You mean you want her treated privately?"

"Of course."

I take very badly to that tone of voice.

I turned on my Gorgon grin again.

"Well, it's not as simple as that. You see . . . " and I gave him the spiel about blood and intensive care and laboratories being easier in hospital.

It wasn't just that my social tendencies were showing. Nursing homes in this burg tended to have a touch of the not-quites when you were playing in that league of illness. It was different in London.

But, also, as I have told you, I can be fair twisted when I like: and I liked then.

You see I wanted my hooks on this case myself.

I looked at the Pixie Sixer. It was her Mummy, not Johnnie's.

"You decide."

"Well—"

I threw in a concession which I thought would clinch it.

"I think I can manage a side room."

I knew fine I could: but softly, softly catchee intellesting patient.

"Well . . . You'll get a specialist?"

He was still trying to keep in the act.

"Of course," I buttered him.

Little did he know.

"We would want the best," she added.

They always wanted that.

But poor sad Sadie I had just left in Govan, she got what was available.

"Naturally," I soothed her.

And I thought of Roddie McAnespie if he was running true to form.

The blind leading the blind was one thing, but the blotto opening the druggo with a Swann-Morton knife was quite another guzzle from the grog bottle.

Still there was a handsome frog all ready to turn into an ugly prince and save the day. Wasn't it midnight? And at that witching-hour did not the glass welly boot become truly mine?

They looked at each other and nodded.

Fine! Great! I had Mummy in my clutches. A real barrow load of experience for export in a few months' time.

At that moment the ambulance came up the driveway.

The attendants trundled upstairs with their stretchers and blankets.

"One more up." I said and went ahead.

George had coped well. I felt under the quilt. Was she a shade warmer? Was the pulse better?

They rolled her in the cosy red blankets and laid her on the stretcher. George held the bottle over her head:

"Don't pull that cannula out, lads! She's not too well off for veins."

I saw the caravanserai downstairs. The police were there by then, their blue light whirling.

"Just like the movies, lads. Fast as you like! The Northern General."

They went down the drive all blue flashity-flashity.

I went back to the room where I had left the girl and Johnnie.

"Will we follow her?"

"Of course. She's going to the Northern General. But can I use your phone first?"

"Of course. It's in the corner there."

"Fine."

It was actually in a dinky little booth so you could be private. It was all gilt and with a velvet seat. The phone was gold and onyx, but the gilt was rubbed, the velvet moth marked and the onyx chipped.

I dialled.

"Northern General."

I put on the seven league surgical boots.

"Is that you, Kenny?"

Kenny took my lines to the bookies for me.

"This is Neil Aitken. Put me on to Herbie Adebaya, will you?"

"S'at you, Mister Aitken? Right away."

There were some bleeps and Herbie's posh voice came on. Herbie's father was a lawyer. His education had been Gordonstoun and Edinburgh University. He was black as the fire box in my Uncle Willie Reid's shunting train at five o'clock on a winter's morning.

He was the Senior House Officer in my unit and we had started receiving ten minutes before.

"Herbie? This is Neil Aitken. Listen, I'm doing an E.T.S. stint. I've just come across a dame with a big gut bleed. But we've got other problems. She's up to the Plimsoll line in aspirin and amitryptiline. Into the bargain she's suffering from exposure."

"That sounds great!" said Herbie.

He wasn't kidding. Herbie was keen as mustard. That sort of thing was meat and drink to him.

"Uh-huh. We'll have a ball. Anyhow she'll be with you in minutes and I'll be right behind. The ambulance driver has some blood in his pocket, so dig out the technician. Second, she's on a Dextran drip. Change that to plasma. Third, get the senior anaesthetist on call. The drugs plus her electrolytes are a big problem. Last, have you heard from Roddie yet?"

"There's a notice on the board. Hold on." He clanked the phone on the table.

As I waited I looked around the room. It was one of those huge second-storey drawing rooms with windows that came down to your socks. I could see the lights of a boat as it moved down the river.

The whole place had been ornate and lush at one time, but the spiders and the mildew had got in.

It was lit by a couple of big electrified candle sconces, all rhinestones and gilt beading. Some of the stones were missing and the gilt beading was hanging loose in places. Over all was this dank unused smell.

I found it difficult to make out the situation. There was obviously a lot of money about, for Johnnie's car hadn't come with a lucky bag, and my favourite Brownie had on a Jaeger le Coultre watch with diamond-set shoulders that had cost someone a few centimes.

It seemed that someone didn't care.

Herbie broke into my wanderings:

"The note says he's at a dinner and can be contacted at a number I've got here. Want me to ring him?"

I grinned to myself. It was all working fine.

"Not yet, Herbie. Wait until I get to you. We'll stabilise the situation first. By the way, is there anything else in?"

The city left all sorts on our doorstep.

"No. All quiet so far."

"Fine. See you in a few minutes."

I went back to Johnnie and the girl.

"I've been on to the hospital. The consultant surgeon will be contacted."

I didn't elaborate on what would happen behind the scenes, or on my part in this. I stated some of the facts, but not all. What I left out gave a different meaning, but I kept that to myself.

"Want to follow her in?"

The Pixie Sixer was ready for beddy byes. She was ash-white and her face looked tiny. I tried to ease things for her:

"You know, there's not a lot of point in doing that. She'll be unconscious for a long time yet. Why don't you go home and get some sleep? Even a few hours would set you up. Ring the hospital at six."

"As long as that?"

"By that time her problems will have been unravelled. You'll get a better prognosis then."

I fixed my eyes on Johnnie and looked at him hard.

He twigged.

"That's a good idea, Nella. We can phone the family now we know what is happening."

She thought about this.

"No! I'm going to stay near her."

She said it fiercely.

Well, that was her problem.

"Good night, then."

As I left I noticed a bar in the far corner. It was ornate: in keeping with the room. It had a fancy mirror and a clock and shelves for glasses and bottles.

Like the rest of the place, it was uncared for. The clock was stopped, the mirror dirty.

Someone had used it: hard. There must have been a dozen dark-green Gordon's gin bottles on the bar surface—all empty—and a regiment of dirty glasses.

There was an indecent look about it all. I wondered who drank there?

The thought of drinking in that big, spooky barn of a house gave me the willies. I left the pair of them making phone calls to the family and rattled down the big staircase, back to George and life.

"How's your pie, George?"

"Sizzling, doc! Sizzling!"

"Drive me back to the Northern before you check in?"

"Sure. No trouble. Three minutes and you'll be there."

I snapped on the map light and scribbled a few words about the last case on the triplicate pad. Then I sorted out the three sets of copies: one for the GP, one for the office, and one for my record just in case of lawyers.

"Who's the controller tonight?"

"Jessie Macdonald."

"Give her these will you? Then I'll get my money."

That was the other thing I did these nights for.

"Sure, doc."

"Good boy. I'll stand you a dram at Christmas."

"Not you, you won't. Not bloody likely.

Not after last year. My wife says I've never to get out with you again. Ever."

We had had a terrible thrash the year before.

George got us to the Northern General gate double quick. As I got out of the glass coach, he said:

"G'night, doc. Hope you're not up too late."

I stuck my thumb up at him.

" 'Night, George. Have a drink for me. An ashet pie and Johnnie Walker. What a supper!"

He rolled his eyes up in agreement.

He drove off.

Maybe he would turn into a white mouse and the car into a pumpkin? But no! I was on my own. I was the only fairy tale about.

But not for long. Not for long. I would wave my own magic wand one of these days, and it would all be for real.

The snow clouds had disappeared and Dame Diana hunted dreams over the city. She was having a thin time. There weren't many illusions left there.

I dived at the flip-flop plastic doors and

46

pushed my way into warmth and my kind of sanity.

I got this peak experience whenever I walked inside any hospital door, but especially the Northern. A lot of me was forged and hammered out there: not in the eutectic way: more the cold bashing of nights without sleep, patients with too much to bear, and a Health Service that made George Orwell seem like amateur night at the scribblers' club.

I waved a hand at Kenny in his box and glanced at the yobboes and drunks on the casualty benches. Over the years they had made such pests of themselves that nobody cared too much any more.

If you were genuine and in trouble you had to pay for that. Still, someone would catch up with you sooner or later and if you hadn't died in the meantime, the treatment was good: excellent in fact.

Kenny leaned out:

"Doctor Adebaya is in cubicle three."

The Northern General is old. It is turreted and castellated and balustraded. It has dungeons that go three floors down and attic rooms with skeletons and mad scientists. It had been a part of the hustling Victorian city that used to live there: but now it looked forlorn, dressed for a party that was over.

Still, it turned over the numbers. The great Glasgow ghettoes, the housing schemes of the North and West, emptied into it. I had supped my fill of surgery from the pathology, man-made and natural, that preyed there.

Everything got sorted out in casualty. It was a railway terminus for disaster and farce. The disaster came from living in that blighted city: the farce was to believe that anything in medicine was going to sort it out.

I walked over the terrazzo floor to cubicle three, slid the curtain aside and went in.

The cubicles weren't big. It was like that cabin scene when the Marx Brothers went to the opera.

Mummy was in the middle of it all. She was having a bad time.

Herbie had her head over the side of the trolley. He had a sucker in one hand and was trying to get rid of more blood dribbling from her mouth.

That meant she was still bleeding. That was bad.

In his other hand he had the mask of the gas machine. Between sucks he stuck this over her nose and mouth and pumped the bellows. Some oxygen in her tissues wouldn't come amiss.

Norah Fleming, the casualty sister, was mixing some plasma gently. Froth and bubbles we did not want. We had problems enough.

A technician was poking about under a heat cage, hooking the patient on to an ECG machine. A nurse was holding the drip bottle I had set up in the house.

Herbie looked up: "Great! Now we can have an eightsome reel. Where did you find this Lulu—and where do we start?"

Sister had the plasma ready.

"Fine, Norah," I said. "Change the bottles."

I would be happier when some grade A, T.T. pasteurised blood arrived: but that was going to take a while yet.

I had been working it out in the car.

"Seems we've got to get her problems in some sort of order, Herbie. See over here."

There was a blackboard for that sort of exercise. I went over to it and drew a flow-chart of her problems. Severe blood loss—shock—still bleeding—drug poisoning—electrolytes ballsed up—exposure.

"If she goes on bleeding, she's dead. If she

doesn't get rid of that muck in her stomach, she's dead. If we wash out her stomach we make the bleed worse and she's even deader. Answer—?"

I looked at Herbie. He was thinking.

"C'mon, doc. Five hundred quid for her life!" I encouraged.

He thought of the cheque he got for a month and laughed.

Then: "She has to have her stomach out."

"Right."

"But that will kill her in her present state. So she's still dead."

"No. The other way she's dead dead. This way she has a chance."

"Not with Roddie doing it. He takes fourteen hours to do a hernia."

I said not a word.

He looked at me:

"Aah!" he said. "Ah-hah!" Herbie was a good guy. He knew the way I was thinking, foxy-like.

"Is she still cold?"

The nurse stuffed a hand up Mummy's skirt and fished out a rectal thermometer. The reading was down near the hobnails in her clogs. She had hypothermia all right. But that wasn't all bad in this case. It had kept her metabolism low. Acidosis would not be so far advanced.

"—She spent hours in an ice-box. You haven't got that too high?" I nodded at the heat cage.

Herbie looked pained.

I smiled at him to take away the sting. I said:

"Sorry, Herbie! I was thinking out loud."

I was too. You don't want to heat them up too quickly. They die. But I wasn't quizzing Herbie. I was quizzing me.

If I hotted up somebody's Mummy all wrong in Memphis, I would be incinerating dollar bills. The only way I wanted to burn up greenbacks was in the Algonquin bar.

At that the lab man brought in the first blood: business was booming.

"Soon as you've got that going, Herbie, get her up to theatre."

He nodded.

As I left the porters arrived.

I took the stairs to the theatre and ran up. I made two steps at a time to pump the blood around my head and take away the weary ache of my long stint in the car.

In the theatre ante-room I put my clothes in a locker. I put on a green cotton suit and the white, magic wellies. The seven league footwear was mine. With one bound I would be free.

Well, not that night: but soon, soon.

I went into the duty room and looked through the glass window.

The theatre sister was a girl called Fay McArthur. She came from the Islands and had the West coast lilt to her voice.

She was in her gloves and mask, but I could see the smile rays about her eyes. She came up to the window.

"It's yourselff. You'll be hungry Hi suppose. Men! Men! You're ahll the same."

"Well . . . If you have a bite?"

"There'ss a student nursse in the changing room. Tell her."

I nodded my thanks. She turned away to her girls who were clattering glass and steel about. They gave me a great team feeling: us against the world.

I put my head around the female dressing room door. I was out of luck. She had the good bits covered.

"Coffee? And rolls? Sister says will you make some?"

"Sure! How many rolls?"

"Two."

She was young and willing. Her feet hadn't stuck in the Health Service muck yet. I left her in her innocence.

I went back to the duty room and sat down at the desk, pulling the phone towards me. I got Kenny again:

"Kenny! Ring Mr. McAnespie for me like a good lad."

"Right, Mr. Aitken."

I could hear the dialling clicks, then the ringing tone.

I should explain about the receiving system.

The whole scheme was a big apprenticeship. First on call was one of the housemen: our Herbie or a mate of his called Dougie Miller. They took the receiving day in twelve-hour shifts. Between them they saw everything surgical, but dealt with minor things only. Their main job was disposal. Did it get admitted? Main ward or observation? Did it want seen by a senior? That kind of thing.

Next was a middle grade chap registrar, or senior registrar—that was me. Last, on back-up, was a consultant.

You made up your own mind about what you could deal with. If you thought it wise or politic you got help from the guy above you. As your experience improved you tried more.

If you got a greedy senior who hogged the work you could get holding forceps for years. Some guys were really funny that way.

But me, I had the opposite problem. I had had it for the past three years, ever since my last appointment.

Roddie McAnespie was my back-up consultant: but Roddie was hitting the sauce something terrible. On his call nights he either wouldn't or couldn't get out of his bed. So I got on with it.

From my point of view, it was the best kind of problem. The amount of surgical stuff I had got my mitts on was terrific. And all that experience was dollars in a future bank for me.

There was a gargle at the other end of the phone:

"Roddie? This is Neil Aitken here. Listen! I've got this old duck with a big bleed . . . "

I told him all about it.

He had been well nourished with Nirvana juice that night. He came up with the idea that she should have a little blood.

54

I thought about Herbie who would be putting it in with a garden hose at that moment.

"What a good idea, Roddie! I'll see to it. But we have these other complications."

I went on with the stuff about exposure and the aspirin and amitryptiline. He went into a blue-funk:

"Can't do surgery on a case like that. Too dangerous. Needs a physician. Get the physicians!"

He said shurgery and cashe, in fact: and he was passing the buck like a potato off the hob.

Herbie had mentioned a dinner. It had been a good one: up to Roddie's usual standards.

The voice changed to a female one. It was Sheila, his wife.

She had been a sister on medical side at one time. She came the dame uppity a bit now her old man was a consultant: but I felt sorry for her.

It couldn't have been much fun knowing that you were going to spend the rest of your life covering up for a bust: and there's nothing buster than a surgeon on the booze. It must have been the less fun for knowing that she had been laid end to end halfway down Sauchiehall Street by a baker's dozen of embryo specialists, including me, before she caught her middle-class ticket.

She gave me a high-hat tone of voice these days. Me, I never whispered we had even held hands.

"Neil? It's you! Roddie has this terrible cold."

It was always this terrible something.

"He's been at a dinner. I told him not to go out. But he did. Now he's caught a chill and he's not at all well. D'you think you could cope? Or get one of the other consultants?"

I thought of the mess on the trolley on its way up. Cope! There was a word for you.

Still! Wasn't I Prince Gumboot for the night? And wasn't this just what I wanted: right in my supermarket shopping basket?

"No problem, Sheila. Get him snuggled up again. I'll cope sure enough."

"Thanks, Neil."

Did the voice warm just a fraction? The phone clicked. I was left to wonder.

The nurse brought my food. Her smile was an extra spoonful of sugar.

As I ate I thought about Roddie and about Mummy and about me.

Remember I told you I didn't drink when I

was working and I would tell you why? Well, Roddie was why: Roddie and a lot more like him.

It was a common enough story in doctors. They had to start so young as students: a lot of them not dry behind the ears. It was not until five years later, when they had nasty decisions to make for the first time, that they got found out by themselves: the not good-enoughs, the gentle, the misfits, the guys who should have been farmers.

But it was too late to turn back. You couldn't sink five years of your family's money in a medical degree then throw it all up. So, they started with a few drinks to help them out.

A common human situation? Maybe! But docs had this extra problem. There was this General Medical Council. If you breathed too much White Horse over a patient, or 'icked up a pail of gin and tonic over his private parts, you got put out: right out in the street, which is very sore on the bank balance.

So the crafty ones stoked up on a couple of Valium from a sample pack, or conned a bottle of Seconal from the ward. There was rarely anything like heroin or morphia. That was too easily spotted. But the cocktails some

57

guys came up with would have won the barman of the year prize in Sammy Dow's any night.

Roddie was on the brandy and barbiturates: and well and truly beached.

But he was safe. He was rocked in the cradle of the hospital system.

Once you got to be a consultant it was easier to shell out uncooked winkles with a pin, than get rid of you. You could be cowhanded, canned, or just plain careless, but the boys would rally round. The whole show could clam up.

Ever tried to find out anything from an NHS hospital? You'll know what I mean.

The ranks had closed around Roddie. He was borne along, his feet not quite touching the ground.

He was steered away from anything major. One of the other consultants vetted his waiting lists so that the secretaries sent for simple stuff for him: appendices, hernias and the like. It was an open secret. He must have known about it. But he said nothing. That made it as bad as could be for him.

He was given his place on the night rota for emergencies, but there was an understanding that the middle-bod on call, that was me, would get one of the other consultants if needed.

But I had taken my chance. I rarely called anyone. You didn't want anyone near you. You had to do it alone to make it stick. So for the past three years I had sweated some blood. I had had the wind up vertical umpteen times. But no-one had died that shouldn't have: and I had learned. Oh, what I had learned. And it was going to run up five bunches of grapes in the fruit machine some time soon.

Mind, Mummy was a disaster all right. I had wondered whether to call Charles or not. Then I thought to hell with it. I wanted to do it on my own.

After I was first appointed, Charles had wandered in a lot at times like that. I had good references, but I suppose he wanted to see for himself. He stood and watched and let me get on with it.

He might ask:

"Where is Mr. McAnespie?"

I would say he had this terrible something or other, whatever had been his wife's explanation.

Charles was a quiet man in all ways. He never said a word nor showed an emotion.

When I had finished he would leave with a nod and without a word. It was a backhanded compliment and I made the most of my chances.

There was more than that, though. He took me to surgical meetings and introduced me around his colleagues in Edinburgh and Aberdeen. He encouraged me to write a couple of papers that went down well in the journals. He was keen that I should join his golf course and the Royal Scottish Automobile Club: but I had shied away from that sort of thing.

For a jumble of such reasons I was not for fishing his sixty-four-year-old bones out of his pit over a nut case gone surgical and a drunken cutter.

And I had given Roddie his place, all proper: asked if he wanted to come. But he was too ill. His wife had said so.

Mummy was in my mitts all fair and square and I was about to put on the rubber gloves.

While I was chewing the last bit of roll, I heard the rumble of the trolley arriving. Donnie Marshall came in then. He was the senior anaesthetist on call.

"Watcha got then?"

I started my spiel again.

He looked at me to see if I was joking.

His pot stuck out. I could see his navel dimpled through his shirt. I poked at it.

"C'mon Tarzan! Let's see you do some clever stuff!"

Donnie was a bright citizen with a taste in bow ties. He had fair hair gone thin. His scalp showed pink through it. His white teeth lined his mouth in a confident show.

We went through to the gas room to see the state of the wicket.

The blood was going in a fast dribble. Donnie did his slick sleight of hand with his laryngoscope and got a tube in her larynx. He put his ear at his end and listened for breath sounds.

"S'easy. Down Craignethan!" and he plugged Mummy into the gas pipes.

He gave me a wink and life suddenly was a lot happier. Mummy's life support systems were under control.

Herbie said:

"Do you want a physician?"

I looked at Donnie:

"The biochemistry worries me a bit. What do aspirin and amitryptiline do to a system? Does she want dialysed?"

Donnie spread his beefy arms to heaven:

"How would I know? Better get a biochemist. Is there one on call? Let's get him out of bed!"

We laughed. It was half relief at Mummy's better prospects: half a giggle at getting sleepy guys out of their beds.

"Who's on tonight?"

Herbie went to the phone:

"Kenny? Who's on duty for biochemistry?"

"Alex McPherson," he repeated out loud and looked round at us.

I nodded. Alex was a solid citizen.

"OK, Kenny. Get him here will you? Thanks."

Donnie watched the black rebreathing bag. The movement was rhythmic enough: but the respirations were minute.

"Right!" I said. "I want a 'scope first. Make sure she hasn't a varix."

Sometimes you get huge bleeds from varicose veins in the gullet: unusual but not impossible. I would look soft if I sliced out her stomach and left the bleed going six inches above it.

"I'll do it in here."

'Scoping procedures were not sterile. I could mess about in the gas room and keep the theatre clean and Fay happy. She went peculiar if her theatre got dirty.

Fibrescopes were the thing, I had been told. They used glass fibre optics with plenty of light. They could go round corners. But we didn't have one. Not us!

We had a Negus oesophagoscope: a steel tube about thirty inches long with distal lighting. A sterling tool. It had saved many lives. But not the most gentle of instruments for Mummy's frail condition.

I got on. I fiddled it gingerly, fingers and thumb, and went down behind Donnie's tube. I poked down gently, gently: sucking out a river of blood as I went.

The gullet seemed clear.

I wriggled it through the cardia into the stomach. With a gush I hit oil: red, coiling blood.

There was a lot of it. The 'scope end is big. The blood welled into it fast.

I eased my head to the side and nodded at Herbie:

"I'm into the stomach. Have a quick suck and a look."

He manipulated the sucker and had a squint as I had done. He was impressed: awed in fact.

"Jeeze!"

"It must be that." I nodded at the drip bottle. It was a night for paradoxes.

She needed blood, but the more she got the more her pressure went up, so the more she bled. And she wouldn't stop bleeding until her clotting mechanisms were restored, for which she needed more blood.

Herbie was almost rubbing his hands:

"She'll need a gastrectomy right enough."

"Yup!" I was feeling good. I had got it all right so far.

"D'you want a look, Donnie?"

"No! No! I've got enough problems."

He laughed and slavered and watched his bag and the green button of light on the portable ECG machine.

"—But you won't be all night, will you?"

To my surprise he was a touch plaintive behind the laughter. Anaesthetists don't like deaths on the table.

Fay appeared on her clean side of the theatre door:

"Wheel, laddies?"

"Right, Fay. We have to get this stomach out."

She nodded and turned away to give orders. Her girls began to open the sterile packs.

Herbie and I went to have a wash and brush up.

I was in theatre snapping my gloves tight on my wrists, when in the door came Alex McPherson. He was in an outsize gown and a pair of plastic overshoes. But what made me open my eyes wide was the sight of a man's figure over his shoulder.

He was in a soup and fish, white shirt glaring under the theatre arc, black tie immaculate. A white muffler and dark overcoat were draped over his arm.

It was Charles Hamilton.

It was the boss.

I wondered what he was doing here.

"Well, Neil? Difficulties?"

"Good morning, sir. A few!"

The sir was easy with Charles. He rated it in my Twinlock file of good guys.

"Tell me?"

I felt like Percy Parrot as I went over it all again. He shook his head in disbelief. He should have heard all of the stories by his time of life, but there was always a fresh twist.

As I spoke to him, Fay flighted around him

like a moorhen with a water rat at her chicks. She managed to get the orderly to take his coat and scarf and dinner jacket and enticed him into a gown and mask, but he waved away the rest of the sterile paraphernalia. Charles was operating long before antibiotics. He had an old-fashioned distaste for the dinkier aspects of asepsis and a biblical trust in the Lord.

I made a cutting gesture with a phantom knife towards Charles. Mummy was so ill, he might feel he should step in.

I still wasn't sure what he was doing there, but his next remark told me.

"No! You go on, Neil. I happened to be at this dinner where Roddie was . . ."

He left the sentence unfinished, but he didn't need to say any more. He had noticed Roddie mouthing at the malt and had dropped in on his way home to give moral support and a hand in a glove if need be.

"Has she got a case sheet?"

The orderly carried it over to him. Charles fished under his gown. He brought out a pen and his glasses and scribbled his name in big letters on the front.

It was like him: a generous, open gesture. He was giving me my chance and was offering to carry the box of eggs. I hoped I could grow to be as big as him.

Herbie and I got Mummy swabbed.

I asked the breathing end:

"You OK, Donnie?"

He said "Yes", but I still had the impression that he was not too keen on the whole affair.

I took a last look at Charles. He had opened the case sheet and was frowning at the notes I had scrawled. Now, my writing is notorious, even among medics, for being illegible, but even allowing for that there was an odd intentness in his attitude. He seemed to be reading very carefully.

He surfaced for a moment and seemed surprised that I hadn't started, as if his mind had been on other things.

"Better get on with it."

Then he retreated into some deep-brown, inner sanctum.

Fay smacked a knife handle into my hand. It was no night for keyhole surgery. I wanted to get in and out fast, so I made a big incision: big enough to let me fish around up to the elbows if need be. Right from the word go we were in trouble. She oozed blood from every surface. Herbie and I needed a palisade of pressure forceps to get the skin and muscle bleeders under control. And when I cut across the great arch of vessels that supply the stomach it was Sweeney Todd time in the Saltmarket.

It was the aspirin, you see, and the blood loss. Together they had loused up her coagulation systems. She simply could not stop bleeding.

Ligatures do so much. You can catch the big fellows. But you can't tie off every capillary. So, under my hands Mummy just seeped blood in a deathly, fine capillary ooze.

In the usual way of things you can get that job done in half an hour if all goes well. I've done it faster. Forty-five minutes is pedestrian stuff. An hour is someone who doesn't know his job.

But that night wasn't the usual way of things. That job took me one hundred and five minutes. It cost Donnie a pint of sweat into the back of his gown as he watched the little green spot on the cardiac monitor do a fandango not yet recorded in cardiology.

I got the stomach out and slung it in a basin.

"Open it up, Fay," I asked.

She took a pair of Mayo scissors and slit it open like a filleted herring.

There was an erosion as big as two fists. The surface looked as if it had been scraped with a cheese grater. There was a gunge of white sludge that was the remains of her drug dinner.

Herbie grunted and I nodded. That bit had been right. But what was left was all wrong.

You depend on sutures, God, platelets, capillary retraction and a battery of enzyme substrates to stop bleeding. Well, her tissues were gossamer fine and wouldn't hold: sutures tore out: forceps came away with fine shreds of tissue in their jaws. God was out for the night. She had bled away her own platelets and the ones from her transfusion weren't coming out to play. Her coagulation enzymes had been strafed by the salicylate in her system.

Alex McPherson gave Mummy vitamin K and blood factors IX to XXIX: but he might as well had given her Robertson's Five Star Ginger for all the good they did.

Nothing made any difference. She bled and bled. You couldn't touch her but another vessel started.

We tilted the table up. We tilted the table

down. We sent for the fire-brigade and the Honourable Company of Edinburgh Golfing Gents. The second battalion of the Highland Light Infantry might have done it, but the rotten Westminster politicians had disbanded the regiment.

Donnie said in a quite voice:

"She's going out."

The ECG bleep had a very sad sound.

Herbie said:

"There's nothing left to do."

He folded his hands on the edge of the green towel, like a half-hearted prayer.

There is an eerie time comes to all surgeons when a patient dies on him. You feel the life slipping away. Something inside goes cold and you know that the life is going.

But the oddest thing had happened to me about a year before. I was salvaging what I could from the inside of a guy whose car had fallen off its jack on to his tum-tum. His gut had been burst all over his peritoneum. His liver was purée and his spleen sausage meat. He was a ringer for Mummy: deep in shock and going deeper. The gas man had phoned his wife to say he would be home for tea: and the attendant from the mortuary was standing by with his body bin. In the front of my mind

I had accepted the facts. I waited for the cold clutch in my crutch to tell me he was dead. But instead of this icy feeling of the threshold of infinity, damn me, I began to glow. I began to blow hot. I felt it come right.

I said not a word. What was there to say? There was nothing to show; nothing to record. I had had a hunch, that was all. Mind you, I felt it physically, this odd warmth. But who was taking my temperature?

I remember the gas man, two hours later, his beans burnt, his toast charred, looking at me and saying:

"Remarkable!"

After that it began to happen more and more.

Don't get this wrong. This isn't some kind of a yarn. I'm not trying to tell you I became a miracle man.

Not me!

Patients died or didn't die, just as before.

But I began to sense what would go and what wouldn't. I got a feel for this. I began to get off with things I had no right to expect.

I took the right leg off a tramp they found in a bothy in Argyll. His blood sugar was high enough to have made candyfloss and the blood supply wouldn't have nourished a tadpole. His flaps should have turned into toffee and melted away.

They didn't. They held together.

I grafted an old dearie whose nightie had gone into the gas fire. This had charred her hip into a broiled steak before the neighbours got to her. Nobody in his senses would have expected it to take.

The graft took like it was charmed.

I took out a cancer in a colon. Drew Matheson, the histologist, phoned me:

"I've had the technicians slice this up from one end to the other. You know you've got this all out with half an inch to spare all round, but it isn't visible or palpable outside of a two-inch radius of the obvious tumour. Cat's eyes?"

I say again, other guys could have done the same, but they would have been pleased to get off with it and a bit surprised, where I had begun to sense the ones that were going to do. This in turn gave me a super-confidence kick. I began to take on things against the odds and get away with them.

I had tried to analyse how it came about. I reckoned it was the same as many physical things of a complex order: skating, gymnastics, acrobatics. The experts practise and practise. For a long time they do it by numbers, by rote. Then it becomes instinctive. After that they compose the poetry.

I reckoned that had happened to me.

Now, that night, right from the moment I got my hands on Mummy, I had had this flash of intuition. That was why I had wanted to get hold of her. I had an instinct that if Mummy came good it would be a touchstone for the future: a down payment on a transatlantic ticket.

With Donnie's words, though, and Herbie's gloomy look, I had a second thought. I had worked hard: given all I knew. The team had backed me to the hilt.

Now I wondered. Was I the biggest balloon in the business? Was it all a myth? Had my ocean steamboat gone aground?

Then, as with other times, it happened. I felt Mummy come good under my hands, though the sensory receptor was in some uncharted viscus.

I shook my head:

"Nope! We're home!"

Herbie looked away: embarrassed. Donnie glanced at the dying dance of the electronic dot with a shrug. Who was I kidding? Me? That was OK by them.

I ignored them. I turned to Fay.

"Give me a hot saline soak, love."

She wrung out a gauze pack in the steaming solution and handed it to me. I handled it until it was blood-hot, then I tucked it around Mummy's internal plumbing. I nodded for a stool to be put against the wall.

"Keys," I said, and sat down. I closed my eyes.

I didn't go clean away. I was aware of the theatre's heat, the hiss from the autoclave. I was also aware of a sense of happiness, of competence, I had never known before.

I snapped awake, got up and went back to the job in hand. I took the pack off the gut. It glistened and shone. It was viable. There was not a trickle of blood on her stitch line. I put swabs in the para-colic gutters. They came out faintly pink.

She was bone dry. I had known it would be so.

Donnie started: a small brisk movement of surprise:

"For Christ's sake . . . " he said.

He peered at the ECG monitor. It was in sinus rhythm, the first time for two hours.

74

Alex McPherson said: "Good for the young doctor."

Herbie said: "Chees!"

Mummy wasn't out of the rain forest by a long sight. She still had massive problems. She would have a rocky stay in the intensive care Hilton for a day or two. But my bit was OK. She would get off the table alive.

As I started to close her muscle and skin layers I looked over at Charles: but he was tugging at his gown ties and heading for the side room.

An odd thought struck me. There had been blinding and swearing and caring and laughter and frustration and disappointment and fascination and finally joy jumping about like electric sparks amongst everyone in the theatre—everyone except Charles. He had not uttered a word. He had simply stood in his corner and watched.

But then it was time to stretch and yawn and pour several pints of coffee into my parched system.

At times like that a party sometimes develops. Folks get high on coffee and fatuous jokes and a live patient.

That night died the death.

Donnie wanted home and sleep. Alex McPherson took him away. Herbie made to stay. A couple of other cases were waiting to be seen, but he reckoned they could wait until he had his cup of Camp. He made to join Charles and me in the side room, but he was stopped in his tracks.

Charles did an odd thing:

"Neil."

"Yes, sir?"

"Organize coffee, then come and talk to me."

Charles sounded serious: no ifs, ands or buts. And the way he said the words excluded Herbie.

Herbie looked at me, but I splayed my hands like Ikey Mo. I didn't know what was up.

Herbie shot me with his thumb and forefinger.

I nodded. Something seemed to be wrong, but I couldn't think what.

I liked Charles's style: quiet, matter of fact, relaxed. Some surgical guys get a perpetual steam up. They yell and blow the stack. Not Charles. I had never seen Charles with his marbles in a scramble. If he got angry, he went the other way: all Olympian and withdrawn, just as he was going then. Any telling-off he had to do was the more effective for its lack of temper.

As I went to hurry the coffee on, I felt suddenly and overwhelmingly depressed. I have a flat cold spot that hits me about four hours into the dawning. It comes on as a physical thing. The lights go garish. I feel cold. I fumble decisions. My fingers don't connect with my brain.

I had come to hate that bad time and the following couple of hours, although after they passed I could go on until teatime.

It was worse than usual that morning. I had had no sleep for twenty-one hours and I was suffering a reaction from making it with Mummy.

I was rocking on my feet when I got back to the side room. Charles was in the shower-room-cum-loo just off it. He was running water and making noises like washing his face and hands.

I sat down and closed my eyes. I fell asleep at once: an edgy surface snooze: just enough to let the synapses slack off. When the coffee arrived ten minutes later, I woke at once. I felt better and more able to stand whatever licks were to come my way.

The same nurse brought the coffee. This pleased Charles. She added sugar to his cup and passed it over.

"Thank you! That's the first test of a good nurse. How to make good coffee at two o'clock in the morning."

She was happy at the compliment and gave us the smile all over again. I suppose the big wheels in the Royal College of Nursing would have had a managerial fit if that had been reported to them. But I had noticed a curious shortage of administrative staff at times like that. Anyhow, the net result of that exchange was that three people felt good for a few moments. That must be worth something.

My good feeling died in bud.

"Shut the door after you, there's a good lass."

"Yes, sir!"

Something to make my ears red, sure enough.

Still it didn't come. He sat back in his chair, still contemplating his brown interior decor.

He came to with a mild question.

"Tired?"

"Yes, I find these E.T.S. sessions heavy."

He made a face. In his day some things had been worse. Promotion was slow: dead men's shoes and luck. His early days had been meagre enough. An honorary to the hospital, he had had a half-crown practice in Maryhill to earn a living while his surgical reputation grew.

But other things were on his side. He had a merchant father to back him. Fees could be slid into the pocket more easily in those days, and they lasted longer.

Still he knew my problems and he commiserated:

"Terrible thing, money!"

That remark sparked off a chain of recollection about the night's conundrums.

"By the by, the patient's relatives wanted her treated in private, but she was so ill I thought she would be better in here. Besides, the house was such a queer mixture of money and neglect, I didn't know if they could afford it."

Charles gave me a startled look. Then he laughed. It was a jolly, ho-ho affair, as if I had said something funny.

His mood seemed curious, but I was

relieved at the laugh. Whatever had made him look so serious couldn't be all that bad.

He said:

"Neil! Tell me the story again. How did you come across this girl?"

Girl? Charles's years were showing.

I went back to the beginning and told him about the Pixie Sixer and Johnnie and the big, sad mansion.

"Can you remember her address? I couldn't read your writing."

"Um. Yes. Something ending in -inver."

Charles suggested:

"Peninver?"

"Yes. That's it."

"Prince Consort Drive?"

He said all of this as if he wanted to be very, very sure about something.

"Yes."

Charles was being courteous and polite, as always. But his questions were bugging the hell out of me. I would be put off no longer.

"Is there something wrong?"

"No."

"Do you know the house?"

"Yes. I've been in it several times."

"Do you know the patient?"

"Yes. As a matter of fact, I do. I used to

know her very well. I was at school with her brother. Step-brother actually."

Such a simple answer: the long shot of coincidence.

It wasn't all that surprising. This West coast belt is very cosy. You can't move but meet somebody's cousin. And at Charles's level of society, the visiting list was rarefied.

Then he cut clean across the lines of conversation:

"Are you still set on leaving the country, Neil?"

This was beyond me. I gave up trying to understand. No doubt he would tell me in his own good time.

"Yes. Arnie Caine—you remember I told you about him—wants me to join him at the beginning of next year."

Meeting Arnie Caine was the slice of luck I had had. He was the owner of the magic carpet that was going to get me out of here. He was the boss—and I mean the no-nonsense, fifty-one per cent stockholding type, fire and hire top man—of a marble and bronze clinic in Texas. I had met him at a seminar in vascular surgery in Chicago where I was a visiting fellow.

We had one of those sudden, chemical

friendships that didn't need to know about backgrounds or credit rating. He was my kind of man. I was flattered and pleased to see he returned the compliment.

Arnie was a great guy in the mould of the fabulous surgeon princes of America. I had a week's break in the middle of my spell. He asked me to spend it with him and his family.

He flew me in his own jet to his ranch, where he raised palomino ponies.

I found the American way of life in that bracket to be quite something. I knew at once that I would adore to have a slice of that cake.

Arnie introduced me to his associates. As a visiting fellow I was accredited and they let me do some stuff for them. We had a few grogs of an evening by his big log fire. I let my hair down a bit. At the end of it he said:

"Scotty, I've had a meeting with the others. I want you to know that you have impressed us. You have a pair of hands we can use. We've seen that you have a definite—"

He paused for a word:

"—flair."

I supped my whisky—a single malt all the way from Islay—and listened without saying anything. But I was excited. It was just about that time the full significance of my optimax operating kick was coming through to me. I was scared to say a word: scared it would fly away. Could it be that it was really showing?

He went on:

"You have an aggressive approach that we like. You can drink your liquor or leave it alone. You aren't a queer or a womanizer."

I had been given the once over twice!

"We have plans for a new wing for peripheral vascular stuff. We need a boy to run it and to pinch-hit on the general side. We should be ready to go in eighteen months. Would you be interested?"

"Can I sign before you change your mind?"

He smiled at me:

"Is that what you want? I'll get my attorney now!"

Now was half past eleven at night: and he meant it. And his attorney would mean it. He would charge Arnie the earth, but he would attend if he was wanted.

That was one thing about the American scene I liked. If you wanted it and you paid for it, you got it.

The people that were going to get me, at the funniest hours.

Then we turned serious:

"Arnie, your offer is breathtaking. The thought of working in this clinic is almost frightening after what I've become used to. I'm certainly interested. But it's a big step and I have this problem with my father."

Arnie listened while I told him about Jock.

"Bring them out here. This sunshine will make a new man of him. And your mother would be a wow I can tell you. A little Scots lady! The town girls would eat her with cream."

I thought of my mother: but I didn't disabuse him. He was so sincere and welcoming.

"I can see you've opened a gang of guts in your time, Scotty. I need ask you no more about that."

Roddie's booze boots were paying me dividends.

"And your microscope work with fine vessels is excellent. Tell me, though, do you see much general MD stuff?"

Emergency services are common in the States. I told him about Benny's organisation and how I worked in it.

"That's good. That's real good. Now, look, I want you to go right on boning up on that end of things. Not every case is referred over here. People come straight at you. If your experience is totally specialized you can miss out. Then you tie up your family problems and we'll get you back here if you still want to come."

His handshake was good and firm. His look was as frank as his promise. We had exchanged Christmas cards. On his was written:

"Looking for you around next Christmas. Let me know by the summer."

I was home and dry on a pile of dollar bills any time I wanted.

I briefed Charles on the up-to-date situation. I ended:

"Though it would have given me satisfaction to get my consultant appointment first, then send my resignation from the States just to show them what I think."

Charles nodded. He said:

"I'm sure you'll get on well, Neil. You have the right attitude for success there."

Charles used his money to keep his surgical end up. He had travelled all over the world, listening, modifying, learning. He knew the States well. His remark added to the signs that were adding up that night. He went on:

"You won't mind me saying that you will

never be an academic success. To do that you have to be more of a book man. Your skills are practical. Besides you have an abrasiveness, a willingness to stand on other people's toes, an unorthodoxy which doesn't fit well here, as I think you know—"

We both knew that I had been passed over for jobs that I might have been expected to get:

"—but I am sure these qualities are what attracted your American friend to you."

I felt my rough edges showing:

"Nonetheless, if you keep out of prison and don't put too many noses out of joint I'm sure you will get your consultant job before long. But—if you do want to go to America, I can't blame you."

He went on in his quiet voice:

"There or here, though, Neil, you have something. There's a load of rubbish in books and films about brilliant surgeons. You know and I know the truth of this. The hardest job is to sit on your backside and read for ten years. Then there's practice and practice and more practice. A lot of waiting for experience that can't be hurried—you've been lucky there."

That was an astute remark, right up to the Charles mark. He had noticed.

"There's a lot of moderate ability around. Most people become competent, even very competent . . ."

He paused.

Then he riveted me:

" . . . but maybe two or three times in my life I've met someone like you. One was a chap I worked with on the south coast after Dunkirk. Another was a fellow I met in Belfast a couple of years back. The best way I can describe it is like a gardener with green fingers. Only yours are red—"

I had an eerie sensation in the inside of my head as he used this phrase. It was one I had never spoken out: not once, not even to myself:

"—for some reason, you have an extra sense. It's more than flair or slick surgery. You have a gift. Tissues take kindly to you. You get away with things. Do you know what I'm talking about?"

Charles was being far too serious and intent for me to play the "Aw, shucks" game.

I tried to answer him in kind: but I found it difficult. I had not tried to put it into words before. I had only felt it as an emotion.

"I know what you mean. I hadn't realized it showed anywhere. I get this—feeling. I feel it come right as I work. But I thought I was just lucky."

"No. It's more than that. There is such a beast as a lucky surgeon. And unlucky ones too—they attract disaster. But these things are extensions of their own personalities. This thing is different. You get away with things you haven't any right to expect."

Charles finished his coffee: put down the cup.

"This isn't to give you a big head, Neil. I know from the little you have told me that life has been far too hard on you for that to be likely. But you should know and realize that you have a gift. A rare gift. Care for it. Don't be too hard on it. Don't sell it . . . "

He waved his hand in a small dismissive gesture:

" . . . I don't mean that you haven't to try to make life as good as you can for yourself and your family. If you think that going to America is what you should do, then by all means . . . "

He rose and began to put on his outer things. He stood over me pulling on a pair of pigskin gloves.

"It isn't just you. I notice it in a lot of you young men. You've become—"

He searched for a word.

"—kissed by the Snow Queen?" I suggested.

He nodded. He understood. We all did. He wriggled his fingers into warmth:

"I've nearly done. I'm ready for bed."

He smiled, but his sixty-four years showed grey in his face:

"You will be a better doctor if you can get something to unfreeze you. Or someone. Perhaps you will find it in Texas."

There was no sting in his remark; no unkindness, but I realized he was making a point of giving me this advice. It would bear thinking about:

"Now I have something to tell you. For this woman tonight you had an answer that she had no right to expect. This operation will have done you no harm at all—"

I perked up. He was going to let me into his big secret:

"—If through this you find a way round the need for going to the States that would be no bad thing. This service is all such a bloody mess. We've lost far too many of our best men for the wrong reasons. We need awkward buggers like you, with confidence in their ability to speak their minds, to oppose this mediocre sham at every turn. We need, in fact, anarchists of a responsible kind. I think you fit that kind of bill well. And you may just have got yourself a patron—"

I had got up to walk with him to the lift. He poked me in the chest:

"That girl—"

He was at it again.

"—is a Taggart!"

To my dawn-dazed mind this meant nothing.

"Taggart?" I asked.

"Taggart," repeated Charles. "Lord of that ilk. Steamboat Willie himself."

My iconoclasm was shown up for the fake it was. In spite of myself my knees did a curtsy: or should I kiss the ring on his finger?

I said "Huuuh?" in strangled surprise and with no originality at all.

"Good night, Neil."

"Good night, sir," I said.

But I promise you it was more than a good night. It had turned out a very surprising night indeed.

I was a pensive lad as I walked to the lift with him. As we got to the lift-well, the cage arrived. The gate opened. Out came Herbie and held it for Charles. We said: "Good night."

Herbie looked me over for mangled limbs or teeth marks. He seemed happy to find me well.

"Much else in?" I asked.

"One query appendix: one certain perforation."

Surgical syntax is scandalous.

I nodded. "Will they wait?"

It was policy to leave what we could until the big theatre started in the morning.

"The appendix will. The perforation won't."

Herbie looked at me.

"D'you want to open it up?" I asked him.

"Yes, siree!"

I had made his night.

We didn't see many of them those days, and the ones we did see often did not need to be opened. You stuck a tube down and sucked off the stomach acid and it healed itself.

The patient was a barman. He had had a pie and peas for a late supper after cleaning up the glasses and ashtrays. On the way home he had been waiting for a bus when his duodenal wall gave out. He had gone down as if Benny Lynch had hit him in the button.

It was workaday stuff. I was glad. We had had enough commotion for one night. Herbie performed creditably. He had good hands. He would be fine, would Herbie.

It was a big inferior hole. Herbie got one or two peas out of his peritoneum: but he couldn't find any pie.

At five o'clock, Herbie and I thought about breakfast.

"Herbie, I'm going for a shower and a shave. Order me some ham and eggs and sausage."

I was ravenous:

"—Can I have a borrow of your razor?"

"Sure, it's in my locker. Here's the key."

"Thanks."

I split for the residency. As I walked along the corridors day was beginning to win. Basins crashed as the first faces were washed. Nurses, happed in the warm inner redth of their blue wool capes, scurried to breakfast.

I wondered if Mummy was still alive.

I found Herbie's razor and some aromatic spirit stuff.

I lathered and groaned in heated delight as the steaming water ran over me. I slapped some of the astringent perfumed stuff about my chops and rubbed some in my hair. Surgical pouffery? Could there be a future for me? I decided not.

With Mummy in mind I didn't go straight to the mess. I went instead to the Intensive Care Unit. There was a side door from the theatre suite. I entered by it and nodded at the hooked-up souls, struggling for life:

"Female. About fifty. Acute admission early this morning. Name's Ross. How's she doing?"

It was my night for smiles. I got a big, breezy grin from a big breezy girl in a Sister's cap.

She looked far too young to be in charge: but she was. She blew the whistle and called the fouls, and did it very smartly too.

"She's doing—just and no more. But she's still with us. Come and see."

We went to view.

ICUs do pull chestnuts out of the fiery furnace: but they don't leave a lot of dignity in the process. Mummy was all hooked up like the rest. She had wires from her wrists and legs. She had tubes through her nose and in her veins. There was a row of scanners and dials on a visual display above her bed like the flight deck of a DC10. If she had been plugged into a set of flashing fairy lights, they could have taken a silver collection.

This stuff was too much for me at that time of the morning. I winked and smiled knowing-like and nodded at the gadgetry:

"All OK huh?"

That was the funniest thing she had heard all night. She laughed with pleasure at the fun of being a first-rate nurse and knowing her job to a tee.

"Yes. The hardware is reading out. All that we can do."

But the wetware was in very poor shape.

She was pinker: full of new blood and electrolytes, but she had been over her head in shock. Her endocrine battery was bombed out and her energy-rich bonds had been declared bankrupt. At times like that you can blind the scene with science but what keeps the patient going is some kind of inner willpower: guts. The whole is greater than the sum of the bits of biochemistry.

I turned to cheery cheekie:

"Fine! Great! Listen, if you're busy, you blow. Leave me be."

94

That was good. She wanted to be ready for the off, and the report had still to be passed on.

I perched on the edge of the bed, avoiding wires and polythene tubes. For the first time I got a good look at Mummy's face. She had the Pixie Sixer's high cheekbones, but the face was thinner. Her hair, too, was straight, but it was of a finer texture. The garish light threw shadows into the radial, prune-skin lines about her mouth. Black smudges telling of her fearsome internal battle, stained the skin under her eyes.

A clapped-out, refined version of the daughter I thought.

Mummy verified this further. She opened her eyes.

I was so surprised I let out a grunt. In that light they were pale grey with black spots. The genie of the genes had put his marker on them, both mother and daughter.

Mummy didn't take me in. Mummy didn't take anything in. Mummy was afloat in life: but only just. Her water wings had sprung a leak: there was a handful of lead in her bikini: and she was too tired to swim.

I had seen that look before after severe

injury. Every physical resource had been used up. The buggeration factor was all that was left.

"I should be dead, but—"

Mummy was out of earshot: almost out of view: but I wanted her to know someone was there. Dying is such a lonely business. Only you can do it. If somebody waves a hanky or throws a streamer as you leave, you might think it had all meant something.

I slid a hand under the bandages and wraps that strapped the support board to her wrist, and got a thumb around one side of her hand, my fingers round the other. I squeezed: not cruel nor pinching but hard none the less.

"You're better! You're all right now. It's over."

The effort was intense. I could see the wrinkles at the side of the eyes quirk, the iris contract. I knew that Mummy saw me.

"It's over! Better! Sleep now."

The nod was almost imperceptible. The merest flick of the eyelids: but we had been in contact.

I stood up feeling sheepish: but no-one had been watching.

I went off to find some grub.

I went back into the corridor through the main door. Then I got my third big smile of the morning.

The Pixie Sixer was there. She was fast asleep on a hospital bench. Her head was laid in Johnnie's lap. He looked miserable. He hadn't shaved. They were flanked by an older man and woman.

I inclined my head at Johnnie in recognition. He looked surprised, and woke the girl gently.

For a minute she didn't take me in. I was dressed like a real doctor for a change, with a white coat and a plastic shield with my name on it to tell me who I was.

"Oh!" she said.

But it was a nice "Oh!"

There were shades of recognition and pleasure that rubbed my pelt in the purr direction.

"—then you're a hospital doctor as well?"

I nodded:

"You get another badge for your sleeve."

Then came the smile: all for me.

We cut out Johnnie. We cut out the older man. They just sat quiet and let us get on with our optic signals.

It was just as well they didn't want to talk,

and that the Brownie and I were conversing in silence. No-one could have squeezed a syllable edgeways into the welter of words being poured over my head by the older woman, who was a very big-life bint indeed.

She was one of those dames who made a study of putting people down. She used various weapons: a frozen face that dared you to be familiar; a haughty gaze delivered down a sharp nose; but the real stopper was her accent. She had the enunciation you can only afford if you have a long acquaintance with the Home Counties and are three generations deep in dividends and capital gains. I supposed it must all go with Lordiness.

That avalanche of affected 'a's suffocated the tiny tendre between the girl and me. We put it off until later.

She said:

"Doctah!" with a capital D as in doubt.

I might well be somebody's kind of a doctor, but I sure as hell wasn't hers. Where were my grey hairs and my striped pants?

I concentrated on this remarkable voice and tried to make out what she was saying.

She ended up:

"—and where is Charles?"

Actually she said "—end wheah is Cholls?"

My answer came out all goose-pimpled with glottal stops.

"The operation didn't finish until four. He went home for some sleep."

The woman looked astounded:

"Sleep?"

Someone was going to have some explaining to do.

"How exactly is the patient, then?"

I loved that exactly. The patient was somewhere between here and the wide blue yonder, knee deep in death: but that wasn't exact enough.

I was about to unbottle a dose of polysyllables from the medical dictionary—you can shut any layman up in ten seconds flat if you try—when I caught Bo-Peep's eyes again. The striking blue with the black spots brought a sharp memory of Mummy. And Charles's words of a few hours ago came back.

I thought: "It's her Mummy."

I spoke directly to her, as gently and as simply as I could:

"She's better. A good deal. The blood she lost has been replaced. The source of the bleeding has been dealt with. And she is on the verge of consciousness. So there is everything to hope for. But she was in very poor shape. It will still be a time before we can be sure."

For some obscure reason I did not mention the drug overdose. I later realized it was because of this older woman and her attitude. It turned out to have been wise to keep quiet.

"Can someone—me—wait with her?"

"Good idea. She's beginning to rouse. Sister will look after you. When your mother does waken, it will help to have someone that she's close to nearby."

The lady with the sharp nose found that member sorely out of joint at this exclusive repartee. She started on me again.

When would Cholls be back? Was I shuah everything was being done for the best? Were other opinions needed? Would I get them at once?

Despite my resolve to sup at the milk of human kindness, I felt my temper tearing like rotten calico, when the quiet gent took a hand:

"Adele! Don't make so much fuss. The doctor knows very well what he is doing."

His voice in contrast to her strident tenor was mild, but there was no hint of allowing dissidence.

He had on a camel coat with a tan velvet collar and shoes from a hand-last. His hair was straight and grey, parted high and brushed angle-wise to his ears. He wore old-fashioned glasses with tortoiseshell rims, and gold legs and nosepiece. These he wore ever so slightly skew. They gave him a soft, dippy, four-eyed look. I came to recognise that this was a subtle disguise. There were no bats in his bell tower.

Behind the squint-set lenses, I recognised the family eyes with the black spots. I bet myself he was Mummy's step-brother, the one Charles knew. I paid myself a fiver later.

Auntie Adele took the pet. She tossed her head, no less. But she stayed quiet.

He turned to me:

"If you could arrange for Nella to wait, doctor."

"Yes! I'll see to it. Come with me and meet Sister."

The girl nodded. Then:

"Uncle Robert, will you see if you can get Daddy again?"

"Of course."

There was a wealth of truth in the promise. If Daddy could be got, he would be.

I took Nella back into the Intensive Care

Unit and introduced her to the cheery Sister:

"This is the patient's daughter. Put her in a gown and let her sit there."

Then I asked "Are you hungry?"

She was like a schoolgirl who has just seen the tuck shop door open.

"Oooh, yes!"

Sister and I both laughed.

"I'll get you some food," and the Sister bustled off.

Then I said a last word:

"She's tired! So tired. And there's nothing more exhausting than speaking when you are ill. Just hold her hand."

Then I went back to the vowels of fortune.

" . . . Charles must be nearing retiring age, Adele. If he was working on Helen for all those hours, then I should jolly well think he would be tired. I know. It's a frightful place—but of all the unbelievable luck that she should land in his hands—I know the decor is—ah—a bit lacking . . . "

He waved his hand at the corridor.

I looked at it through moneyed eyes. It needed a scrub and paint job, did it? It was all right for sad Sadie but it wouldn't do for Mummy.

He went on:

"You had best come home with me. It was good of you to come. All I—we—all of us would expect. And I know Helen will appreciate it too—"

He turned towards me.

"—When would it be reasonable to return?"

I was all off toffs because of Auntie Adele's attitude. I gave him a winter type look.

"Say midday. Four hours is a long time in this sort of recovery situation."

"Thank you."

The eyes with the strong family markings did seem to mean it. I supposed he couldn't help being rich.

I put a thaw in my nod. Then a happier thought made me feel quite spring-like. Adele the awful had mud-coloured eyes. Maybe she wasn't a blood relation.

I went for my sausages. As I munched my way through a couple of McKellar Watt's meatiest I also reflected that the family all seemed to think that Charles had operated on Mummy: not me.

I thought it might be as well if we left Auntie Adele in that fond belief.

2

I GOT into the first theatre of the day at the back of nine. We had collected a milk boy who had fallen under his lorry and ripped a square yard of skin from his leg; a man with a strangulated hernia; a young, nursing mum with a breast abscess; and a couple more citizens with hot appendices: all good clean fun.

Herbie joined me and we got stuck into it.

There were two tables in the big theatre. About ten Roddie came in and took over the other table. He had dried out. He was more or less himself. By twelve we had it all finished.

Then I was done—in more ways than one.

I unbuttoned my feet. I took my mind out. I hung them up in the lobby for air. I wouldn't need them again until blessed Monday. Oh! I would put in an appearance on the Sabbath day: but that was a courtesy affair. No work was indicated. There would be a walk about the policies and a chat about the chirurgical affairs with Charles followed by a sherry from a bottle he kept in his drawer. He was good at that kind of civil gesture.

As I changed out of my greens Roddie asked:

"Quiet night?"

I was beat by then. I kept my words flat and my face from snarling.

"Routine. You know."

You could see Roddie relax. His shoulders came down. His eyes were less wary.

"We'll have coffee then."

Quite the little consultant giving his royal assent and all.

I had just soothed my gullet with a few gulps at the brown brew, when Charles appeared at the door.

"Morning."

"Morning."

Everybody said it to everyone else.

Then very brisk and with never a glance at Roddie:

"How is Mrs. Ross now, Neil?"

"When I saw her before nine she was improving."

"Let's go and see her then."

He turned on his heel and left. I was expected to follow him double quick, no doubt about that. He was in his Chief's warpaint that morning, with his best feather headdress. I shrugged into a white coat.

Roddie's face was red.

"What's this all about?"

"Family friend of his was admitted last night with a big intestinal bleed. Charles just happened to come in."

"Why wasn't I told?"

He spluttered as he said it. His tone accused me of betrayal.

Well, I had set out to con him a little bit: but in the end I hadn't needed to. He had been too pissed to open up a mealy pudding.

His bluster rang a sour response on my own temper. I turned on him.

"C'mon, Roddie! This is the case I phoned you about. Sheila took the phone because you weren't feeling well. She said you said I had to carry on . . ."

I waited a long second: then I slid a carving knife between his ribs, right up to the hilt:

". . . remember?"

Of course he didn't remember anything of the kind.

He gave me a look of jealousy and hate. Then his soft centre showed. He looked down. His face went glum.

Any triumph I might have felt fizzled out on the spot. I felt no contempt. I didn't feel sorry for him. He was just an awful warning.

I did a sprint that would have brought me fourth at Powderhall on New Year's day and caught up with Charles. We walked to the Intensive Care Unit.

When we got there Uncle Old Fashioned had returned and was waiting on his own: Auntie Adele was absent.

He got to his feet:

"Hello, Charles. Jolly nice t'see you again. What a small world."

"Hello, Robert. How are you? We're just going in to see Helen."

"Nella is with her. The doctor . . . "

He nodded at me.

". . . was kind enough to arrange that."

Charles said:

"When I left her early this morning, Robert, she was very ill. But you've been told?"

Uncle Sir Robert indicated me again:

"Yes. The doctor has explained. I have gathered the full story. But Charles—I haven't passed it all on. Not the bit about the pills. Most distressing. And worse if Adele gets hold of it."

It was clear that Charles and he had been buddy-buddies in some rose garden of the past. Many unsaid things were being said. He went on:

"But this is a tremendous stroke of luck, her landing in your care. We were vastly relieved and reassured. We had heard that you had retired."

Uncle Robert didn't ignore me, not in a nasty way. But it was obvious that Charles was the surgeon of the moment, and had been so to that family for many years. I assumed that Charles would reinforce the idea that he had been the genie of the scalpel at Mummy's guddle. It wasn't that anyone would tell fibs. It was just that no-one would say anything. It was an accepted convention when a junior was gaining experience.

In fact I was just as pleased.

I was happy that Charles had let me go to school on Mummy, but I was more than a little out of my depth in all of this heavy heraldic caper.

But then to my astonishment, Charles gave the game away.

"You must understand, Robert, I did nothing. I'm too old for this sort of thing now. You heard half aright. I have given up private practice completely. My job here is more supervisory now. I merely watched Helen's operation. If she lives it will be due to this young man."

I took a mesmerized bow by inclining my head forward half an inch:

"Robert, this is our Mr. Aitken. Neil. Let me introduce you to Sir Robert Taggart."

I said gargle, gargle and put out a hand like a week-old haddock.

Uncle Sir Robert put his specs on straight, a simple gesture that had a sobering effect, as his new orthometric gaze was very clear indeed:

"Ah!" he said.

There was a pause as he rearranged his ideas. While he did so, some unsorted, scrambled memories filtered into the front of my own recall: scraps of newspaper articles, snatches of telly chatter.

He had the same misfortune as people like Max Aitken and Hugh Fraser: big enough in their own way but with the ombrous eminence of their old men forever in their sunshine. But, though Lord Taggart was still alive, the financial and social tic-tac had it that Uncle Sir Robert was a very likely lad indeed and well up to his paternal knocker.

He stood aside as Charles said:
"Excuse us, Robert?"
"Certainly."
But the look he gave me then, seemed to be a pass of some kind.
We left him and went to see Mummy.

You could tell.
How?
That's more difficult.
The meters and dials read no different. The dots and lines on the chart had stayed the same. They told nothing in their detail of what Charles and I had reckoned in a glance: some ineffable change you couldn't argue with.
We looked at each other momently. We both knew.
Maybe the grey smudges were less like the clown of death's grease-paint, perhaps the face had a hint of peace, as opposed to the mortal grimness of a few hours ago. She had colour: a tinge of pink.
I reflected for the umpteenth time that medicine and science are curious bedfellows: there's always this ghost sleeping between them—the thing you can't explain.

As Charles and I approached the bed I noticed something.

The girl's eyes were closed and she had clasped one of her mother's hands in both of her own. At first glance this seemed conventional: the giving and taking of comfort in silent, tactile messages. But then I noticed that even in her light sleep, the girl's brow had a furrow of concentration.

She was willing her mother to get better. Fanciful?

I couldn't argue with you on any scientific ground. But I had had enough experience of the unexplainable not to try.

I thought only:

"Good for you, kid."

Once more I marked her out as special: out of the ordinary, under the mini-skirt and the bold looks.

Charles put his arm around the girl's shoulder. She jerked and opened her eyes. Joy and welcome spread over her face. He was obviously a great favourite.

For the second time in twenty-four hours I had a small, irrational spasm of jealousy at being excluded from this love stuff. I would have to get a hold of myself.

111

"Uncle Charles! I knew you would be here soon. How super!"

In fact she said soooper like a ten-year-old getting a Macallum on a hot June day.

He made avuncular noises at her and they patted and cuddled one another.

That was not my deal. I studied my shoes: they needed a polish, as usual.

The girl turned towards her mother.

"How do you think she is?"

Charles went close to the bed.

"Helen!"

Then again:

"Helen!"

Sister had told us that the patient had been having lucid moments. She had one then, summoned from her limbo by a remembered voice.

She knew him. Her lips were caked with flaked skin and dried mucus. She still had a tube down her gullet. It made her palatal voice sounds poor. Her words were croaked and clogged:

"Charles."

The merest grunt.

Talking was an effort. She tried to smile. The centre of her lower lip cracked open. Blood showed fresh in the split. She winced.

"Helen! I don't want you to try to talk. Just listen. You are doing well. A few days and you'll be up and about. Soon have you playing tennis again."

A shaft of understanding shone between them. As with Sir Robert, Charles was dipping into an old world. He looked at the tubes and dials and made a moue of distaste:

"Have to get you out of this. Back home."

She nodded at Charles, and twitched up her lips in that little smile again.

She slid a look at me. Her glance was languid: uninterested. She was exhausted by the effort of listening to Charles. Yet, in the last instant of her gaze, before she gave up her hard-won consciousness, she looked puzzled.

Then she closed her eyes. After all, where in her world would she have met the likes of me before?

Charles said to the girl:

"You can leave her now, dear. You've done your job well."

So he had noticed the emotional transfusion as well. Pity we couldn't bottle that invisible stuff and store it in a bank like blood.

Relief and tiredness rushed into her face as

she relaxed her effort: happy tears and bleary eyes.

The three of us walked back to the corridor. Uncle Sir Robert got up again. He nodded at Charles, but then turned to me:

"What can you tell me?"

I glanced at Charles. He looked back at me with polite interest: said not a word. I realised that Charles was indicating and the knightly relative was accepting, that Mummy was all my own work: my patient.

Those striking eyes were direct in their message. He wanted the news hard and straight.

"I do think she's going to be all right now. There are complications—pneumonia, paralysis of the bowel, blood clots—that are liable to develop in such cases—"

I was aware that the girl had turned her eyes on me too. This blue-black barrage was all getting a bit much for me:

"—but we'll keep a careful watch. These problems can usually be got over."

I paused: then remembering his remarks about the drug scene I added:

"The tablets which she took—well, she lost so much blood that it emptied her system of the drugs before she went too deep. That bit

114

of it is over. I've—ah—edited my operating notes and her case sheet. It can be kept quiet. No need for anyone else to know—"

I looked at the girl:

"—I take it your boy friend can keep his mouth shut?"

"Who? Johnnie? Oh, he'll do what I tell him—"

I had to laugh at the assurance of the brat:

"—but I thought it was Uncle Charles who op—"

Robert cut in:

"We've been into that, Nella. I'll explain later—"

Then to me:

"—and thank you, doctor—for everything."

Better than a cheque, those words: well, almost.

He walked away from us and stared at the wall of the biochemistry building while he blew his nose.

When he came back he looked as if the rectangular patterns of brick and mortar had had some pleasing prospect:

"Charles! Would that you could prescribe strong drink for me, but I must take this child home to Cleveden Drive."

Miss Independence changed her name on

the spot and had us meet Miss Indignation:

"Uncle Robert! I've had my own flat for a year now. I can get myself home by taxi—"

Then she added in a tone that indicated no such thing:

"—thank you very much."

Sir Robert was flummoxed: all this youth going its own way: not like his day. Still, relief also showed:

"If you're sure—"

Charles added:

"We could have lunch, Robert. The Malmaison? Haven't had a chat with you for far too long."

Robert liked that prescription even better:

"Will you join us, doctor?"

There was no doubting the sincerity of the invitation.

"Thank you. No. I must get to bed. Besides, I go near the West End. I'd be glad to drop your niece at her flat."

The old lads beamed. The girl was comforted. And I could draw this conversation short and get to my stricken bed.

Yet Robert was troubled:

"You've been at it all night?"

He looked at Charles for confirmation.

Charles winked at him.

"Good for him!"

Then at me:

"Isn't it?"

I nodded.

"You can give him his drink another time, Robert. He's far too young to start at this time of day. Aren't you?"

I nodded wryly: That was the second free drink I had passed up in twelve hours.

Sir Robert reached out his hand. I shook it.

"We shall raise these alcoholic matters again some time soon," he promised.

Charles and he departed for grape country. I went to the changing room for my mackintosh, then took the girl to the lift. Downstairs I slammed her safely into my elderly Mini: if you did it hard, the door stayed shut. Then I spread a carbon trail to Great Western Road, blasted from the thirty-two holes in the colander it used for a smoke-pipe.

I had expected chatter: release from her first near experience of death. But she sat silent: exhausted. When I stopped the car and leaned over her to get at the catch, I got a kiss for all my pains.

I could see it coming: all shiny and full of gratitude. I expected it to be breathy and brash. It was in fact chaste: and of a flavour not known for a long time: sweet. I waved her goodbye and fizzed like a home-made rocket for the far side of the Kelvin.

I was going to have me the biggest sleep since Snow White ate the Mackintosh Red.

In Nether-Maryhill, near the hospital, I sublet a room from one Rahmin Passoud. I cohabited in chaste neighbourliness with a widow lady called Jenny McLean.

I let myself in with one of the seventeen passkeys that Rahmin had had cut cheap for bulk. He was in the hall, his shirt out cooliewise:

"Well, you little brown wog-type bugger! How many of your illegal family have you ferried up the Clyde today?"

His smile was all white teeth and pink tongue and gums. It looked eatable.

"Mye Godd!"

He was straight from the Spike Milligan show.

"Mye Godd! I onlee managed one bowat load today. Busyness is verri poor!"

His smile disappeared into a frank, happy laugh for all the money he was making:

"Mye Godd! Yess! I have onlee been twice to the bank today!"

There was so much truth that the tears ran from his screwed-up eyes and he held his belly to enjoy to the full his own mirth.

"Listen! When you become the first Paki king of Caledonia, don't forget your poor white friends."

"Goodness! Noa! I woan't! Eye'll find a place for you in mye kitchens."

He wiped his tears away with the clubs of his spatulate finger ends and licked at those he missed.

"You shall be my Grand Vizier, nothing less!"

There is a vast Asian fairy tale, a cross between Ali Baba and the Thousand and One Nights. He had been raised on it. He was forever quoting magic spells and sorcerers from it. He loved the unending, fantastic invention.

Mind, there was no fantasy about the way that little brown gent beavered at the business of the day: all day and every day. He strove. He schemed. He squirrelled. If I could have bought shares in him I would have paid a premium.

And all his sisters and his cousins and his

aunts, they worked too. They rubbed and scrubbed and polished up the brasses on the big front door: and if they didn't watch what they were at, they were going to end up owning the Queen's navee.

He conducted a corporation bus. He owned, in some sort of family partnership, a Granny a' things. It was open twenty-seven hours a day. It had a stock that would have shamed Sir Marcus Sieff.

You wanted it?

It might be foosty, full of holes, covered in cobwebs, pickled in cat's pee, stale, rat-nibbled, or rancid: but they had it. Into the bargain, he sublet corridor space, spare couches, and camp-beds to an itinerant army of tax-dodgers, and immigration fugitives. He also let rooms to Jenny McLean and me. We were special. We were permanent. We paid weekly: forehanded though: no favours. He shared a stall at the Barrows on Sundays, where he sold saris and cheese cloth shirts. He made a killing on his children's allowances: but I wasn't sure that some of the heads that were counted might not have been on loan from a pal down the street.

He was a great guy. I loved him and his family and particularly his wife, who was an absolute pet in a rather solemn way—until she smiled: then the sun came out.

I took a strong breath of Indian cooking:

"What's it today? Yak steaks and Brahmaputra gravy?"

He was away again. At least I was good for a laugh.

"Mye Godd! We will be making you like our food yet. You must keep on trying!"

Actually it tasted fine. I was coming to enjoy it.

Little Ranji, his wife, kept poking plates of the stuff at me with that beautiful smile:

"Would you like to try?"

"Lubbly! Just lubbly!"

That made her laugh too. Jack Point hadn't a patch on me.

But that day was a feast day. Family jollity was the in thing. They were too busy for me. The place was alive with brown bairns, busy with bangles and bells and incense burners and those God-awful garish posters they fancy.

I fished in my mackintosh pockets and found the remains of the liquorice allsorts:

"Catch!"

I threw them up the hall. They went for the wax paper bag like whippets after a rabbit.

"Eat the black ones, now. I don't want you losing your tan!"

I closed the door on the razz ma tazz, pulled off my tie and peeled off my shirt. I took my toes to the heels of my shoes, dropped my trousers on them in a crumpled heap, and fell on my bed in my Y-fronts. I knew nothing until seven o'clock.

At seven Jenny gave me a knock.

"Y'awake now? Don't fall over again."

"No. I'm on my feet."

I collected my wits. Not all of them. Not enough to feel pain. Just enough to tell me where I was and the time of day.

The first question was easy. I was in my Paki pal's Victorian palace.

With all this stuff you read about Glasgow being Europe's biggest slum, you might find that difficult to believe: but it's true.

In the bone-work of the carcase of slummery, you find more fine nineteenth-century tenements than you can shake a stick at.

There are stairways of sweep and dignity, balusters of wrought iron, doors of finest wood, rooms of noble proportion, knockers and bells and letter boxes of best brass, and, tiled entrances of tone and distinction in elegant art nouveau designs.

I know, I tramped up and down hundreds of them.

I wondered. I marvelled. The like of those would not be seen again, ever, on this earth. And that seemed a good reason for knocking them down. As soon as they showed signs of a crumble they caught demolishers' distemper. It will be the same thing when they kill the last whale.

Anyhow, Passoud's pad was an example of what had been best of its kind. The city that had once been there seeped out from under the curry smells; and now and then from behind the garish paint a thin smothered plaint sounded in my sensorium.

When I woke, I found the heathen feast going well. The spicy cooking smells were thirty thousand olfactons to the good.

The thought of viands revived me. Tea was wanted. A visit to Jenny was the thing.

I had an elderly towelling robe I wore for such occasions. If I bent the wrong way, however, I gave a provocative display of dangle, so I slipped on my dress jock-strap: the one in Royal Stewart tartan.

Then I went acalling.

Attired in this boudoir best, I fought my way through assorted Passoud brats in the corridor. I picked up Shulie, my best three-year-old girl friend and knocked at Jenny's door.

"It's your neighbourhood health care adviser."

"Come on in, Neil."

I walked in, looking forward to the happy feel of the room. Jenny was one of your natural home makers. There was a strong nesting instinct eager to get at the moss and feathers. Although the right man had come her way, he had died before she could give it full expression. Jenny's bed-sit had a big window. It looked over the leads and chimney pots towards the Kelvin. Lights shone in spider spangles from the enclosing urban environs: but the overall feel was of air and sky, even at night. A gas fire puttered in the ornate tiled fireplace. And for some reason, I never smelt curry in that room: more a clean smell of soap.

I put Shulie down on a rag rug made of dyed nylon stockings. Jenny had made it.

"Kettle's on. Would you make the tea, please."

Jen made crochet work as a side line. She had a steady trade for a boutique in Drymen. She was finishing an intricate flowers and leaves centrepiece.

I was glad I had met Jenny in this big world.

She was a sturdy soul: nothing willowy about her frame. She was of the same stock as the girls that had sailed from the crofts to Canada and hacked a living out of the permafrost and the lonesome pines alongside their men folk.

Nothing willowy about her mind either. She wore her black hair in a braided bun that acted as ballast for a level commonsense.

I went to the cooker. It was hidden under a hinged box. I made the tea and left it to infuse. Then I went back to the rug and lay on my back. Shulie climbed aboard my stomach and began to row the Atlantic, using my arms as oars. It was an old routine: very health-giving to the abdominal muscles.

"How's my girl? How's my Shulie?"

She explained in detailed gibberish how her world was. I nodded. I was in there with her. We rowed into the setting sun in happy accord.

Jenny said:

125

"This was one of your long stints, Neil?"

"Yup! Got to pay the bills. But, oh, I'm getting too old for this two jobs caper."

That was true. Of late I had developed an ageing of the bones: and the mind was feeling a bit elderly too.

"Come across anything interesting?"

"Yes. There's always something."

I rambled through the night's E.T.S. work. Then I gave her a real surprise. I wound up with my climax.

"—and listen! Guess who got in on the big time. Your modest neighbour. Guess whose apron front I got to open up."

Jenny finished a flower and bit off the thread:

"Tell me."

She wrapped her work in a clean linen towel. She got up and made cup and saucer sounds as I retold the saga of Mummy, the house in the 'Shields, and all that money.

"Milk?"

"If you had a lemon I could drink a quart of tea."

"I've got some lemon essence."

"A bottled brainwave!"

She turned to her pouring.

I unshipped my oarsman and set her on a

buoy in mid-ocean. To keep away the sea-sick man I gave her some of that white coloured chocolate I happened to have in my robe pocket.

When I came to the Taggart bit, the part where I found out who she was, Jenny's reaction was all I could have wanted.

We did the vaudeville crosstalk bit.

"Taggart?"

"Uh-huh." I buffed my nails modestly on my hairy chest.

"Lord Taggart?"

"The very same."

"The big boat noise?"

"As ever."

"One of his daughters?"

"So I'm told."

"Well!!!"

Jenny was impressed. That in turn impressed me. Jenny had had life impressed all over her, very hard, in her time. It took a lot to impress her.

She said it again:

"Well!"

I felt like somebody's c'ever ickle boy-boy.

I was called to the sea once more. Jen digested her biscuits and my news. My scuppers were awash with regurgitated tea as

127

we sculled away over the knotted nylon rug.

"What'll that do for you?"

We ground to a halt over the Newfoundland banks. Shulie looked for monsters.

"You know, you're the second person who's said that to me. I can't think what it's supposed to do for me at all. I mean, she lives or dies. I think she'll probably live. Bully for her. What's that worth? A bottle of Scotch? All right, her old daddy's a lord. So a case of Scotch! So what? Lords were all very well in their day—but they're out of fashion now. And patronage in the Health Service? That went out long ago. Money helps. With it you can cushion the whole affair. If I was a lord's son, I would have green parkland where I could pop off at partridges, and have a guy buttle me brandy to order. But my daddy's noble aspirations were limited to a trip on the *Lord of the Isles* when he was six. No. I can't see that helping me."

"It can't do you any harm."

"So? So? I can't see it doing me any good. No. I'm taking myself off in a few months to do me my own good, remember?"

"Still definite?"

"After all I've told you in the past year! What do you think?"

At fifty, Jenny was a mixture of persuasions common enough hereabouts: nationalism, socialism, and Protestantism.

But she was not one of your nutty Nats. She was more a couthy Celt: happy where she was. A week spent south of Carlisle brought on a paralysing homesickness.

Then she had been a rebel like many of my family. My memories of the remains of this town dated from the forties: but she remembered bed-bugs for pets, fever vans for thrills and vicarious death, and groups of fathers, brothers and boy friends holding up the corners of buildings all day long. I wonder why they never had a Che Guevara in Garngad.

But when the war came she got married. The fires of rebellion were used to heat other passions. Now she was dismayed and disillusioned by what had happened to the old Scots values in her life. Was this the promise of socialism?

Most important, she had been brought up a Protestant. Rectitude and propriety; punishment and righteous anger had been the daily meat and drink of her soul.

But it had all gone for nothing. No-one got

punished for anything now. Anybody could shit on your doorstep.

Weighted down with all of her pastness she weighed in at me with her old colours amast:

"You don't think you could do more good where you are?"

I cocked my head at her.

"Good for who—whom?" I never could get that case business right. "Me? Or the peasants? My country is going to be the one that can afford me."

"That's not an argument for someone with your education and calling. It sounds so selfish."

"Jenny! I've tried it as it is. I've known nothing else. All I've ended up is pockets to the breeze."

I dropped my voice a bit: tried to persuade her again.

"Look! If I was the star striker of the Shettleston Sure Shots, with fifteen hat-tricks for the season, you wouldn't expect me to hang around when the talent scouts signed me on for the big time. That would be my passport to Atletico Milano for a transfer fee of two hundred G's and my best boots stuffed with lira every time I scored a goal. Who

130

would say I was wrong? Not the citizens of this burg for sure."

I tied up at the Statue of Liberty. "It's not just the money, Jen, although that for me has been a disaster scene, what with Jock and all—"

She looked at me with an intent face. The depth of her understanding about Jock was clear enough. She was on my side for that bit of it.

"—the difference that attitude makes over there is almost too difficult to believe. Their docs are bred to be winners. Oh, sure! They win out in the spondulicks, all right—and I intend to be there when they pay out. But the patient wins out in the end: and I mean *all* patients in the long run."

She looked at me in disbelief.

"It's true. Over there, all of the guys try that much harder, because there's so much to go for. Here, they're losers from the word go. Gloom and depression three times a day after meals and remember to shake the bottle."

Jenny didn't thaw:

"That's been quite a speech. Why don't you *do* something about it?"

We had been over that before. I shrugged

the shoulders of the it-can't-be-me-I'm-too-busy brigade:

"I'm doing something now."

"You're quitting!"

"A good soldier learns to run and fight better another day."

It sounded lame, even to me.

Jen's non-smile became nonner. The wind went all Bleak House-wise. I cut the cold draught short:

"I have to go and give Jock his tea."

"How is he?"

That made us friends again.

I had Jock. Jenny had her loneliness. Everybody had something. Still, Jen and I didn't cry on each other's shoulders. We just got on with it.

"Not good, Jen. Not good. Hey, Shulie! I'm off now. Give me a kiss!"

She scrambled on my knee and gave me wet kisses and white chocolate goo all over my face. She wrapped her arms around my neck and squeezed. I groaned at her great strength. She squealed and squeezed with her pudgy arms all elbow dimples.

I bought my ransom from her with a tube of Smarties I happened to have in my other pocket.

"You spoil her, Neil, but you are good to her."

"God!" I was shocked. "You don't think I try to be kind to her, Jenny? This is a *friend* of mine." I wobbled my cheeks at her. "Don't say things like that."

She walked to the door with me. I held out a hand for one of hers. She gave me both of them.

"Seeing your sister tonight?"

Her sister's second marriage had not been all that big an improvement on the first. Her new man ran second baton in the Royston Road wine circuit. Jen went to help repel boozers on a Saturday night.

"Mm. As usual."

"Will you win?"

"Oh! We'll try hard."

By God, but I would put my money on that girl.

"Good luck! Now I'm off to see Jock."

I kissed the backs of her hands with respect. She kissed my cheek in return. For a moment I wished that some girl would come around: a girl in Jenny's mould. Then I might be tempted to try putting my feet in the water of love.

Not the whole corpus, you understand:

nothing that would involve the liver or bowels: just a little bit at the edge.

Startled by the whole idea, I beat it before the notion took any further substance.

I went back to my room, gave myself a buzz with a battery shaver I had got cheap from the Japanese, and put on my trendy gear: the leather jacket with the Redskin fringes.

Pity the car didn't match that image.

I vroomed westwards in a shower of soot. The remains of the old city lay behind me. The future of it lay in front of me: a peripheral housing scheme the size of Perth and as desolate as the satellites of Saturn. You went in one road, and you came back out by the same one. Very clever for the no through traffic but very trapping for the soul. And in those boundaried square miles of corporation convenience there were bedrooms to spare and baths that you couldn't put in front of the fire.

What there was not was a park, a pub, a picture house, a pool room, nor a Punch and Judy show to enliven the whole of that twenty-first-century project. Such esoterics as flowers, trees, butterflies and dicky-birds were also in short supply: and not just because it was winter.

But fine I knew from my nightly forays on behalf of Benny McIndoe's percentage that similar sized native quarters all bright, shiny new and suitable for the punters lay North, South and East of me—all in real life grim: and some of them grimmer than that.

Ever been in Darnley? Don't bother.

And the best of it was, they had built these things in triple reinforced concrete: last for a thousand years they would.

It was the more difficult to bear when an hour in any direction would get you the finest scenery in the world: East Neuk golf courses, Ayrshire farms running to the Atlantic, trout burns in border hill folds, and the great Highland bens staging Northwards to the clan lands.

But no! We had to live in this.

I drew up in the front of the house and behind a Mercedes the size of a charabanc. It said GG1 on the numberplate. No. Not a civic dignitary: not yet anyhow. It was the logo of an old pal of mine: Glassy Gallagher the Catholic.

Our mutual respect had been forged before the priests and the lodge masters had got at

135

us. Time was our families had lived across the landing from each other in a real close and shared the same mid-stair closet that our mothers had kept in a state of scoured sterility. We had tram rattlers for lullabyes and shipyard arcs for night lights.

In our day Glassy and I had taken lumps out of each other. Then, together, we had taken on the world. We had ruled every wash-house roof for a square mile around. We extracted blackmail sweeties from the soft marks. We held the Co-op to a yearly ransom of nicked Spanish oranges that must have taken its dividend for a month. We had Kensitas coughs when we were ten, by twelve we had been marked out by the police as troublemakers.

We went to different schools of course, segregated by our elders. That was divisive enough: but more came. Glassy had to quit at fourteen. His pay was needed. Along with the other eight children's. Their old man had to be kept in booze. While me, I had got into this books palaver. I was a queerie up my close I can tell you. I was still at the school when I was seventeen.

Now, by the death of the old buildings and the rota of new houses, the Aitken and

Gallagher oldies had moved within a day of one another to neighbouring houses. It was not that they had ever lived in one another's pockets but it gave comfort to have someone you know nearby. Such luck was entirely coincidental. It was a well-known corporation pastime to move friends and neighbours as far away from one another as computers and ill-will could devise. It made Glassy and me a bit happier to know there was a familiar face nearby and someone for a crack about old times. Most old people in those schemes had to live on canned beans and telly. The spice of talk; the malt vinegar of the real life they had known, had gone forever.

Glassy and I saw each other seldom now, but the old respect still held. He was leaving his folk's house as I arrived. We met on the pavement and shook squeeze-grip hands, wee boy style. It was still a draw.

"Gilbert! Howsa boy?"

I called him by his Sunday name, then. The Glassy incident was old news.

His old man had taken the buckle end of his belt to his wife one night. The back swing had flyped the lens from Glassy's eye. The juices had spilled on the floor. He had viewed the world with a china-brown impassiveness from that eye ever since. But the other one made up for it. It danced and flashed and winked.

"Neillie! How's the sawbones?"

"Ankle-deep in blood, Gilbert. What about Mary? And all those wee Fenians?"

Gilbert had married a compliant girl. They had four boys. He had become a model for a husband and father if I ever needed one. Past times I had not; but that night, standing in the cold, nattering about his family, and with Jenny's touch still on my face, I let myself wonder again if there might be something in this love and marriage affair.

We both shivered.

"Better get on into the house," said Gilbert:

"So I will."

"Neil, will you tell your mother and father that my folks are moving soon. It's just newly fixed up and I'd like them to know from one of us: not second hand. I've got them a bungalow in Lenzie!"

Lenzie was a pretty town in the foothills to the Highlands: very residential. I was glad for them. Glassy's mother had had a hard time with his old man; although a stroke had put him off his stroke, and belts had gone out of fashion those days. It was like Glassy's straight ways to want to let us know himself.

Glassy had started his career by knocking spare wheels. He had extended his field to bumpers, and bits of engines: and on a couple of occasions, whole cars. He then surprised everyone, himself most of all, by finding himself legitimate. People began to ask him if he could get this or that. He went to the scrap auto people and scrounged. He got known in the trade. A year or so before his name had appeared on one of those show rooms off the boulevard. He had an Oriental type franchise: velly good value: velly good money made in rubbery paper just like real pound notes. Glassy didn't put it on though: at least not with me.

"I'm real glad about that, Gilbert. I'll go and say hello before I leave tonight."

"They'll be glad if you do that. They're lonely out here."

Lonely among thirty thousand bodies: can you imagine?

"How is the sergeant?" he went on. "Still the brightest buttons on parade?"

"Aye, Gilbert. Still ramrod straight—but what an effort. I wish the poor bugger was out of it."

For all his early mayhem Gilbert was a good Catholic now.

"You shouldn't say that, Neil."

But he punched my bulge to show he was still on my side. We went our ways.

I went up the wooden ramp they had built for Jock's wheelchair and let myself in with a latch key which I had in my pocket.

Time was, when I was six, I wore a droplock key on a string around my neck. After school I would climb the close stair and let myself in.

"How's the wee sodger?"

I had to be inspected back and front and made to salute:

"Will I make the tea, sir?"

"Carry on that man."

Big Maisie would be in later with her string bag full of dividends and her idea of what was nourishing. But Jock loved a cup of tea.

I would nod my head at him. Glee sparked between us. Happiness was easy with him.

He had a broad face, with eyes the colour of a faded Rangers jersey and a Clark Gable moustache. A grin habited his facial muscles, ready to crease into action at the least excuse.

When I was about fourteen and interested in how you proved manhood, I had wondered if its ready appearance might be a sign of fecklessness or of weakness. I had come to realize it was an earnest of his ability to endure.

After the tea I would fuel up for the night: a pail of coal for the evening blaze and a shovel of dross for the blacking. Last, I would set the table.

Then I would climb in beside him and curl up in his arm for stories of derring-do about the sodgers until Maisie arrived.

But that was past. It had been a long time since he cuddled me.

I did not visit him as often as I should have. Partly that was because Jock could look after a lot of things himself—the lights, the telly, the fire—from a panel of switches by his bed. Partly that was because I couldn't stand it any more.

But that night was a must: Maisie's night out. She couldn't be allowed to miss that.

I opened the door to find her in the hall. She was giving a final twitch and pull at her dress and finery. She was in full racing colours and ready for the off. Her coat and boots were ready to don.

Her slate-blue eyes looked at me with their usual off-puttance.

"Aye. Is the bus there, then?"

"Hello, Maw."

I hadn't been allowed to kiss that face for years: and as for being held close to that fierce-prowed breast, I would have got more comfort from the paps of Jura.

I understood. Maisie had retreated into an emotion-proof dugout in life. Not so much to keep it out, though: more to keep her own under control. If it had gone off, ever, the blast would have ripped us all apart.

But we had worked out that it was all right for me to hug her. I hugged her that night.

I waved a bunch of hot-house freesias at her. I had got them on Great Western Road from a late night Paki—yes, another one—cut price, for it was Saturday night and even he couldn't make them last until Monday.

"Put one of these behind your ear."

She squeezed me back, hard as any man.

"You shouldn't have. They're that dear!"

Then she stepped to the mirror and matched a flower to her hair. For a moment I held my breath. God Almighty! What had I done? But no! Not that night: but I wouldn't say that again.

"He'll be that pleased to see you. He's been waiting."

Ah! But was *she* glad?

I liked to think so: but she never said. I was never a dear nor a pet. Sometimes I might be son: but it was more a nickname than any bond of blood or emotion.

"I've got all the fixings here."

I nodded at the paper bags I had brought.

"I've got a nice supper for him. I'll give him his meal and stay a while."

"That's fine. See if the bus hasn't come yet?"

I opened the door and looked out. There was no sign of it.

"Excited?"

She flashed a look right at my eyes.

"Oh, aye. I always enjoy my nights out."

Was there a touch of irony? Or of scorn?

That wouldn't have been like her. As I said, she kept all of her emotional aces close to the chest, did Maisie. One busted flush in hearts was enough for her lifetime.

"Give me up my coat, eh?"

But the final lilt of that rhetorical question answered my own mental query. It was all right. We were chaffing.

As I helped her into her brown simulated fur coat, Big Maisie came over strong.

She didn't stand out in the crowd did Maisie: she jutted above the stream of life like some figurehead painted to frighten the sharks. You had better slide round her, or break in spray before her. Any encounter—be it love or anger—and you got a deal of pain for your pains.

She had been born with hair which curled and sprang, carroty and glinting. As she grew older and the colour faded, you might have looked for some middle-aged modesty. You didn't know Maisie. She had it dyed and stained and burnished. The mariners would find their way by that top-knot.

She had been born, too, with a handsome, bony face. Its equine length had once been split by a generous wide mouth grin. But jollying Jock along for twenty-five years had riven hatchet lines into her face on either side of her nose and mouth: and the smile had been turned into a thin-lipped gash.

Maisie had been a vexation all of my life. But no matter that she might embarrass me, every time I set eyes on her, I had, by God, to admire her.

I kneeled and held open the zipped boots

with the shiny uppers and the man-made sheep-style lining. I watched as she pulled on gloves made in pretend pelt to match the coat.

I thought of the night outside. She wouldn't be too warm in all that plastic, I thought.

"Never mind, Maisie. I'll buy you Bo-Peep's flock and a Siberian bear all to yourself. See if I don't."

She gave me a mocking look:

"What are you going on about?"

I sometimes do that sort of non-sequitur: voice a sequence to a train of thought. It can be worrisome if you don't know me, I'm told.

"Never you mind. Listen! I think I hear the bus."

"Can you see it?"

I opened the door and looked out again.

"Yes. It's just arrived."

"Good."

She banged on the door that led to the living room:

"I'm away then."

I heard Jock's muffled response:

"Aye. Ta-ta!"

I said:

"Have a good time."

I reached for another hug: but I felt her muscles tense. We had had enough of that for one night. Instead, she gave me a smile, just the permitted amount, and she was off in a whirl of perfume.

I stayed at the door for a moment. The bus was there, brightly lit, its engine running. There were the shrieks and giggles that liven up parties of women when the men are safely out of the road. She ran towards it. She still had a high-stepping girl's run, the feet throwing up and out.

"Here's Maisie! Big Maisie. C'mon hen! In beside me."

And that was the acme of Maisie's life: her big night out. Clickety click and two rums and cokes at half time.

We said little about these nights out, did Jock and I. They had never been a subject for discussion. But the air between us was thick as fog with guilt: his because his accident had been such a stupid, needless affair: mine because I could do nothing for her.

Not that she asked for pity. It might have been better if she had. That way I might have been able to help.

Listen! Want a laugh?

She worked in the big bakery out by

Balmore. I met her and some of her pals once. I had been working hard at the books and this summer day I thought: sunshine, fresh air, a walk. There was nothing conscious in my route. I took a bus. I got off. I walked.

Well, there she was, my own mother. They were all out in their white coats and bandannas picking up rare Scots sunbeams when I saw her. She was arm in arm with two or three pals. I went to stop, to say hello: but she gave a tiny shake of her head and passed by.

I asked her about it later.

"Well, since you've gone to the University you sometimes speak different, sometimes use big words. My friends might have been embarrassed."

Maisie's perfume matched her persona.

That night it was Parma Violets.

It kept my scenticles stunned for merciful seconds while I hung up my jacket and furled my shirt sleeves short. But when I hurled open the living room door all camouflage from Maisie's fragrance was gone. The smell of Jock fizzed up my nose like an instant fuse: and that blew twenty-odd years of mind stores all over the inside of my head in a mess of memory.

I stamped into the middle of the room and did my thumbs down the seams of my pants bit:

"Evenin', Sarn't."

"Evenin', Corpril."

We had been a military household for years. When Jock had finally realized that the future had no place for him, he had sent himself call-up papers for the past, and went on to fight life from a bed-fast HQ.

From then on his world had four walls. They were covered with army photographs, souvenirs and cap badges. The wartime paper gave the prints a harsh, grainy quality. You could feel the rough serge: and the weapons had the dull sheen of deadly utility.

One photograph in particular did him proud.

I could just remember Jock on his pins. Mostly, though, I remember him flat on his back or wobbling on his air cushion.

This picture showed him at his upright best. He wore his kilt, the badge of the fighting Scot. It was snug at his hips and neat to his knees. The ankle puttees were rolled inch perfect: the boots polished to a glitter.

148

Even in that faded brown and yellow you could tell that his shoulder sash was of red importance: and the silver knob on his cane head glinted authority.

But above all was his black-cock's feather. It was the regimental mark of the colour sergeant, King's company. It gave him a foot in height and an extra foot in some inner stature. The glengarry tails had been whipped forward by the wind. The full porcelain complement showed in his big grin. There was no doubt about it: he was pleased with himself.

"The Brigadier says to me, he says 'You're the best I've seen. A real cock o' the North!' And he had a set of feathers mounted on a solid silver badge for my very own."

He had made the grade in an elite society of small, hard men. Now the memory sustained him.

In our old home he had sometimes managed to sortie out from that entrenched position in a wheelchair raid on the Teuchter's Arms or the Cunarder: but these forays had needed time and patience and the help of a strong friend or two to carry him up and down the stairs. Of late, those sallies had become rarities. Oh! Maisie and I both tried:

but the grind of looking after him was immense. Not that in itself: but after you had earned a day's hard living and then found your way to the middle of this barracks of a housing scheme, there just weren't enough hours to go round. Then, too, a lot of his old pals had got lost with the tramcars: and social service workers were curiously shy about working after opening hours.

That night, though, I had with me some warlike material that would set him up in a strong defensive position. I took one of the string-handled bags over to his bed for inspection. I tumbled out some cans of McEwans Export, and a bottle of Haig Dimple.

"Ammunition up, Mistah Aitken!"

He looked admiringly:

"Now, Corpril. That'll keep us busy for a bit. Carry on!"

We exchanged a glance that held all of the glee from my childhood days. Big Maisie was away and I could spoil him again.

"What d'you fancy to eat, Sarn't Majah? Got a nice bit of chicken heah. How about that, sah!"

I had had a talk with some of the physicians about his diet: low protein and all that stuff.

But we decided it wasn't worth it. He should have what kept him happy.

I took one of the cans, the Dimple and the other bag, which had the eatables in it, and headed for the kitchen.

I split the gold cap on the bottle of whisky, put about two fingers into one glass for me, then filled it to the brim with water: I had a long night ahead. For him I poured three fingers and a big thumb, and added a pinkie of water: we didn't want to spoil anything. I poured him the can of Export as a beer chaser and carried them in to him. Back in the kitchen, I took a long belt at my own whisky and snuffled the malty brew up my nostrils. I needed that. Jock's smell, you see, it got worse every time: but a sniff of John B. Arleycorn always helped.

I cooked his meal on a black iron pan that had come from my Granny Aitken's. I walked back and forwards to the door and we talked about that awful problem of all men who belong to Glasgow: Partick Thistle: the enigma of football: the Society Jokers. Beat Rangers out of the park one week and lose to a team of wee boys from Ecclefechan the next.

I could mind the early days like this: when

151

I got back from school. You could imagine there was not too much amiss.

The fair hair was still wiry and crinkled then. The grin easy and good-natured. The face moved all the time with life and with effort. It creased without cease. Puckers of glee, wrinkles of amazement, grimaces of concern followed each other fast in a ham's display of emotion: but you could never doubt his sincerity. He suffered and laughed with you. He could get angry: but he loved for you and with you.

In those days his shoulders and upper arms had bulged and ballooned. His soldier's muscles were still able to heave his frame about on the chain that dangled from the steel gantry over the bed. The blue and red tattoos wriggled and rippled. Scotland was the brave, his regiment was faithful, and Maisie was his true love.

The whole picture told of a love for life, forever coiling and rewinding.

There was vitality in that frame to last forever. Just a little something would put it right, surely?

A magic spell? Spit three times on a black slug and call it granny. A Sunday School prayer? Or could it be a special doctor? But it seemed that doctors were all bums—with me the biggest one of all.

How things had changed. The voice for one: it had a husky, feeble quality. Then his hair had thinned: and the disuse of those thirty years had reduced his chest and arm muscles to string under a doughy fat. It was a struggle for him to pull himself up: and when he grinned, it was a rictus of real effort, the easy good humour paid away in an overdraft of living beyond his use.

He wasn't through yet, but the moths had got at him bad.

Although it had not been a great season for miracles, whisky was better than nothing. By the time I got the chicken fixed, we were both feeling better.

Maisie was good to him, but she was never what you would call a cook book. Jock got his calories all right: but it was as likely to be pies from the baker's or delicious dishes just like mother made straight out of the deep freeze store.

In self-defence I had advanced from tea. By then I was a dab hand at catering. I set a tray: tried to tempt him.

I had put the bunch of freesias in a vase:

but I broke off one flower head and put it in a glass of water beside his cup.

I put the tray on his bed table. "Corpril! You'd make a fine messing sergeant." The whisky had sharpened his appetite and turned his cheeks pink. He made a great show at working with the food.

I sat myself in an easy chair. Now and then I sipped my drink. And we had the soldier talk all over again.

We had had it a dozen, a hundred, a thousand times: but he honest to God seemed to have no idea that he had ever told it before. It was all he wanted to do: or had done for all of these years.

I replenished his Export and added more whisky to his glass.

Some of the old easy confidence of his grin came back as he talked. That must have been how he looked when he controlled men on a parade ground: never taking himself too seriously: the assumed ferocity ready to be bought off with a laugh.

It must have been his attitude in the fighting:

"—but I'll tell you, Corpril, I was never so feart in my life. There we were on a dirt road outside Dunkirk. I was in the Bren platoon.

154

We set the gun up in a ditch. Some Jerries came along the hedge opposite. They didn't know we were enfilading them. We caught them right. Gees! They wondered what had hit them!"

He had killed them, the enemy: but he hadn't been able to hate them.

He sat back and pushed his tray away.

"I fair enjoyed that, Corpril. But you made too much."

He gave me a quick look to see if I would comment. I did, too:

"You did fine," I said. "You'll get fat as a pig if you go on eating like that."

He seemed relieved.

Remember I told you about hope? If it was all I could do for those others, it was the least I could do for my own old man.

I lied cheerfully and comprehensively, for he had eaten the merest pick.

He had more whisky and we had more about parades and guns.

About half past nine he began to tell me about the action in which he got his blighty one: this hellish hurt he had. Then I knew he was stiff enough to get the night's shame over: that same private shame he had had for all those years.

It was the only time he depended on make-believe: and he had to be drunk.

It involved a tracked vehicle and the honour of his uniform. But the final and awful indignity was this: the tracked vehicle was a red bicycle, and the uniform that of His Majesty's Mail. The action had involved cycling home after a few drinks to celebrate the day's deliveries. He fell off at the close mouth and transected his cord at the level of the fourth thoracic vertebra. He lay and roared like the Bull of Bashan because he couldn't make his legs work.

That had been the beginning of Jock's second military career.

When he started on this maudlin make-believe I knew it was time to clear away. I washed up, then dried my hands: but I left my sleeves rolled up.

I got out the big, plastic basin and put a bath towel to warm at the fire.

"What about Jock the cock, then? Will we get him out for his airing?"

"Aye! Aye! Let's get the poor wee man out. Let's get it over."

I pulled the bedclothes clear of the bed. Then I bent towards him:

"Hup!" I bellowed in soldier command.

He held tight. I eased up his bottom and slid the towel under. The kilt-proud thighs of the photographs were stick-like now. The kilt-swinging hips were helpless. Jock the cock was reamed by a rubber catheter which led to a bottle slung from his bed-frame. I undid the connector.

The hircine reek was almost visible, so thickly did it clog the air.

You see, Jock the cock had got infected. Despite toiletry and anointings, despite powdering and barbering, and antisepticing, and antibioticing, he was in a bad way. He was a scalded, lobster-red. The foreskin was puffy, and there was a drool of pus at his pipe. The bladder and kidneys had become sumps of sepsis. Bacteria had smashed his kidney filters and his system was filled with his own waste.

That was why he couldn't eat. That was why he was so weak. That was why my soldier daddy was dying.

I bathed and washed him yet another time. I rolled him over and slapped Eau de Cologne about the saucer-sized sores on the cheeks of his bum. He should have shouted in pain at the sting: but Jock lay in passive mastery of

157

his pain. He felt nothing from the waist: had not done so since his fall.

It was something.

Jock had been in and out of hospital many times. Each time helped for a while. But the last time, two years before, he had made us promise he wouldn't go back again: ever.

Maisie and I had promised. The least we could do was let him die in his own home if he wanted. But the way of his death was so minutely slow.

I greased his sores and gummed him up in his tube and fastened him into a clean bottle.

I slipped on a clean pyjama top and gave him a comb and mirror.

Then we had the final inspection.

I leant over him again and we clasped one another. We held our close embrace as I heaved him upright. That way I could blink my eyes over his shoulder: and he could say:

"Hold me! Hold me!" with never a word passing his lips.

"C'mon now! Get ready for inspection!"

"That's it, Corpril!"

"Stop wavin' abaht like a ship in a bloody gale. Hold still! 'Few don't hold still, I'll have you scrubbin' out latrines for the rest of this bloody waah!"

He winked and shook his head:

"That's it! That's good! By gees, I'd have made a sodger out of ye!"

"Don't talk on p'rade! Keep ya bloody mouth shut!"

I glared at him.

He held on to his steel chain. He stayed straight and upright. I inspected the rest: heels and elbows for blisters: toenails.

Then I remade the bed, hiding that outrage to his parenthood, his soldierhood, his once upon a time manstandhood.

"Haw, Christ, Corpril! What an end for that fella."

He was right. He should have fathered so many more than me: so much better: so much more in his own mould.

But that was all he said. He didn't complain. It wasn't in his great good nature.

But other poisons were getting through to him, beside the biological toxins. Though they were bad enough, they were not the final stopper.

Deep inside him, Jock had fetched up short. He was faced with his own mortality: and that fading into death by the day.

The photographs were still there: but the long exposure to light had made some of them the merest blur. The silver cap badge was tarnished black. The black-cock's feather was drooped and dusty.

Outside and in, Johnnie Aitken was all coming to an end.

"Hey-up!"

I snapped him a salute. He returned it.

"Want the telly?"

He shook his head.

"No. I feel good, lad. Fine to see you again."

"Another dram?"

"Well—maybe."

I poured him a last drink.

He looked at me in admiration:

"That's what sodgers like!"

Then I left.

There was an ache at the back of my eyes. And see all of that jazz about Jenny and the kiss on the cheek? You could forget it: and so could the whole human race.

I should have learned from my own experience by now. I should have learned from Maisie.

For the one millionth time in my life I vowed: never. I'll love no-one again: not any time: not ever.

I simply couldn't stand the racket.

3

NEXT morning I decided to walk to the hospital. I washed and shaved and put on the suit from the old habit of the Sabbath.

I looked at the bits of me I could see in the mirror: but there was no difference. Funny how you think there might be one day: Sir Galahad or even Rob Roy McGregor.

I let myself out and cantered down the stairs to have a breath of Presbyterian Sunday. There was no mistaking the spare, grave quiet of the city streets. I treated myself to a few seconds' nostalgia at the close mouth. That morning, however, there was a tremor in my peripheral vision to disturb my memories of peace.

In the disused basement of a building opposite, a bunch of junior mayhem merchants had set up stall. They had been there all night. The pavement was an environmentalist's nightmare: lager cans, boxes half-full of cold rice, the debris of a dutyless world, in broadcast contempt.

Their lookout got his eye on me. He gave the clan sign. The others came to inspect a possible prey.

The boys had short hair that put the Barlinnie barber to shame. The girls were made up like Coppelia's doll. They all had black, vacant eyes. You could see right into where the soul should be.

Not one of them was more than fifteen.

They worried me even in the calm light of the Lord's day.

I met their silent, indifferent hostility with an eyes down that ceded all territorial rights to them.

As I walked away I mused on this unexpected product of our welfare society.

I had known wee tough boys by the score when I went to Faifley primary school: some had grown into hard men of ivory quality, both about the carpals and cranium. But there was always some reason, some emotion—be it as dim as a candle up the Cloch lighthouse—behind their fury.

But this lot seemed to need no rhyme nor reason for their hate: no aim in their appetite for hurt, except to inflict it.

Overnight the wind had got up. By then it was blowing in a steady stream. It soon drove all thought of the weirdo waifs from my mind.

The constant needling of that Arctic draught brought on a neuralgic ache over my eye. I was glad to get indoors into my kind of heat and smells again. Hospital life breeds soft docs.

I was on the floor first. That wasn't surprising. The lads had become very unenthusiastic about Sunday mornings by that time: nobody bothered to say thanks any more. That sort of thing has a dripping water effect on keenness: it wears away slowly, but oh so surely. A lot of white coats would be left on the hook that morning.

I went to Charles's room and put on the one-bar fire the hospital allowed. A staff nurse had seen me come in. She poked her head round the door:

"Tea?"

The word had a cheering ring to it.

I put some coins in the box and nodded.

"Could you find me some codeine tablets as well?"

Her grin told of a conspiracy between us.

"How many?"

"About twelve!"

"Ah-huh!"

She winked to show she knew all about these hangovers. I wished that I had had such a reason.

I knelt down and warmed my hands at the fire. Then I held my palms to my face. That brought some ease to the neuralgia.

The tea came and I set out three cups and saucers. Six codeine tablets were in a little plastic dispensing box. I poured some tea for myself, added powdered milk, then drank some of the hot liquid, using it to wash down two of the tablets. I folded the rest in a hanky for later.

Charles and Herbie arrived one after the other. They said "Hoo!" and "Haa!" in satisfaction as the steam rose to thaw out their cheeks: and the hot, thick cups, held two-fisted, took the white from their cold nipped fingers. The drug and more hot tea soon made amends. I felt better.

We chatted about this patient and that operation: but the main issue of interest was still Mummy. Charles said:

"I looked in on Mrs. Ross for a moment last night. She was still very sleepy—but improving by the hour. I told the family to go home. I said we would talk to them this morning. Let's go and see how she is."

We went along to the Intensive Care Unit. When we turned the corner we came on the hard wooden benches that sat outside the main entrance. Three people sat waiting.

The Pixie Sixer was there: pink-scrubbed, simply dressed, and fresh as April shoots. The sight of her sublimated the codeine in my system to a happier grade of opiate altogether. I felt even better: and the migraine sparklers went from inside my head into the smile I had for her.

Uncle Robert was there, too, his glasses awry as before. He got to his feet with a welcome of real pleasure and warmth.

"Charles! Mister Aitken! Good to see you both this morning. You did say we might come along to get your news in person."

I had another hard look at Uncle Sir R. I guessed that not too many Uncle Sir Anybodys would have kept his backside to that kind of hard vigil. I doffed my mental glengarry to him.

While I was lifting the headgear in his direction, though, and while listening to the old pals greetings between Charles and him, I was taking the third figure aboard my conscious mind with some effort.

Uncle Sir R went on:

"As you can see, we've found Murdie."

He nodded at the other figure on the bench, who this time managed to get to his feet. It was his third try. It was quite a performance.

He held himself erect by some memory of how he ought to feel in an upright position. Any present notion as to where his various members were in relation to space was fortuitous. His head stayed on his shoulders purely from force of habit.

Now I have had lots of experience, both personal and vicarious, in the by-ways of strong drink. But at that, I had never, ever seen a guy so stoned.

I guessed he must have been at it for weeks. As it turned out it had been a two-month binge.

He had been crying as he sat. He made no attempt to wipe away his tears. That was just as well, for he needed all his hands to keep him upright.

He blubbed and sobbed. He made no attempt to control himself.

"Daddy! Do stop! Please don't go on so! Here's Uncle Charles. And the doctor who did the operation. They'll tell you. The danger is all over now."

She turned to us:

"Isn't it?"

Then in an exasperated voice:

"He's always like this if there's illness or an operation. He goes to pieces. Imagines the worst."

The girl was matter of fact about the whole affair. Her voice had a bored, admonitory tone about it: the phrases simple and emphatic. She had been through this sort of thing with Daddy many times.

At that he exploded in a splutter of spittle as he tried for the complicated control that makes for speech.

"Heaow'ss she?"

He got the words out with a sort of mangling effort: like chewing linoleum with false teeth that didn't fit too well.

Well, well, I thought. So this was the Pixie Sixer's papa! No wonder she hadn't known where to turn for help.

And, of course, he was Mummy's other half.

Her problems were not entirely medical then. Perhaps a few years of being connubial with this soak was reason enough to try an overdose.

Charles made with some non-abrasive chit

chat while Herbie and I watched in wonder. He was worth remembering.

He was an impressive figure: not over-tall, but with a strong, lion's face looming over a forty-four-inch chest, though that had slipped and folded over a crocodile skin belt in big bulges of flesh.

He had pop eyes. In salute to his weeks on the bottle, these bulged out like button mushrooms. Thin margins of pink on yellow sclera ran round the irises. His skin had a violaceous look as if he had been parboiled. He breathed a mixture of degraded alcohols over us that made tear-gas obsolete. His liver had packed up the unequal task of detoxicating his system weeks ago. He was, in a word, pickled.

Tissue tendrils in their thousands washed about in a blood alcohol that would have powered a motor bike.

Charles ended up:

"Now do sit down, Murdie, like a good chap. We'll be back shortly with the news."

You could tell from his dry tone that Murdie wasn't his good anything. It occurred to me that if Charles had known Uncle Sir R since his schooldays, he would have known Mummy as a kid. And for him to have watched her marriage to this lush might not have been all that pleasing.

Murdie tried speech again. We gathered that he wanted to see his wife.

"They don't like too many people in the intensive care ward, Daddy. You can understand that."

It got through. He nodded twelve times to show himself as well as us, that he understood.

Tears still streamed from his eyes.

Charles and I went into the ward.

Mummy was doing all right: better than expected.

It was now clear that the faded looks had been fine at one time: delicate: to the point of weakness? The outer show of a mind not up to living down to her husband?

I reflected that her daughter was a shade thicker in the bones: a handful bigger at the squeezy bits: a thought tougher in dealing with the truths of life.

The very traits she had inherited from her father made her more able for him.

Charles slipped down his mask: kissed her cheek.

"Charles. It is you. I couldn't believe—. I'm so asham—"

Charles drowned the word before she got it out.

"Soon have you out of this—"

He gestured at the tubes and dials in distaste. Charles's scene was chloroform and carbolic.

"—I thought you should know. We've found Murdie."

Mummy did a clever thing. She asked a question without making a sound or moving a muscle.

"He's not in the best of shape."

She looked past him. I felt I had been caught peeping in the keyhole.

She shook her head. It was the tiniest of movements, but two years of RADA and a crash course at the actors' workshop couldn't have produced the effect of that minuscule gesture.

It told that the peace that had been left with her, the contentment that had been won as an accidental by-product of her overdose, had gone. She was back in the big, real world.

But then she belied her fine looks: showed the toughness that underlay: gave two lady-

170

like fingers to the fate that had nearly unzipped her from life.

She, plain and deliberate, removed Murdie from her mind and from the conversation. He was not going to exist for her until she was in command of herself again.

She turned all of her attention on me:

"Where have I seen you before?"

"This is our Mr. Aitken—"

Should I roll over and get my tummy tickled, I wondered? But I couldn't deny I liked being Charles's our: anybody's our for that matter. It was unusual in my life.

"—He operated on you. You should know he saved your life."

"Ah. Then I want to thank you. Most sincerely. I want you to know that I'm glad, very glad, to find myself alive—today."

There was an inflexion on that last word. A few days before hadn't been so hot.

"But—don't I remember you holding my hand?"

Charles looked startled. I went red. That wasn't my recognized style.

"No. Must have been a dream."

"That must be it. The memory is vague. Funny, though. It was very comforting."

After that she insisted on small talk and

inconsequentialities: no more deep discussions allowed. There had been enough delving into her private world.

On our way out of the unit I saw that Charles still looked troubled. I said:

"The patch on her panniculus is fine. But the one on her psyche is thin. What should we do about it?"

He was vexed for this "girl" he so obviously liked. He was worried because he was only happy with things he could cut and stitch. Psychiatry upset him.

That's a common feeling among surgeons. I shared it. The mind was a whole other thing.

"Would you like me to get Abie Rosengard to see her?"

The Northern General had no formal psychiatric department. Abie was a peripatetic nut-cracker, based on the big bin out near Anniesland. He had a remit to interview all attempted suicides who were brought in. It was standard form that he should be told about all such cases: but because of the way I had handled things he hadn't heard about Mummy yet.

"Hum—" he said undecided.

172

I waited for a moment, but he still didn't reply. I suggested:

"It would mean everything reasonable had been done."

He looked his relief at my rationalisation:

"Yes. Yes, of course. But—ah—you will get him to be—ah—"

Charles had visions of the dragons that might be dredged from his girl's subconscious:

"—gentle. And to keep it quiet."

"Of course. I'll phone him tomorrow. He's off somewhere at a conference this weekend."

We told the assorted relatives our good news: but kept the nut bit to ourselves. The word psychiatry scares the hell out of other people besides surgeons.

Uncle Sir Robert and the Pixie went off for a moment or two to say hello to Mummy, while the rest of us kept Murdie boxed in. Then, the visit over, they went their way to dry out Daddy rubberlegs: and we continued with the ward round.

By the Monday we took the tubes out of Mummy's insides. By the Tuesday we got the drip out of her arm and moved her to one of the side rooms off the female ward. This was the big favour I had promised the night I came across her: the bait I used to get inside her apron front.

Some deal!

It was a cell of surpassing gloom. It looked into a narrow shaft of four walls. This well gave reflected light only from a lining of white, glazed tiles. Direct sunlight never entered the room.

If you went to the window and peered up you could see an edge of sky. If you looked down you could see the litter and debris of a hundred years.

In the days of laudable pus, of wet gangrene, of mutilating surgery, of the aesthetics of pain dimmed only by laudanum, the white reflected light, the white covers, the white enamelled bed-frames all must have given an austere sanctity to the anguish that went on there.

Perhaps that stark orderliness gave a comfort, a paradoxical appearance of holiness to the frightful deeds of the doctors. In such surroundings prayer may have seemed appropriate. You might even have believed it could work. In such a clean, scrubbed sepulchre God could surely be coaxed to mercy.

But by the time Mummy got there it was different. The Health Service had come in one door, and God had gone out the other. I suspect He went with never a backward glance, thankful to be out of that lot.

A coat of pastel paint now covered the walls, with the door and window frames in contrasting colours. You could now die in psychedelic splendour and be borne aloft on a painfree cloud nine, full of ingenious pharmaceuticals.

A piece of modern hospital furniture, only slightly battered, in the corner: a bit of hardboard over the old fireplace and we were in the running for the frontispiece of *Ideal Hospital*: and who needed God anyhow?

But you could tell something had gone. Not that more people died: in fact fewer did. It was just that the place they got better in had this lack: this empty feeling.

By the time Mummy got to it, it had been transformed yet again: courtesy and insistence of Uncle Sir R.

It was subtle though: nothing to hit you in the eye.

I had seen fancier flower arrangements: but I had never seen bigger blooms: an unsuspecting bee would have bust his buzzer with pollen overload. I had seen more fruit in a bowl: but at that time of year peaches came from far away at something like a pound a throw. I had seen a smaller television set: but this one was so advanced that Spock could have used it on the *Enterprise*.

The hair-brushes, mirror and comb that were set out on that chipped chipboard chest were heirlooms in heavy, worked silver. The perfume bottle that stood in back of this was unpretentious: plain even. But that musky scent must have cost a whole colony of civet cats their lights.

Amongst the luxuries that Sir Robert installed was one which had an unexpected result. This was one of those coffee pots which percolates itself and then switches to a keep warm station. It was supposed to be for herself and for the important visitors she would have. But from the hour it arrived, it was kept going by her bedside in a business-like bubble.

It started so simply.

Mummy's room was dusted and mopped by a cleaner called Peggy McDiarmid. Peggy was a rickle of skin without teeth. Her face had a scone-mix colour. It had died the death of a thousand wrinkles. She helped carry the

Northern on a thin, humped back of porous bones you couldn't have given away to the dog-pound.

She always had a spare effort to carry the sorrows of any patient under whose bed she crawled. You didn't prick Peggy to make her bleed, she did it spontaneously for anyone who needed help.

She did all of this with a consistent good nature that even seemed a bit gormless: but in the face of the kind of life she had, it took a courage that shamed me.

For her pains she got to wear second-hand shoes from the Barrows, and one of those pink and white striped wrapovers that the hospital got from the Gulag Archipelago, designed to show her permanent imprisonment in the fifth grade.

Peggy was your complete democrat: but you didn't descend to her, you rose.

I had gone into the side room to check Mummy's case sheet about something. The Pixie, who had set up a home from home there, had the percolator bubbling its caffeine song. Peggy was on her knees beside it, with a rag and polish, when it switched off.

She sat back on her haunches:

"Here! That's a rare wee machine. Does it just work itsel'?"

She champed her gums:

"Here! That's a lubbly smell, so it is. That's bewtiful."

The Pixie turned to her at once:

"Would you like a cup? Do, please, join us."

Well, bully for the kid, I thought.

Peggy considered her and the prospect.

"Oh, here! I'm no' supposed to. The supervisor would chase me. But it does smell awful good."

She looked at me then.

Peggy and me, we knew all about rules. We broke them every day. Rules were fine for the folks who made them. They were the sort who could afford to keep them.

"Are you having one, then?"

"You'n'me both, Peggy. And her. And her. A party!"

The girl clapped her hands for delight. She was always that obvious: gullible almost, despite the would-be sophistication.

"Doctor. Would you please—?"

She gestured at a chair.

I placed it at the bedside for Peggy. Then one for me. Peggy sat all proper. Mummy, too, held erect against the pillows. I sighed inwardly and straightened out my slouch. See posh folks!

The Pixie rushed about with cups. She was the hostess. It was her party.

Mummy started a dialogue with Peggy.

When she expanded to Peggy's edentulous entente that day, I realized that this was a home-spun therapy that would do nothing but good until I got the horse's word from Abie.

Those parties continued from then. The Pixie became the coffee queen of surgical three. When I let it be known that fly cups were on the house for deserving souls—nurses, ward-maids, students—every last bod who might have reason to go into the room slipped in for coffee at any time of the day. It got to look like the late snack bar in George Square.

All of this made Mummy hold court from her bed: made her manufacture small talk with strangers: helped her own determination to get a jump start back into life.

But a sad and unexpected by-play unfolded: played unconsciously by her daughter.

Under the mini-skirt, under the swinging sixties soignance, was a wee girl wanting back into the play room: needing to be reassured that her Mummy was safe. She haunted the side room day and evening: used her *kaffeemädchen* kick to the last bean, just to see and hear and be near her mother.

And she had all day and every day to do it in.

I realized that this was a therapy for her too: for an expensive, pretty, and quite aimless life.

Next day I phoned to leave word for Abie Rosengard. He had been at a nutcracker nosh and rave-up somewhere in the south. But his secretary said:

"Hold on. He's just here."

" 'Lo, Abie. Thought you weren't due back until tomorrow."

"Nor was I. But I had had enough."

"Knew it all, anyhow, eh? That's what I like. Confidence."

Chats with Abie were long affairs. He always knew the latest rows and jealousies in pointilliste detail:

"Listen! Have you heard . . . "

It was going to be a good story. I could tell by his enthusiasm. But I had to stop him.

"Abie! I'd love to. But I haven't time to blether. Not right now. I'm due in the P.M. room five minutes ago."

"Ah! Pity! It's worth the telling."

"I'll bet it is. And I want to hear it."

I did too. I got on a treat with Abie.

"Well, what's your problem?"

"We've got a pill plugger in the ward. At least the side room. Name of Mrs. Ross. She's some kind of an aristocrat. Youngest daughter of Lord Taggart."

Abie sounded surprised.

"In the Northern? Hardly her scene."

I laughed:

"It sure isn't! But there wasn't a lot of option. It's a long story."

"Two good stories going a-begging."

"That's right. But on top of all that she's a family friend of Charles Hamilton. He asked if you could let him have a professional opinion on the pill taking bit, but without making it too—ah—official. For various reasons it's being kept quiet."

He was intrigued. I felt gratified.

"Is she depressed?"

"Well, not so far as I can see. At least not the deep down melancholic miseries. But I get the impression that she is unhappy. And

181

there is an idea among some of the family that she's been quiet lately."

"Anything else?"

"She has been on amitriptyline from her family doc for a while."

"Did she try hard?"

"Yes! It was a good effort. She just got off with it through a funny combination of events."

"What sort of dosage?"

"She swallowed a real tubful of amitriptyline and aspirin: sixty of the one, a hundred of the other."

"Sounds realistic. We're sure she took them?"

Sometimes fruitcakes leave the bottle around for effect. They take some of the tablets, just enough to give them the woozies and frighten the hell out of hubby-hubs. But the rest go down the lav.

"Yup. I know that for a fact too. It's all in the long story."

"Can I talk to her now? Has she recovered enough?"

"Yes. Any time."

"When is she due to be discharged?"

"Not for a few days yet. She has a big wound. I want to make quite sure that it's mended. Charles wondered if you would take it easy on her."

"The people all love me for my gentle ways."

He mocked himself, me and all the world with his gravelly laugh. It went with his marvellous chutzpah. But there was a depth to Abie that transcended brashness.

"I know that, Abie. But she's not your usual sort of cookie."

Abie spent his life holding hands with the hopeless: delving the depths with depressives: sitting by salvaged suicides.

He tried to follow them up at his own unit, but not too many patients from the Northern kept these later appointments. You need a certain background, a basic minimum of means and motivation to be a successful psychiatric patient. And a future to hope for.

As a rule our clients didn't rate too highly on any of these: so Abie usually got to watch them slide back into the mud of whatever psychic slough they had been inhabiting.

He had been well immunized, though. He kept cheerful:

"I shall slide quietly in and have a talk with her sometime today. I'll remember that she's a friend of Charles and that he doesn't want the skeletons rattled unnecessarily. But I'll see if I can get at definite problems."

That was just what the boss wanted.

"Then suppose you come up to my place. Say the back of six. It's a while since we had a meal together. I'll cook us something. We'll have some wine, and discuss this patient. Then you can relay all of it to Charles. How would that do?"

That would do just great. Abie was a gourmet of distinction. He did his very own thing with skillets and skewers.

"I've gone all gastric juicy at the thought. Six o'clock it is. Shall I warn her you're coming?"

Another laugh:

"Let me surprise her. Her defences will be down."

I wasn't so sure about that from what I knew about Mummy, but he was the expert.

I climbed the stairs to Abie's flat later that evening. There the smells and savours of Kosher cooking took over.

I was ravenous. I rang the bell and walked in. That was Abie's long-standing instruction. I took off my coat: hung it up.

"It's me, Abie!"

He was in his kitchen. The wall between

this cookery and the living room had been taken down. There was now a counter top with an inset hob and an extractor canopy above. That way he could stand and cook and talk to his guests. They sat on bar stools on the far side.

"Open that Manzanilla, Neil. Pour us some. On a tray by the window."

I went over to the window. I poured us both a gill or two from Jerez and looked out at the winter night.

Abie lived near the BBC. It was in fact not all that far from Rahmin Passoud's place: but while Rahmin's place had caught bulldozer's blight, this had been refurbished.

Glasgow is one place where smoke abatement paid an early dividend. I hadn't seen a fog—not the choking, sooty kind of my boyhood—for years. Here and there in the city, people had started to clean up those marvellous Victorian stone houses, at least what was left of them. They stood out incongruously in a sort of permanent *déjà vu* effect.

Abie lived in one of these.

He had done a lot to the inside too.

There was no overall style, but he had a flair for what you might call *objets*: jades, glass, bronzes, ceramics from Europe and Asia crammed the room. A scatter of rugs in the deep reds and purples of Turkey matched heavy, damask curtains.

From this warm richness I looked out into Glasgow. I knew what was down there: but I was up here and supping sherry. Haul up the hawser, Hughie! I'm aboard. Everybody should have a gangplank to his own self, and a great bloody cutlass to chop you up for sharkbait if you didn't behave.

I took the drinks over to the bar: put my elbows on it and sniffed slowly. My nostrils widened at the tang of garlic:

"Gees, Abe! Will you marry me?"

He thumped at some steaks, thick as his wrist, on a beech board set into the worktop.

"Listen, I was going to tell you about Ernie McLean—"

He went into a long rigmarole about this McLean character, who sashayed around the Cardiology department and knew all about the funny squiggles on ECG recordings. It seemed his own heart had led him to the wrong bed one night and thereby hung the story.

I leaned my jaw on my hand and indulged Abie's lust for gory detail.

He was a big, fleshy guy, was Abie. What was left of his hair he wore in wispy strands combed frontwards over his pate.

There was a picture of him in his bedroom, taken at his graduation: slim, dark, intense good looks. You might not have known he was Jewish then. All right, *you* would. Me, I have this blind spot.

But there was no doubt about Abie by the time the steaks were spitting that night.

The lids had thickened. The nose had fleshed into the hook that has haunted history. And the eyes had saddened with the archetypal agonies of his race.

He was Kosher now all right.

He was the one guy in the world I had met who truly gave not one damn about what anyone thought.

He got to the end of Ernie McLean's saga in the sack, and laughed, shaking his head at the infinity of human folly.

"Like to pour the wine?"

There was a bottle of claret with the cork drawn. It was soaking up gentle warmth to release the pressed scents of France. I wrapped the shoulders of the bottle in a paper napkin and poured the wine.

The table was already set. Abie brought the

starters. We sat down: sipped and supped. There was "Try this then": and "Have some of that": and "Your glass is empty".

Eventually we got the table pushed back, the coffee on the hob and the brandy between our hands. We got to the business of the evening.

"How did you get on with Mummy?" I asked.

"Who?"

"Mummy. *La dame des Aristos*."

"Mummy? Ah, yes, Mummy. But why Mummy?"

"That's all part of the long story."

"I'm all attention."

So I told him all about it: the Pixie, Johnnie, the funny, rich, neglected house.

The thing Abie did so well, was to listen—ears, eyes, his whole lined, Semitic visage furrowed in on your story. Every few moments he would say:

"Interesting."

"Ah, yes."

"Really!"

And you would wonder what part of your subterranean soul you had revealed to him.

I got to the end of the surgical bit:

"That's my side of it. What about yours?"

"As you said—"

He gave me the big smile again: the one that had taken all that the human race could dish out, and still managed to love it.

"—she's not obviously depressed—very perceptive for a surgeon—but I think we must assume that's at the root of it. What caused it though, I have no idea. You were quite right. I didn't get to first base with her. She's embarrassed about the fuss. Very grateful for it being kept quiet. Even a little irritated by her own incompetence in making a job of it. But the incident is finished. Closed. She doesn't want to think about it."

"Will she try again?"

He drank some brandy: cocked his head at the fire.

"Who knows? But I don't think so."

"Hunch? Or did you find reasons for thinking that? I'd like to reassure Charles if possible."

"Hunch, yes. But there is more. At her time of life women often suffer from loss of identity. They can't have any more babies. The sex drive is going off. Their children don't need them. That sort of thing. Well, I think that she had been suffering from that sort of crisis—"

"Had been?"

"Yes. What she did gave her an awful fright. A sort of self-induced E.C.T. if you like. A whole lot of things fell into perspective. She got a dose of instant insight. And the daughter has been a help."

"The youngster? How?"

"She left home in a teenage tizz about a year ago. Couldn't get on with her old man. His boozing was too much for her. Set up a flat out West—"

I nodded.

"—I met her in the mother's room. Had a chat with her later. She realizes what she did. Moved out and left the mother to take on the husband alone—"

"Have you met him?"

"No. Is he all they say he is?"

"And then some."

"H'm! Anyhow, there are plans afoot to renovate the house and set her up in a sort of penthouse with her own entrance. They were both most enthusiastic about it."

"She's like that."

"—So that between her new insight and having her daughter next door to knock through to, I think the outlook is better than it was. Although—"

He paused and reflected on his talk with the mother:

"—I think something extraordinary sparked her blow-out. But I don't think we shall ever know what."

"So I just tell Charles there's nothing to be done."

He looked startled: then laughed at me.

"Now, that's a typical surgeon's remark. Of course there's always something to be done. But—"

He gave one of those massive Yiddish shrugs that says so much.

"—*I* can't help her. They've got to *want* to see you in my game. You know that, Neil. No. I wasn't her man. Besides she would almost need someone to take her on one to one. I just don't have that kind of time."

Abie was a whole time NHS bod, like me. He had to spread his wares very thin sometimes. Rationing was essential to preserve the inner man.

But I was sorry for Mummy as he wiped her name off his slate.

I used to think that Abie's job was a washout, and there was no doubt you wouldn't have got me to be a nutmeg grater, not for all the gold in Tobermory Bay. But I had learned that Abie had a lot to give. The psychic punch-ups produced by a few centuries of Glasgow miseries were really small beer beside the two thousand years that his forefathers had suffered.

Just to look at the lines of his face was to see a blueprint for surviving any damn thing.

It was a pity that Mummy wouldn't get to use it.

Charles also had his coffee in the side room in the mornings. Good brew in a hospital was not to be missed. I got to tag along with him.

In the two weeks that Mummy was with us, Charles's morning coffee became an occasion. At the end of the ward round he would dismiss his white-coated cohort:

"Time for a break I think, gentlemen . . . "

And the lads would troop off for a cup of instant dissatisfaction. Then:

"But Sister and Mr. Aitken and I will go and see Mrs. Ross."

And off we would stroll to our percolated perfection.

The Pixie was there every morning. Uncle Sir R was also constant. Murdie too was in daily attendance: at first as an embodied ament, his mind lost on some ethereal plane.

But as his skin regained a colour associated with life on this planet: as his eyes sank some way back into his skull: and as his breath became merely fruity with juniper juice when he got down under a bottle a day, the manner of the man came through.

In place of that awful blubbering whine he sported a hearty voice and a deep chesty laugh. He sucked cigarettes into half-inch cylinders of ash at a breath. He made points with his big ham hands. He balled them into fists for punching home ideas. He jabbed the air with a roly-poly, manicured finger. He bellowed in a self-confident certainty that what he said was important and made so much noise about it, some people thought it was. I noticed that he rarely spoke to his wife directly. She was included in the general *bon-garçonnerie*.

But I caught him looking at her once with an uneasy expression. I had a notion that he would have liked rid of the rest of us, that he would have liked to say something private, like a promise or an apology. But he was walled into the persona he had forged for himself and in a few seconds he had tuned his performance back to stage ham.

Apart from those three daily visitors, however, the Family began to arrive in dribs and drabs, along with a few friends who were rotogravure material for the *Scottish Field*.

Right from the beginning I thought of the Family with a capital F: and not just because Grandpa had a purple nightshirt.

The whole Taggart saga was folk-lore to me: to anyone who had been brought up in the basin of the Clyde. The name was the same sort of mind-mark as the Suspension Bridge or Hampden Park.

Lord Taggart of Toward, Scotch Baron, Laird of the Clyde, Steamboat Willie himself was always being quoted as news in the local papers when I was a boy. He would be seen patting a race horse that had just won enough corn to stand off a seven-year Egyptian famine: or beaming at some dearie with a feather in her hat as she broke a bottle over his newest boat: or sitting top-hatted and frock-coated in his Silver Ghost at some *cours d'élégance*.

The press and photo boys gave him the full measure. The telly had run programmes on his gardens, his yards and his industrial museum.

It should be said that the news items—even

the spicy ones—were presented without too much malice. This was because Lord Willie had been for years a genuine and generous philanthrope: although he didn't favour charity charities. He liked to help people who were helping themselves.

Like most other people in this small battered nation of ours, I took a little of his reflected glory on myself.

Apart from the Book of Remembrance at Edinburgh Castle, the Wembley Wizards and the view of the road to London, there didn't seem too much else to get worked up about. It put a bracer up your trews to think there was one Scot whose boats reeked lum for lum with the best of them in any world port.

All that much any home-brewed punter could have told you. But Charles was able to fill me in with some of the background colour to the early days.

"Used to give the most marvellous parties at Toward Craig. That's his place on the hills above Greenock. In the summer they would have weekend parties. Tennis. Or off on picnics and toss for who got the dickie seat with his girl. Dancing at night. Chinese lanterns. Champagne. Charlestons. An army of servants—"

He sounded wistful. I wouldn't have minded a wist or two for memories like that:

"—all different now, though!"

"Down to their last Swiss bank, are they?"

He gave me one of his Olympian looks.

"Oh, no, indeed! Still very wealthy. No! What I meant was that at that time it was all Willie's ball game. He was *big* Willie in his day. It was his pitch, his pavilion, his referee—whistle, pea and all. He *was* the business. Tremendous personality. But now, what with tax and all this socialist buggering about, the company has been hived off into small units and it's all run by the money men. Robert keeps his hands on the reins very successfully, but—well—there's just not the same flair, the same panache as when Willie was at his peak. The old man was a real dynamo in his day."

It was not often that Charles got himself so enthused: I thought that this old boy must be some warrior. I wondered if I would ever meet him. But Nella had told me he had a virus infection, some 'flu-like affair, and at his age of ninety-something, it was thought wiser for him to stay at home until it was over. It seemed likely that Mummy would have left us by then.

During those first coffee mornings, the Family overwhelmed me by its sheer complexity. There were cousins, and stepsibs, and in-laws and out-laws in a family tapestry so thick that I could not make out the genealogy tree though the foliage of relationships.

Charles helped me out:

"The old man married three times, y'see. Buried three wives. All remarkable ladies in their own way. They had to be. He had six children. Two by the first wife. Three by the second. His last marriage was supposed to be one of convenience: comfort for his old age. She was over forty at the time. Well, she turned out to be the great love of his life. After two years she presented him with Helen—that's your patient. Sadly, she died in the giving. Two of the children divorced and remarried. One—Helen again—was widowed and remarried—"

"Was she though?"

I was startled into the rhetorical remark. Mummy had a lot of problems to shoulder on her frame of fine bones. I wondered what else her closet hid.

"—There were grandchildren from every one of those unions. When they all get

197

together—as they do every year for the old man's birthday—it's some mélange I can tell you."

I could imagine. I was having the most awful job of trying to sort them into some kind of order.

He went on:

"Nella—your Pixie—is Helen's youngest child. Murdie's only offspring. And she's her grandpa's darling, I can tell you. The sun rises and sets just to please her."

I began to place the septs of the Family better after that. I noticed that the Quink trade-mark of the eyes stamped some of them. It turned out to be the grandfather's marker: the old Lord's very own Mendelian seal.

It was a striking badge of membership. There were Taggarts, of course, with Colquhouns, Frasers, dun cow Browns, and small d Macdonalds as a result of the second-generation marriages.

"Where is your brother—step-brother?" I asked Nella one day: he had not appeared to visit his mother so far.

"He died some years ago. Went overboard from a sailing boat off Hunter's Quay. Silliest damn thing. I—we—miss him a lot."

The girl flashed a quick, scared look at her

mother. She wanted no repetition of the pill game: nothing to upset her beloved Mummy's recovery. Going to a flat of her own had only ever been a corporeal move. She had missed the comfort that thin breast could bring: would not risk losing it again.

I was shocked at this news. It didn't seem right that someone so well protected against life had had to take so much stick: a solecism on the part of fate.

Once again I wondered what could have sparked off her response of despair after having endured so much. But even Abie Rosengard couldn't solve that one. What was a mere surgeon to do?

I went back to this game of wealthy families with Nella as Miss Lolly the rich man's daughter.

It turned out that the others had spread county-wise into the tweeded domains of Perthshire: or South to the Home Counties, with connections that ensured a smooth flow of position and patronage from one generation to the next. Their visits were one stop affairs. It became clear that the old Lord, Murdie and his wife, and Nella formed the Glasgow holding battalion of the Family because the company was registered there. Otherwise the city was of importance nowadays only to the old boy: the place he had made his money.

Once they got over the surprise that the likes of me had anything to do with their relative, they were all rather jolly.

For fun I let myself sip a little of their rainbow juice. It was heady stuff. A few mouthfuls of that multi-coloured liquor and you would no longer care. There was no war where that lot lived on the far side of the great divide: money. And I would be joining them soon.

I soon realized that the attitudes and mores that had kept me right side up in Ruchazie for thirty-odd years, would get me wrong side up with the trend-setters of Texas. There I would be guilty of inverted snobbery. I would have to learn to deal with them on their own expensive level.

Well, guess who became my tutor in chief in this gentle art?

None other than Charles?

At first I couldn't believe what he was doing.

He breezed into the middle of this high-hat scene like an acrobat taking the spot light. He tramped up the red carpet they rolled out for him as if he was going to perform on the trapeze. His feet danced over the pile.

I felt as if I was up to the knees in the stuff, and very awkward to begin with. But I soon came to see how you could get to like walking on that particular rug.

For all the time I had known Charles and had worked with him, for all his quiet liking for elegance, he had always been a very plain, straight guy in his words and actions.

Now he was putting on an act.

He would sit down opposite Mummy's bed and cross a fine ankle over a knife-edged knee. He would produce his slim, gold cigarette case with a flourish: then offer round, and select from, a full row: then snap a light to it with complete assurance that it would fire first time. Which was all very surprising for Charles had become forgetful in his sixties. He could never remember to get new flints, or a refill of gas: and his usual supply of cigarettes looked like Dopey's tooth.

After this display, he would inhale, lean back, blow smoke in the air, and enjoy his coffee. Meet my friend Charles Coward.

There was a pause each morning as the visitors watched this performance. After it the buzz of conversation went on a full key into the treble. You could tell they were happy.

I recognized what he was at. He was showing the spoor mark of their society. The Family and their friends were satisfied that Mummy had one of her own kind to steer her through this place where all the other sort of people came.

And he reassured them about me.

He insistently introduced me to each new arrival. Every time he left no doubt that I had opened and shut the zip-fastener in Mummy's tummy. I shook hands all around and basked in a sheepish afterglow.

Uncle Sir Robert backed him up. I realized that I was being imprinted as hard as I could be by two senior bucks in the herd. I was being put up for membership.

And because of these old boys I was accepted.

Perhaps there was the odd reservation about my Possilpark *paysanneries*, but I was in: no question. I thought that one of the Family should have had a closer look at the set and length of my bicuspids and run his hand through my curly coat. Despite Charles's training I was an odd, vulpine recruit for that sheep fold.

But it was only a fun game now. I was off to Philadelphia some day soon. They were quite safe.

I hauled down my red flag for good.

Truth to tell, it didn't seem to have done an awful lot of good for me or for the country I was about to leave. But I didn't throw it away in disgust. I folded it and put it in my memory locker. I might want to take it out sometimes to remind me who I had been. I looked around that costly company and mused that it might become difficult to remember through a lot of money.

Well, since I wasn't going to run that pennant on my yard arm any more, I had better learn the signal flags of wealth.

I drank coffee and watched Charles to learn this new code.

During the morning sessions I could contribute little to the conversation. It was full of family jokes and in references from the owners of the casual minks and the inhabitants of the well-preserved tweed suits. So, after my bow to surgical fame had been applauded, I found myself talking to Nella: intimate conversations bound by the shared experience of the night of Mummy's secret. I pulled her leg and made fun of her. Johnnie, it turned out, was a clock-watcher: of an upper echelon to be sure, but he was kept busy in office hours. He never joined these mornings so we had ourselves to each other.

I got a thing going for this straw-haired kid: a true liking. It was your genuine baby sister stuff. There was no blue-flash at my sexual spark-plug, despite all of her anatomy being in the right place and of a proper size and texture.

I didn't think much about this at first: put it down to an ennui, a malaise that had been affecting me for months. This was not a primary botheration of the bollicles: but a secondary result of working too long and too hard with nothing to show for it. It had jaded my action-man to the point of indifference. I began to understand how impotence could happen.

Then it dawned on me there was more to it where she was concerned.

The trouble was that a one-stand roll in the hay wouldn't do with her. It would need a season of haymaking: and maybe take in a spring-sowing as well.

You see I had this funny thing about the

ladies I lay with. I couldn't love them—I was afraid of that—but I had to like them. And I liked this kid far too much. Any relationship with her would have to be deep: far deeper than any I could afford right then.

It was a time for severing roots: for storing the corms of caring: for tying old friendships into bundles, like drying herbs to spice my colonial life.

So I kept it strictly on a chums from St. Catherine's level: teased her about getting sleeve badges for every heart she had broken.

She lapped it up. Glissandos of giggles alternated with moues and pretty pouts. She gave out with bright, teenage chatter: and looked at me curiously.

It wasn't that she didn't know what to make of me. She didn't know what to make of herself: what role she wanted to play.

For the moment she was happy to take my big-brother, little-sister lead until she got her beloved, beleaguered Mummy the hell out of this funny-smelling mausoleum.

I was chaffing away with her one morning when I wondered—just for the hell of it and just suppose I wasn't bound for a commission in Caine's Cutters—how you might turn such a situation to your favour.

I let some idle strands of the supposes warp through the woof of maybes. I let the weaver of commonsense—that rough, unyielding material that had clothed my mind so far—go for a tea break. I let Puck of the Paisley patterns—the rich, coloured stuffs of imagination—take over the shuttles.

Right out of nowhere, he spun a whole new design: unexpected: attractive. On a background of white damask there were silver wedding bells: and alternating rows of £ signs.

A bastard? Me?

I often am: more often than not.

But not that time.

It wasn't deliberate scheming: only a day dream: no worse than winning the pools or the Irish sweep: and as unlikely.

Besides, I knew myself for a marsh-mallow at heart. No-one would ever get me into a marriage bed unless there was at least the illusion of love: even if the thought of that word made my toes curl like I had put my fingers in the toaster.

I looked at her again.

Suppose love grew? I had heard that it happened.

Then I wouldn't need to take a plane for

fame and fortune. It would all come true like the fairies said.

Well, I knew all about fairies.

I pulled my head out of Noddy-land: shook myself free from staring and immobility.

Risk love on a spoiled brat—be she ever a riot? Give up my great American dream? Settle for a subsidized life in the Great Service? Live the rest of my days a handout man in a begging-bowl country?

Come in Eliza Dolittle.

Time I was in America.

I glanced around, feeling guilty.

No alarm bells had rung: no-one had noticed. No-one, that is, but Mummy.

I caught the tail end of a look from her: thoughtful. She flicked her eyes down at once: retreated to the private gardens she so often walked in.

But I was left in no doubt that she knew I had been peeking at the iced cake in the larder.

One night before Mummy went home, she and I and the Pixie took one another by surprise: and at that unwary time I got more involved than I meant.

It was broomstick time. I had been snuffling about this Celtic conurbation all night on an E.T.S. session. The sins of the city had etched my mind like the picture of Dorian McGray. I was tired. I had seen enough of life and human nature to last me through the next three incarnations.

I wanted to tamp down Macadam behind a tarry boiler: plod clod-soled behind a plough: lay brick on brick and bond them with uncomplaining mortar: anything but deal with another bodily ailment wrapped in a story of life and spirit nourished by living in the fine New World, our Harold's white heat of frustration.

The framework of gristle and guts was a wonder of wonders. God must have stayed up half the night inventing it. But He must have got tired towards morning for He sure left some problems around for Adam to solve.

What was wanted was a belt at a square bottle I had in my locker. I knew I had let supplies run out at Passoud's, but I had a spare laid by that would smooth out the wrinkles in my brow and bring comfort to the crenellations inside my cranium.

I had been with George again that night.

Once more he dropped me at the hospital gate.

I ran upstairs to the wards. I went to the nurse at the duty desk. She was knitting a Fair Isle cardigan under the shaded light. The ward had the usual background of snores, moans and grunts: and from the screened patient in the corner, an explosive fart brought a sigh of relief.

"It's only me. I'm going into the staff room. All OK?"

The nurse was from an agency. I had worked with her before. She was a married girl with two children. Her man was a service engineer. She did a regular three nights at weekends. If she did more, she explained, she and her husband only met in the mornings in time to put the kids out. This way, they got to sleep together weeknights.

See moonlighting? It was the national sport. Up every close were moonbeam folk. Sleep got squeezed in among the money-making somehow, somewhere.

"The wean's in here on the couch, doctor. My man's got a job on the side. He's asleep in the bedroom. You know?"

I knew, I knew! Join the flakers' fraternity! Heads down at any time of the day. Everybody needed two jobs to stay alive in this damn country: with the wife out as well.

Beside her was a Mills & Boon romance with a handsome doc on the cover: all clean-cut nobility, starched white coat and stethoscope. I rubbed my hand over my face. The stubble felt grimy, the sweat greasy. I wished I looked like the picture. More, I wished I felt like it.

"D'you suppose he starches his combinations?"

She gave me a smile that made me jealous for a moment. It was for the guy she got to bed with sometimes: and those kids. This seemed my season for the green-eyed bugaboo. Nobody, nowhere, had a smile like that for me.

I went back into the corridor: into the staff room: opened my locker. There, sitting on top of an old copy of Pye's *Surgical Handicraft* was the instrument of the Scotsman's faith: and I was needing a transfusion of spirit very badly indeed. My own had laid down to sleep somewhere a couple of hours before and I hadn't seen it since. I grabbed the bottle like a Covenanter clasps his Bible.

As I came back into the corridor I noticed a line of light under Mummy's door.

I had had enough of the caring scene for one night. All I wanted then was someone to take care of me, as for instance Mr. John Walker, complete with red coat and top hat. But—well—she was a pal of Charles, and I did have this special interest in her.

I rapped a row of finger nails along the door and eased it open. I poked my head around the edge.

"All right?"

I said it quietly. I put a whole sentence into that one word. All she had to do was give me a sleepy nod and I would be off: duty done, conscience clear.

But no such luck.

The green shaded light on her locker threw a bright epicentre on her face and shoulders and reduced the rest of the room to a deep gloom.

She was sitting upright in bed, her shoulders covered by a lace-fine, woollen bed-jacket. One hand was outstretched into the green shadow at the edge of her bed. She was stroking gently at the hair of her daughter. Nella sat on a chair, but had leaned shoulders, arms and head on to the bed in the trusting sleep of a babe.

Mummy and I swapped speculative glances. She said in a murmur:

"I envy her. I haven't slept like that for years."

"Shall I get nurse to bring you a pill?"

"No. I'd rather do without. Thank you all the same—"

A curious bird this Mummy. A week ago she had been scoffing chemical candies like my sweetheart Shulie ate Smarties.

"—last week was exceptional."

"You're quite a battler, aren't you. It's taken a lot of guts and courage to put on the face you have done over the past week. A pity to bury it all in a box before you have to. I'm no expert in how minds are wired up. That's Dr. Rosengard's field. But I reckon it must have taken some overload to make you want to blow your life fuse."

"Yes. It was horrid. But it's over now. And I know it wasn't meant. At the time I was a bit—shocked is the only word."

So there had been something: and something horrid.

"—You've been kind and if I ever told

anyone in the world, I think it would be you. You give me—"

She indicated the girl with a nod:

"—You give both of us—confidence. I think it's your manner. But it's over. I'd like to forget it."

The buzz of our words began to disturb Nella. She stirred and muttered in a coming-to preamble.

We stopped talking: watched the girl surface.

"Oh, hello. It's you."

I'm not being big-headed. There was just no doubt that I was pasted in her scrap book beside John Wayne.

"Time you were in your proper bed."

"What about you? What are you doing here?"

"That's a long story—"

Then to Mummy:

"If you don't want a pill, would you yell and scream if I was to suggest a small snort?"

They both looked startled at that: anxious even. What kind of an eejit had they here?

"Are you serious? Is it allowed?"

"In your case I shall make a personal dispensation. No. Honest! You're all riveted up tight inside where it matters. You know you've been on a normal diet for a day or two now. Besides, I'll make it well watered."

Mummy looked interested then: the Pixie—you've guessed—clapped her hands.

"Is that whisky?"

"Kilmarnock's best. Very soothing for the small hour fidgets."

"Don't think me rude—but—whisky isn't my favourite nightcap. I prefer brandy. And Robert brought me in a bottle for my visitors. Won't you join us?"

"Brandy? Not a stuff I'm all that used to—but I'm willing to learn."

"It's in the cupboard."

I stood Johnnie Walker's face to the wall so he wouldn't be offended. I poked behind the coffee machine and cups. I found the bottle. In fact it was one of those flat, medallion-shaped bottles of Armagnac: Clos des Ducs:

"Good for Uncle Robert."

I frowned at Mummy:

"She doesn't get this, does she? Far too young?"

"Stop it!" with a stamp. Was there behind the laugh a hint of impatience: like would I never take her seriously?

"OK you're in on the booze."

I took out three of the fine coffee cups. I poured them both three fingers.

"Water?"

"Yes."

I added the finest tap water in the world to make fifty-fifty: handed them over.

I made my own fist-sized: and neat. Well, they weren't all that big cups: and, oh Christ, I was tired.

Mummy plumped up her pillows: lay back. The girl kicked off her shoes: sat on the hospital armchair, feet tucked under her bottom: knees chubby and scrubbed through the fashion tights.

I fetched a chair up to the central heating radiator: turned it so I could lay my back and shoulders on the warm surface and ease the neck strings.

We talked.

The talk was inconsequential. It was no more than fluent chatter. But the point was its fluency: as easy—easier—than I had ever talked to anyone except my Granny Aitken.

At first Mummy took my attention: we were still on an open line from our talk before the kid woke up. She was quick and sharp and cultured: and by that last I don't mean precious. She didn't posture: rang true as a bell. There was a sophistication to it all that only personality can bring. Her money had helped to give it gleam and polish: but the grain was bred in the wood.

It all went with lace at the wrists and the throat: the movements, still graceful despite the nodules of rheumatism that ruined her slender hands: the fine structure of her face.

Besides these, Nella was as raw and wholesome as shredded cabbage despite the sex-pot image.

But as we talked I realized that, seen alongside the differences, the similarities were even stronger. The same high cheek-bones giving a stamp of resolution: imperious almost. The same strong, mottled eyes, full of truth: and seeking no less in return.

For a second, hazed by lack of sleep and the effect of the liquor, I imagined a resemblance right out of Spooksville: the more eerie for happening in the big, echoing, green-shaded room.

I rubbed my eyes and it vanished.

But even after it had gone I was left with the notion that once the puppy stage wore off, the girl would fine down like her mother— only stronger: and a lot more fun.

I could feel the Armagnac filtering into my

angst cells. The tautness, produced by a night's hard grafting at the griefs and gruesomes of the city, relaxed its hold on my shoulders, my neck muscles.

I breathed in the pot-pourri of the past week: the prime coffee, the rich scents, the aroma of best cigars: and now this spare, rare spirit.

What a lovely way to die!

But what an even better way to live. You could sure as hell get to like this sort of life if you could find a seat on the gravy-train. The guards van, even a buffer ride, would do.

I almost groaned as my mind-movie sprocketed this unwanted trailer on to the screen again.

Suppose? Suppose? Suppose?

"Suppose no supposes, you silly bastard," I told myself. "Get yourself the hell out of here."

I lurched to my feet.

"I must go. I'm asleep on my feet."

"Oh, of course. Thank you for stopping by. It was kind of you to spare the time. My! You *are* nearly asleep. Hadn't Nella better drop you off?"

It dawned on me with force that she was right. What with the neat spirit and the lack of sleep my gyroscopes were on the wobble. I was rocking on my feet. I looked at the girl:

"You know, that is a sensible idea. Would you?"

"Glad to return the favour."

"I would hate to be stopped right now by the road patrol. I wouldn't turn the balloon green: but I'd have one hell of a job with the chalk line."

Nella got up. She put her coat on: went to her mother for a kiss.

"Thank you again . . ."

I waved Mummy quiet. I could see she was going to go on about being nice and all that rubbish. I cut in:

"That's all right. All part of the service. Good night."

"Good night."

As we went down to the car park I was feeling happier about the mother. It wasn't the emotional breakthrough of the century, but I had managed something. Not bad for a knife and forceps man.

Nella had a white MGB with an off-centre speed-line along the bonnet and over the hard top.

"Very smart!"

"Mm. It's supercharged. Would you like to drive it some time?"

"You betcha!"

She drove like the dame in the *Avengers*: all skirts up her thighs and zoom zoom.

"North End of Winton Drive. Where it meets Maryhill Road. I'll con you from there."

She got past the old Empress theatre all right: but after that was punter-land and not her geography at all. She tried to make it sound as if she just needed a little reminding.

"Next corner? I remember now. It's a while since I've been around here."

But she had never been there before: physically, or in her dreams. What was a couple of miles to a hoody crow, was a space journey as our lives flew.

She stopped opposite Passoud's place.

Written all over her face was curiosity about how I lived: and could she get in on this unusual life, at least for a bit?

But I had been through all that.

I got out. I ducked down to knee height.

"G'night kid. This makes us even. But I want you to know it was a real help. I think I would have fallen asleep at the wheel. Listen—"

I was going to say a piece about her mother, but from behind me a voice said:

"Here! Come and see the magic wee motor. And here! There's a wee bird in it for the big fella."

I sighed. I strained my sacroiliac joints until they squeaked: leaned well into the window: murmured:

"Nella. Listen once. Then do as I tell you. There's half a dozen heroes behind me. No real interest in me. All in you and your car. When I stand up, just go. At once. No panics, but get yourself out of here."

My earnestness got to her:

"And you?"

"My weakness is you being here. Understand?"

"I see. Right."

"Put it in gear. Now!"

I stood up. She left sensibly: quickly, but with no spinning of tyres: no shrieking of rubber.

The bravos reached the kerb too late. The car gone they turned to me. But they knew me: I was poor sport: a feart.

"Is that the wee ride, then? In up to your knees, eh? Christ! You're lucky."

They ranged around me: curious, baiting—

yet indifferent. Gadflies: yet their sting was liable to be Sheffield steel.

I dropped my eyes: ritual surrender. Made my way for the close. A foot in a basketball boot got in my way. I dodged it: avoided all contact, all trouble. I would pledge me no more commitment of *any* kind before I left.

I wasn't worth even a good going jeer. A single cat-call followed me upstairs.

I thought that I must warn Jen and Rahmin's wife about their handbags and their washing: but in the morning the gallant lads had gone and I forgot all about them.

When I got into the musty, curry-and-spice staleness of Passoud's hallway, I was having a future day sensation. It comes on when you have lived too long into the next twenty-four hours to make sleep worthwhile.

I put my friend, with his red top-coat still unbuttoned, on the table. Beside him I found a letter addressed to me. It was stamped with US eagles. I wondered if I would be getting patriotic about those emblems some time soon.

From the postmark I guessed the letter was from Arnie Caine. I was in no state to take in the written word. I decided to have a few hours' sleep, though I knew that the waking up would be hellish. The letter would have to wait until my painful awakening.

In what was left of the night, I had troublesome dreams. I sweated through the oddest scrapes from Montezuma to Tripoli thru Tallahassee, Apache Wells and the Bronx. I woke feeling wretched and depressed.

Even as I lay, sucking the parrot's perch I had for a tongue and squeezing sleep out of my eyes with bunched knuckles, two betterment factors began to operate in my life.

First, Jen came in with a tea-tray. She was ready for work: had on a hat and an unfastened coat.

"I thought maybe you could do with this."

"Jen! What will I do without you when I go?"

"There's an easy answer to that."

She put the tray handy for me, and left. I lay on my side like a frowsty Roman: propped my head on my fist: took a long swallow at that brew for all occasions. I reached for the letter and opened the envelope with the apostle on the end of the teaspoon: shook out a sheaf of papers. I pawed them about and read them piecemeal.

That brought me to the second bright spot of the very young day. It was from Arnie, as I had thought. His letter read:

"Scotty,

It has become clear over the past month or two that the shutters are going to go up on overseas medics some time soon. It is not certain what form this will take, or how drastic the shut-out will be, but there is no doubt that it will not be so easy for someone like yourself to get over here.

The boys and I have had a meeting, however, and we have decided simply to bypass the whole affair by advancing the date on which we would like you to join us, by six months. This gives you a clear three months to tidy up your affairs.

You will find enclosed a suggested document of contract. With it you will find an independent legal assessment, since I don't suppose you will have anyone over there who is up to our local procedures.

Read them and sleep on them. If there are any comments you want to make, or any changes you wish to suggest, let me know. They will be given every consideration.

If there are none, book your flight for early

June. You will be put on basic salary for that month. That will let you get over here, find a place to live and settle in.

You will be scheduled to start work on July 1st at 7.30 a.m.

> Best wishes,
> Arnie."

There was another letter written under the heading of a law firm in the same city.

It verified that the contract was legal and equitable. At the end of the typescript a signature was scrawled over the firm's name. But a PS in the same handwriting had been added. It was laconic.

"Doc,

I play skittles with Arnie Caine once in a while. He is a regular guy. This deal is copper-bottomed. You can put your shirt on it. You had better grab your chance and get on over here. We'll teach you to play skittles as well.

A.S."

The contract was enclosed: a sheaf of flimsies.

Before I left for the hospital I wrote a reply.

I hoped to get to New York by June. I was going to hire a car and take a closer, longer look at his big country. Unless I was completely disenchanted, or burned up in the Mojave desert, he could look for me as planned.

I put all of the documents Arnie had sent into a Manilla folder: I would study them at leisure. Then I put my reply to him in an envelope and stuck the Queen's head in various colours on to it.

Maybe, I wondered, I should sing the National Anthem, and follow it up with a couple of verses of "Scots Wha Hae"?

But, no! My time for all of that was past. I would never again sing the old Scots psalms:

"We wuz robbed!"

or

"We had them beat, but then—"

These tunes were sung forever looking back, the gaze fixed on the might have been.

Me! I was never going to look back again.

I put the envelope in my inside pocket ready for the post.

4

I WAS operating that morning: a straight general theatre. At the break, I excused myself. I changed out of my greens into a white coat.

Herbie grinned at me like two octaves of C major.

"Not staying with the peasants then?"

"When I can hob-nob with the twice-born? Not likely."

Then I told him:

"I'll be back in half an hour, Herbie. You can start the next case."

He nodded and looked pleased.

I wanted to speak to Charles, to get a definite decision about Mummy's discharge. In a funny way, the letter I had written and posted made me want to clear my feet of her problems. I met him in the corridor. He was in a sports jacket and was carrying an overcoat.

"Morning, sir."

"Morning, Neil. Coming for coffee?"

We went towards Mummy's room. I

brought up the question of her discharge.

"You'll need to decide for yourself, Neil. I'm off."

"You're off?"

I said it as in mutton-head, with the mouth slightly agape.

"Yes. For a couple of weeks."

"Where are you going?"

I was still trying to get on to his tram-lines.

"Madeira. My wife had an awful 'flu about Christmas. She's never really got over it. And my own bones are just too old for this damn Scottish winter. I had a whim for some sunshine."

He looked at me with the same expression you get on a plate of custard.

I thought about his remark, and his pudding-faced look. I wondered what the hell this was all about, for Charles was not a whimsical chap. Consideration and forethought were the orders of his day.

"When are you going?"

"Soon as I've had my coffee. I looked in only to sign some letters and to say goodbye to Helen Ross. By the by—"

We had reached the door of her room by then. He put out his hand to the knob: but paused:

"—you will look after her for me, won't you? Do the—uh—proper thing?"

I looked back at him attentively. He was making a strong point gently: but I wasn't sure what it was.

I supposed he was asking me to give her special attention when she came for her out-patient follow-up. I supposed all wrong, but I didn't find that out for a few minutes.

"Of course."

"Thanks, Neil. I take that as a favour."

We went into the room. For once visitors were few: the Pixie, Alistair Taggart, a cousin, and Uncle Sir Robert was all.

Then Charles stabbed me, right in the solar surprise:

"I'm off today, Helen. I'm taking Molly to Madeira. She has been poorly since her 'flu in December."

There were oh's of commiseration: wishes for her recovery. Then he went on:

"Neil—Mr. Aitken—thinks you are about ready to go home. Perhaps tomorrow? But I'm going to leave that in his hands."

"Charles! That will be good. I've arranged with Robert—" she gestured at Uncle Sir R:

"—and Father that I'm going to Toward Craig."

I noticed Murdie wasn't quoted.

"I couldn't think of anywhere better, Helen. An ideal choice. Neil will tell you when—"

Then came his fixeroo:

"—and you won't need to come up to town. Neil has promised to drop down and see you."

Uncle Sir R said:

"That's very good of you, Mr. Aitken. I appreciate that very much."

Mummy and the Pixie also thought this was a good idea.

I suspect that I glared at him: the sly, conniving old bugger.

I owed Charles a favour for teaching me how to charm the rainbow tasters of this world, but this was carrying things a bit far.

Charles stood up to go. I rose with him. I said to Mummy: "I'll check your wound later this morning. If all is well, we'll say home tomorrow."

The blue in her eyes had turned cobalt. The black spots were iridescent. Well! Hospitals are good places to get out of.

"Have a good holiday, Charles. My love to Molly."

He kissed her cheek and left the room. I

went with him. I walked him to the hospital entrance, then out into the yard to his car. He got in and rolled down his window.

"You know, Robert asked me if I would speak to you—"

So there had been an old boy ploy:

"—but I told him there was no way I could *tell* you to do it. I said I would ask. I made it clear that it's unofficial. That you are an S.R. and not entitled to do this. That it would be a favour to me—"

He went on:

"—It's more than just her stitch line. It's all this business of why she took those damn pills in the first place. Especially since Abie Rosengard couldn't help."

"But Charles—"

It slipped out in my exasperation:

"—of all people. Me? I'm no psychiatrist."

I had done not too badly the night before: but that was the extent of my expertise in the field of couch-work. Beyond that I would be floundering.

"Neil, you're a *doctor*. Somebody has to try to help her."

I felt a surge of shame: just like he meant me to:

"Of course. I'll do what I can."

He looked relieved again.

"I suspect that you won't find them ungrateful."

I gave him back one of his own, down-the-nose looks, except mine had got bent in a small affray in back of a betting shop: but that was a long time ago.

"That was unnecessary, I know. G'bye, Neil. See you in two weeks."

He rolled up his window, waved, and was gone.

I went back to the ward and got hold of Pansy Miller. She was the Sister on the female side.

"Well, Flower, if you can get me a nurse, I'll have a look at Mrs. Ross's wound."

"I'll come myself."

She sent a probationer for the dressing trolley. We went back to Mummy's room: got rid of the visitors.

Pansy pulled down the bedclothes: fished up Mummy's nightie: took off the dressing.

The scar was good. The suture line was sound.

I said: "You can go home tomorrow!"

When Pansy and I got back into the corridor, I tried for some sympathy.

"Imagine! The boss had the nerve to say

I'd go see her. All the way to Greenock!"

But she was on their side, too.

"I should think so! She's had a hard time—and fine you know it."

She flounced off.

I hoped the strings of her starched cap tie would cut her throat. See liberated women!

That night I decided to report the news of my posting to Arnie's overseas command to the colour sergeant. To give a hint of the coming goodies, I splashed some of the future I was to draw in dollar bills on an elegant supper from Ferrari's: they did it all up dinkie in tissues and cardboard boxes. I would do them something real proud before I went: and after I got them over there, I would astound them. But this would do to show the way forward.

I loaded the Mini and drove to the four-square, roughcast, one in a line headquarters of Jock's home based army.

I rang the bell with my elbow. I waited for Big Maisie to open the door. Over the parcels I would smile. I would say:

"Mother! Wonderful news! And a celebration!"

She would smile back. For once she would open her arms to me.

"How marvellous! Come to me, my clever son. Let me hold you."

Well, no. Not exactly.

She opened the door: but then she stood back, well out of the range of any unpremeditated acts of affection.

That was a bad sign.

"It's yourself."

There was a mistresspiece of emotional commitment for you.

In face of this the best I could manage was: "Hello, hen! How're you?"

That was all right. I could tell from her look. Nothing soppy there. I made a sort of pucker with my lips and poked my head over the parcels: but she laid not a peck on any part of my person.

"No' bad."

By God, but that's a phrase for you. It is, I should guess, the most utilitarian understatement ever worked by man. There is a classic perfection about its meiosis: polished as any Latin epigram.

But it was not worked on a dozen sheets of crumpled notepaper: rather wrought on generations of battered Clydesiders. Then abraded and sanded and buffed to the sheen of polished steel by wrestling for a lifetime in this West coast welter and never being beaten: well not quite.

It meant that you didn't have a King Cobra up your kilt: nor had Nessie decided to have you for a snack. But short of that sort of disaster anything else was—no' bad: the chimney on fire, your man lifted for barratry, beaten five one at Hampden. Such things had to be endured.

I could tell of an inner distraint from the hatchet lines in her face: deep and dark and pained. That night Big Maisie's enduring was hard and bitter.

One thing above all other upset her like that: Jock. He must be worse.

I inclined my head to the big room door.

"Did the nurse come in to him?"

"Aye! Two of them. They're very good. They give him a bath and that."

Then she mumbled on in a most uncharacteristic way for a couple of sentences:

"I can't manage it myself. I can only do so much."

Maisie tramped a terrible treadmill on Jock's daily existence.

She had rubbed and scrubbed, had Maisie. She had washed blankets and sheets: had them flapping before her eyes instead of sheep when she was awake in the night. She used Dettol and Jeyes fluid by the gallon. I helped when I could: hauled carpets and chairs into the sun: let summer zephyrs fill, and great winter gales howl through the rooms. We raised Airwick flags of distress. But you could make nothing of it. That smell soaked into the carpets, the curtains, the wallpaper, the woodwork, the very paint.

No wonder Maisie got lines in her face. But that night there was something more.

She shook her head at me. For once in her life she seemed defeated.

This was not a good augury for a midnight blow-out in the dorm. I tried to breathe enthusiasm into the evening which was as brightly lit as a bonfire of wet bamboo shoots.

I stamped round the door with my square bashing bellow:

"Na' then! Sarn't Majah! A bit of hexhiting news!"

But when I saw him I knew I had a hard job on.

At my last visit there had been expectation

and excitement: Maisie going out: me coming to visit with a bit of cheer.

The HQ platoon of that Command Post had seemed operative and fighting back: the morale factor high.

But that night you could tell the dugout had had a hand grenade through its letter box.

Oh, Jock struggled upright: said hello: told me I was a great sodger. But his eyes had a heavy droop to the lids and told of a mortal wish for sleep.

I rustled around to a bright, whistled tune to see if I could whip up a bit of whoopee and distract attention from the pulverizing blast of that infernal machine.

"Prawn cocktail for you, Maw . . . and here, Jock, this chicken has been cooked in wine. I'll make coffee . . . have a drop of this brandy. Now, I want you to hear my news . . ."

And I settled to tell them all about it. But even as I talked the effects of that explosive device smashed at us with inexorable power. And the force that crushed them, the blast that left them with fractured grins on their faces, their lives shattered into shards, like some comic cartoon cat, was want. Want begotten over the years. Want begotten by not quite enough, sired out of me not making the money grade.

Not that we had ever suffered poverty. Amongst us we had avoided the obscenities of that state. I sometimes wondered if that might not have been easier to bear. That way you could give up.

Jock had his welfare. Maisie baked potato scones by the thousand. I had had my grant. Besides which I did my stint for odd bobs. You should see me single turnips, hump hundredweights of coal, or skin the froth from a handful of pints. And I was glad to do it.

But my casual work got casual pay. You have to bake an awful lot of pancakes to make bread. And Jock got no hero's pension for falling off his bike.

On top of all this was the extra straw. In fact it was the whole bloody haystack.

Jock's infirmity. God, how it sopped up care, and time, and patience, love—and money.

The regular monies needed to build betterness for the three of us had never been there. Any we got in our fingers fell through them in patchy operations of daily make do and mend.

After the cap and gown ceremony things weren't a lot better: a houseman was still looked on and paid as a sort of apprentice. And then I had to drudge around as a registrar for years. It doesn't matter how good you are—or how bad—you wait your turn in the queue: and the trail of young hopefuls is endless.

Even now, as a Senior Registrar, there was nothing like enough money to make up for those lean years. There never had been enough to buy anew the trappings of domesticity: to freshen the decoration: to refurbish the whole outlook on life.

But that would end. There was a dream in view. It had been there since ever.

Somehow I would get Jock better. Somehow I would camouflage him: from himself: from us. I would dress him up: get him out and about: give him some pleasure in, some reason for, living. I would find surcease for his misery. I would cosset him: anoint his ulcered body: shield those puny, muscle-wasted buttocks with the holes. And above all I would get rid of that plague mark, that tide wrack of my failure so far: that awful bloody smell.

By Christ and I would!

Well here was I that very night, the white witch doctor of Dobbie's Loan. Was I not coming to the rescue at the head of the Seventh Surgical Cavalry? Was I not a tantivy trooper tootling rescue on his trumpet?

" . . . and I'll have you out in the sunshine as soon as I can get a place for us all to stay. Jock, we'll get a chair with a motor, and a cigar lighter, and a wee bar at the back. And, Maw, they've got great dentists out there. You'll get bridge work set in diamonds."

They nodded and shook their heads in amazement:

"Aye! That'll be great. Sure enough."

But I was conscious that my act was dead as the Band of Hope on a Friday night at the Queen's.

I fell silent. I looked at Jock.

In the peace that replaced my chatter he nodded away: but it was no longer in agreement. It was the start of sleep: a deep, toxic sleep.

I felt the shock of sudden understanding. What I had not wanted to know was now clamant: could not be gainsaid.

Jock was beginning to die in earnest.

Later, in the hall, Maisie said:

"You must go. I can see that. And he wants

it too. But he'll never leave here unless in his box. He's not got long to go."

I nodded and said nothing: but I thought plenty. I might kid myself on I was a medic, but in terms of life and seeing straight my mother had me beaten out of the park.

"I might come later. To visit. That would be nice. But I could never leave here. I would be lost!"

I put on my coat. I looked at her and nodded again. I left the house without touching her. I doubted if I ever would again.

I was too late.

She had seen it. He had seen it.

Only muggins me hadn't seen what was under his very eyes.

The whole idea had been far too late, right from the word go!

The letter from Pixie Perjink was as leavening as a pound of yeast.

I was in the mopes about Jock: Charles's urbanity was missed in the unit—tempers were running a bit short. I was over the ears in a blue rinse that beat the time my Uncle Willie Reid washed his boiler suit with his wife's white sheets.

It was proposed that my first visit to Mummy should be an occasion: dinner: and if I please, why not stay the night.

I couldn't think of a better idea. So that Thursday morning I pressed the pants of my gent's nattiest: and took out the worst stains with some Trilene from the anaesthetics trolley. At lunchtime I nipped downtown and bought a new white drip-dry shirt along with a gravy and soupless tie.

When my hair was combed with water and my shoes had a shine from a swab, who could outsmart me?

I grinned to myself at the self-satisfaction of looking pretty for the first time in months as I bowled along to the out-patient department.

I went early for a no sweat session. Finished about half-four I thought: then drift downstream to Greenock to sip at some very dry sherry before din-dins. I could be talked into being a toff.

But that afternoon I was clearly shown my place in the other ranks. See my prickles? Every one of them stood straight up. I would have given a bad-tempered porcupine a run for its money.

We were supposed to be four up. But Herbie came in looking doleful to tell me that

Roddie had been lowering gin and gins for lunch and had struck out: then the resident had gone to Edinburgh to do a teach-in for his fellowship.

Well, you can't say "Keys", or walk out, or throw a faint: and no-one on the administrative side is going to take off his jacket and pitch in.

You soldier on.

Herbie and I were the whole army. Between us that day we saw sixty-eight patients.

Sessions like that cook up an atmosphere all of their own.

You don't want chat. You don't want their bottoms even to touch the chair. You just want them to levitate on to the couch with the sore bit already bare.

By half past four I knew a sullen and utter exhaustion. I no longer cared one damn if they lived or died. The same message was written large on Herbie's cherry-blossom face, and the piano player had shut the lid on his keyboard smile.

Once might have been all right: or twice: or now and then. But this sort of caper was an accepted way of NHS life. Some mug will cope.

From the waiting room, from the

impersonal cubicles where the most personal parts were presented for this perfunctory farce, the dull acceptance, the helpless patience of the waiting bodies, rolled in in a wave that was sentient.

But there was their cruncher: if we had nothing left to give, they had nowhere else to go.

It would have been better to be honest.

Better to have said "Go home": take an Abdine: see a herbalist: hold your breath while you count to five hundred. If you're still alive you're OK! Anything but expect to get help for their problems in that place.

If one of them had a hernia, or a carbuncle, or a gall bladder with stones in it, they were quids in.

But they were only a few.

Most of them suffered from life. For that we had no help, and certainly not a kind word: not that day.

They got sent to Physiotherapy, or to X-ray, or to have their fart velocity measured: anything to get rid of them.

I should have done something with my anger: resigned, blown up the Houses of Parliament, shot the Minister: something. We all should.

Did I tell you about the local MP? He needed his toenails pared: or his foreskin cleaned out: a five star red emergency. He phoned the medical superintendent, who phoned the out-patient sister, who told the consultant. It was an afternoon like the one I've described: even worse. So help me, this old git was ushered along the corridor like minor royalty to be seen at once, and the sweaty masses who voted for him had to wait that little bit longer.

I was only a junior junior at that time, with a short, white jacket to show my lowly status: but the shame of not having kicked his pompous parliamentary behind lives with me to this day.

That afternoon I caught myself snarling at some old biddy because she wasn't giving me the answers I wanted.

Oh, she was a shiftless, greasy, witless sycophantic old tramp: but that was her. She was a product of her life, her times, her background, her upbringing, same as me. I was no better: only different. She couldn't help it. Nothing this side of death was going to change her: and at her age death wasn't that far off.

I caught her looking at me: frightened: real upset.

"Doctor! I don't know what you mean. Honest!"

I blew the whistle on myself: stopped the game. I went out of the rear door of the clinic to a back stairway. I sat on a step and let the cold concrete cool the seat of my soul to a temperature that would let me handle patients with safety. For the first time in years I had a real yen for a fag: I would have smoked it through in one long draw.

I looked out of the big gothic window. It was clear as Dixon's blazes used to be from Cathkin on a November night that I was getting out none too soon. Then a wry thought struck me.

Suppose when I got to the States I found that the thick end of a few thousand dollars was not the thaumaturge I needed: that the name I was going to make for myself was carved in sand?

My oh my: where the hell would I go from there?

I got out of the department at a quarter to six. "So long, Herbie."

He was sitting at a table writing up his last notes. We had only words for each other: no cheer: no chums in adversity: no emotion of any kind. That was all away down the plughole like Monday's suds at the wash-house: every last bubble.

" 'Bye, Neil."

I got into the Mini and motored to the Tail of the Bank. During my journey I managed to regenerate enough life potential to let me function at a social level—raise a smile, shake hands. But I still felt like death: drained of charge: my will swinging without polarity.

The acknowledgement that Jock was six down with only injury time left for play was getting through. On top of that awful afternoon, the coming evening had turned as exciting as a visit to Ardrossan beach on a wet Tuesday in February.

Greenock is built on the side of a cliff. You pant your way up goat tracks. A policeman showed me the particular precipice I had to drive up to get to my dinner. I went along, high up over the bay, among the stunted trees that leaned away from the weather. I came at last to a modest sign: "Toward Craig".

I drove through the gates, which had a lodge house on either side. They weren't

exactly gingerbread houses: but even in the
beam of my lights, past in a blink, they
seemed unusual: attractive. I coasted down a
driveway lined by a plain iron railing painted
white that bordered a park on either side. I
came round to the front of the house.

The Pixie appeared at the door, hands out
and running, before I got the door open.

She took a tomboy Tarzan leap at me from
three feet and wrestled with my neck:

"It's sooper to see you again."

I fended her off: held her back to have a
look at her. She had left off the cheap and
nasty image: had reverted to kind: a very
expensive species.

She had on a heavy, silky wrapover dress in
dull gold. It was cut with an elegance that was
just too old for her: but you could see it
wouldn't be long until she would match such
an outfit.

That night it intensified her youth, her lack
of defence.

I said "Look who's all growed up. Very
glam indeed!"

She beamed: "Like it?"

"Two badges on your sleeve—one for the
dress and one for looking so pretty."

If I had been eighteen, or even twenty-eight, it might have been different. As it was the kid showed through every shimmer so I locked our arms behind each other and we skipped back to the door. Scotch horses could hardly be considered a sexual overture.

The entrance was through a double door of small glass panels set in wood. I guessed that through them in the morning you could see Bute.

There was a fireplace that would have taken a yule-log. In fact it was burning up a load of sawn-up baulks from a pier. The tarry, tangy smell was welcoming.

But what made me pause to warm my hands at the fire, then my backside as I swivelled around, were the dozen ship models set in a frieze of little alcoves just under the low cornice.

She crowed:

"All you men are the same when you get your eye on those!"

She was right. The little boy in me, and some of the elderly gent I was fast becoming, too, wanted his hands on those.

"I've seen things like those in the Kelvin Hall. I'd like to get one into Victoria Park pond."

She scoffed: "They don't sail."

"I could play Titanics."

"What! With your trousers rolled up?"

"All the way to my white, hairy knees."

We did this brother and sister thing again.

"These were some of Grandpa's ships."

I admired them, taking a little tour round.

Similar glass-panelled doors led from either side of the hall.

One led to a dining room. A table was set with a promising array of silver and napery. The other, through which we then went, gave on to a sitting room that would have taken the garden party at Holyrood: yet it was made intimate by the low height of the ceiling. It had a huge, gently out-bowed window the whole breadth of the room. A knee high window seat ran along it. An old-fashioned brass telescope was mounted, ready to give minute detail at a glance. I could sense the huge panorama of the Firth that must spread before it.

There was a Chinese carpet that would have cost Marco Polo a fortune in mints. There was a scatter of comfortable chairs and couches covered in matching chintz, faded but gleaming from recent laundering. A sister fire burned the rest of the pier. Two golden labradors lay in front of it. They lifted their heads, but I wasn't worth a sniff.

A small Family party was scattered about the room in various displays of well-padded comfort. They prized themselves erect and made a gauntlet of goodwill which I ran. The strokes of warmth with which they scourged me were encouraging.

Uncle Sir R gave me his hand. His wife, Faith, was a plain but gracious lady I had met briefly in the hospital. She had a sat-back line in observation, and a deadly recall in mimicry. She jemmied the Pixie loose and took my arm:

"You know everyone else, but come and meet Father."

On my way across the dragons I nodded at Johnnie: and from a table of glasses and decanters, Murdie waved his fat hand at me and made pouring signs. He pointed to the whisky. I nodded and he got busy about the welfare of my empty right hand.

At the end of this avenue of welcome I stepped on a curly serpent's tongue to meet the old man himself. Mummy got up from the arm of the chair.

"Daddy. This is Mr. Aitken. The one you've been told all about."

I wasn't too sure about how you would parse that sentence: but the sentiment seemed well placed as was the smile.

I said: "You look well."

She had on a short velvet dinner frock the colour of pomegranate juice and black sandals with glacé straps.

Then Lord Taggart of Toward, Laird of the Clyde himself, leaned forward and gave me his hand. He gave me a Mason's grip: men of his age did that as a matter of form.

I gave it back. He gave a gratified nod. But I cheated. I had never been near the goat. I had learnt the grip from a drunk one night in casualty. Still, it smoothed paths.

"It's difficult for me to get up. I'll not rise till it's time for my dinner."

I almost started, I was so surprised. Vowels a fancy there might be scattered through his family: but Willie Taggart was as blunt and Scotch as a bucket of salt herring. His tongue had all the twists of phrase: all the lilt and fall of an Ayrshire doric that ran back two hundred years to Robert Burns. It had been schooled by a Presbyterian application to the three R's, into a punctilious correctness that seemed stilted.

I couldn't help it. I said, "You talk just like

my Auntie Watson, my mother's sister."

"Where did she come from?"

"Patna."

He slapped his knee:

"Dammit! I was born in Mauchline. I quoited in Patna often."

Quoits were a favourite miners' pastime.

"Did you win the money?"

Fierce betting went with it.

"The men liked to take me on. Beat the Master's laddie, they thought. But I backed myself to win. And I did!"

He wagged his head at me in certainty.

"Draw up a chair till I talk to you."

Mummy settled back beside him. I sat down in front of him.

We paused and appraised one another. I felt the familiar response to those striking eyes: attraction. But there was an extra drawing power to Lord Willie. Indeed there was a whole new physics that I had not met before in the magnetism of his character and will. He was old: somewhere in his nineties; but better not get too near his dynamo qualities. You might get sparks coming out of the oddest places.

I supposed it was natural that he should

reek of the iron he had bent his way to make his several fortunes.

He still had a full head of hair, the grey of cold ingots from the smelting shop. Some slight variation in the genetic colour pot gave a darker, blued-steel shade to his eyes: gun metal. An iron will sat his frame erect despite the arthritis that crooked his hands and tried to bow his shoulders.

But all of this hard determination could not gainsay some small strokes of age.

His hands trembled. It was slight, though, and had not yet gained the dimension of indignity. And he was failing. Recent months had obviously stripped his frame of flesh. His skin, his suit, his shirt collar were all half a size too big for him.

But there was nothing soft in old Willie's head. Even at that age, when thickened arteries often shrink the brain and turn thought into a jelly of non-sequiturs, his cerebration was impeccable.

"So you're Mr. Neil Aitken?"

"Yes, sir."

There were now two men in my life I could call "sir" with no difficulty. Shades of my rebel days: foundered on Health Service shoals: and now drowning deep in the blue blood waters of Debrett.

"I know that you saved my daughter's life."

I shuffled my feet at that kind of talk.

"I understand, too, that you've had to break some sort of damn fool regulations to come down here. Well, we'll talk about it later—but I want you to know that I'm grateful. Very, very grateful. Mistress Ross means a lot to me. Now, here's your drink."

Murdie arrived at my hand. He put a glass the size of a milk pail in it. It was filled with a rare export whisky. I sighted it at Murdie, then round the room: "Slainthe."

I took a steady, appraising drink.

"Ah!" I said: then when my whisky buds appraised this pleasure, "Aaah!"

I caught the Baron's eye. He nodded:

"You can tell a lot from the way a man takes his first drink. You're not a sipper, sir. Nor a gulper. You give it due respect. I like that."

His eye slid over to Murdie, who was in the act of lowering the couple of neat gills he had in his own glass in a oner.

But Lord Willie's glance showed little

admiration. And his wife looked ever downwards.

I thought I should direct attention elsewhere than Murdie's exercise in gulpology. I turned to Mistress Ross:

"The view from that window must be magnificent."

She was glad to have something else to think about. She rose:

"Come and have a look."

The old lord was pleased too. It was a favourite topic of his, that panorama:

"Finest view in the world, laddie."

The Pixie came over. I walked over to the huge window with the two women.

The big booming night echoed up the cliff from Cardwell Bay. The street lights of the Kyleward towns—Dunoon, Inellan, Rothesay—gave a pinprick, winking, civic topography to the wind-filled blackness. The lights of a ship moved through this void with startling speed and confidence.

I said:

"Para Handy and Dougie bound for the pub, no doubt."

This raised a laugh, and started a conversation about puffers. It turned out that if I had been Marconi I couldn't have tuned nearer the old boy's wavelength. Puffers had made his first fortune before the Great War.

Although I knew a bit about his general history I had not known that. I was fetched back beside him and we talked about the little Clyde coasters until dinner was announced.

When we got to the food, I was once again sat next to Lord Willie.

The dining room reflected the same, faint east of Suez, west of the twentieth century look as the lodge houses. The design motif on the fire-irons was repeated on the door finger-plates, the light sconces, and a hardwood inlay over the fireplace.

I said, "I do admire your house."

That was yet another way to a lord's heart. He made a noise like the MGM lion getting its ears scratched.

"You like it?"

"It's a Mackintosh house, isn't it?"

He slapped his thigh in a great gust of glee:

"Folks all say that. But they're wrong. It was built by Herbert McNair. Same time. Mackintosh got the kudos. But McNair was better, in my view. It was built for a fellow,

Morrie Morrison. He was in the China trade—"

In fact he said filla and tred: I almost hugged myself at the quaint Lallans that kept breaking through the upper crust.

"—He went bankrupt—"

For the first time I had a glimpse of Willie Taggart, the big wheeler. He used the next words like a white-hot blade:

"—I had to sequestrate him—"

The gangrene of the business world had to be excised: cut out: cauterized. There was no question of mercy: no talk of leniency. Such a man had to be seized and put to the knife before that damning contagion brought ruin to all it touched.

Clean cheques and bills read to old Willie like a manifest of health.

I nodded and listened to him with admiration: like when Jock told me stories about the soldiers.

But our strictly two man table talk was not allowed to go on. Faith prized us apart.

"Not tonight, Father!"

She used the more formal term, as befitted a daughter-in-law.

"—and you can have Mr. Aitken—"

I chipped in: "Neil, please."

"—very well—Neil—again for your stories. You know—" she went on to me, "—once he gets started on the old days, he just goes on and on."

"But I find it fascinating."

I did too. There was nothing difficult about it: no simulation: no sycophancy. My sincerity must have been written all over me like arrows on a W.D. sign.

But she would not be put off:

"No! No! Party manners please."

We all laughed. Then I said to him:

"Next time, then. You have an eager audience."

"Right, lad!"

The meal was simple: plain: and came to us piping hot. It was also quite excellent.

It was served by a housekeeper, an old retainer called Susie: in her sixties I would reckon. She had the same Ayrshire doric as her lord and master: and she called him Maister William. She had got her tongue around that in her young days, and when Lordiness came to him, she had been too old to change.

I had been a bit self-conscious about the lack of mots with which I could be bon: but I needn't have worried. We floated along on a raft of family gossip. And thanks to Charles's tuition and the sessions in the side room, I knew enough to keep my end up.

Murdie was quieter than you might have expected: especially with the tankful of assorted booze he had managed to load. I noticed the old man got his eye on him from time to time with a shade of scornfuls. I thought that must be a choke lead around Murdie's neck.

The real bomb of the evening, though, was the Pixie.

Now that her mother was safe, her family around her, her background secure again, she did the whole teenage thing: squeals and giggles, wheedles and cajolings, languishing looks and laughter at her own jokes. She teased her Grandpa: put Uncle Robert in his place: kept her father in some sort of order: contradicted everything Johnnie said.

And she flirted with me. Out of my white coat I was no longer scary. I wore trousers just like the rest. And I was the quarry on her home ground.

I wondered about Johnnie. But he was the most awful bloody bore. She had nothing to lose: and it might just jack him out of his stodginess.

But I refused to take it seriously. It was not for me. I was cheery cousin Charlie from Camlachie, out at his Auntie's for tea.

At the end of the meal Faith again stepped in:

"Nella! These men have had enough of your chatter. We'll leave them for a while. Coming, Helen?"

We rose.

When they had gone, Robert stayed on his feet. He sized up Murdie. That didn't take long. He turned to me:

"D'you play billiards—or snooker?"

Does a cushat dove croon to its love?

I had learned my game in a parlour of pitted slate beds that had once been covered in baize. The cushions were made of chewing-gum: and anything further away than two feet you potted blind through the fag-haze. But it was a long time since I had played.

I allowed that I knew the blunt end of a cue from the sharp one.

The knight's night looked up.

"Care for a game?"

"Yes. I'd like that."

Johnnie said:

"Good. He doesn't like playing with me.

No contest you see. I'll go and sit with the ladies."

Murdie collared the remains of the wine: pushed his chair back to cross his legs and give himself ease.

"I'll just sit for a minute."

"Coming to watch, Father?"

"Aye! I'll watch for half an hour before I go to bed."

Elderly lords knew how to take care of themselves. It was just on nine o'clock.

I went to the old boy: slid his chair back. But you mustn't make as if to help him up. He did that himself: insistent.

Uncle Sir R led the way through a smaller door on the far side of the dining room. It led to a games room. This was in the same style as the rest of the house with all the motifs to match.

There was a leather settle raised on a platform; a scoring board with brass slide and markers; a cue rack. At the top end there was a sideboard with a three bottle tantalus and glasses.

"Billiards or snooker?"

The former was the gentleman's game. The multi-hued game has always appealed to the gambler in me:

261

"A frame would be fine."

He fished under the table for balls and set the triangle. I picked a cue, checked the tip.

"Heads."

I won. I said:

"You start."

Robert straightened his glasses: the game was serious stuff to him. He kissed the left angle ball like a Cabbage White, then came back down the table to nestle behind the green. He had had a lot of practice had Robert.

The frame went down in an amicable manner that was strange to me. There was no money on it: no money that I couldn't afford to lose. He put most of the balls past. All I did was line up my sights and hit the ball in the middle until I got my eye in. The knight was a careful, competent player, but I thought he might be a bit short on the aggro you needed when the heat was on.

At the end he said:

"Ten bob on the next frame to give it spice? Fifty pence now, I suppose. I'll never get used to this new money."

Well, we wouldn't raise a lot of heat on that, but it would help to pay for my petrol.

"Sure!"

He bent to reset the balls.

The old man said:

"Will you get me my night-cap, lad? A finger of whisky and two of water. I'm allowed that by my doctor."

"Sounds as if he knows his job."

I did fixings for the three of us and handed them around.

"I hear you know your job, too."

What d'you say to that sort of thing?

I said:

"Is that enough water?"

But he persisted:

"I hear from Charles Hamilton that you have great talent, but that you're off to America soon—"

He said Americky.

"—for want of opportunity? So that you can make money?"

It was my play; but now there was cash glinting on the sideboard. I screwed the cueball off the top cushion and laid it along the back row of reds like a whisper. Well, here was a business man: hardest nose in the West in his day. He understood:

"That's about it."

"I could never understand how you doctor

fellows let the politicians get you in such a mess—"

That made two of us.

"—still, that's not the point. Tell me, if you had no money problem would you really want to go?"

There was a conundrum, one I could not remember asking myself before. I thought about it while Robert sportingly broke up the pack.

"I don't have that option."

Robert had left me just enough room to work in. I began to put away reds and blacks:

"But if you did?"

I wondered just what the hell was coming next?

"I don't suppose I do."

"I thought as much. Well then I—Robert and I—the whole Family—"

Even he used the capital F unconsciously.

"—owe you a great deal. Now Charles Hamilton tells me that he is to retire soon—"

Charles had been nattering about that for a while, I knew.

"—I think you know that you have his full support and that you will very likely get his job."

I was bent over my cue, stroking balls

home, when I realized what was coming. My ears began to sing like I had been in a plane too long. I stood up slowly: broke the rhythm of my break.

It just couldn't be as simple as that—but it was:

"—I can speak to a man and make sure for you. What would you think of that?"

I hadn't believed Charles's hint: and hadn't I laid into Jen about the impossibility of such things nowadays. Yet there was in the old man's tones no hint of senile wanderings: quite the opposite. This was a powerful man, sure of the levers he could manipulate.

I shouldn't have been so surprised. It was the way of the world. You could bleed from the pores from sheer effort: or you could land lucky. I had just drawn three aces to a pair of kings.

I swallowed a lump of anger the size of an orange: not at them: more at myself, the eternal dope from Vinegar Hill.

I stood up as if I had a poker up my jaxi:

"Very kind of you. But I couldn't do that. It would have to be on my own merits or not at all—"

The old man chuckled and cut across my words:

"Stiff neck, eh? None the worse for that."

He seemed pleased at something. I went on:

"Besides—"

I bent to the table again: measured a long pot at the blue while I considered all my besideses: the fear of drowning in the Mare Nostalgia of Caledonia; "Wha's like us?" The dread of being never more than a matriot, when the motherland had lost all dignity and could only whine for pap and reach-me-downs from the English? The gut-gnawing certainty that if I didn't get out from under I would catch the parish pump pandemic: that infection of all Scots who had been nowhere and seen nothing. I saw the results of its bane every day of my life: paralysis of the will: a life spent watching match-flame pictures.

And the final sinker: if I took the old Lord's offer I could never be my own man again.

But there. He was only being decent by his way of things. Whatever I might want to declaim on a soap-box in my own midden, this sure as hell was no place to vent my personal revolution. I was going to vote with my feet, not my voice: up the embarkation steps of a PanAm jet from Prestwick.

I went on with the weakest besides of the lot:

"—I'm committed to go. I've promised a man."

"I like a man who keeps his word. I always keep mine. I put my word in a contract. D'you have one of those?"

"Yes. But I haven't signed it yet."

In the middle of that citadel of commerce, there could be no buts of that kind. Contracts were the very stuff of his life.

"Your wish to keep your word is commendable—but based on sentiment. Contracts are drawn up to be acted on according to facts, not fancy notions. And you'll not make much money either here or over there if you forget that. When are you due to go?"

"I've to be there for the summer."

"That's months away. There'll be plenty of time for him to get someone else."

"Even if I agree, there's more to it. You see—"

He waved me quiet:

"Aye! Aye! Charles has told me all about it. Even consultants in the Health Service don't live all that fat and you've an ailing father. You need another income. A private practice maybe. Well there's a wheen of us Taggarts and there's always some damnt thing wrong with one or other of them for a start. And we're needing a new medical man for the parent company. There's always some fellow being flown back from Sumatra or Singapore and needing to be got on his feet so he can get back to his ship. They go to London just now, but we can just as easy route them to you up here."

The implications were quite stupendous. I wanted to sit down. I looked at Robert for confirmation, but I had heard aright:

"Tell you what I'll do. You have a try for Charles's job when it comes up—on your own. If you get it, we can talk again. If you don't get it, or if you still want to go abroad, there's no harm done. Think about it, laddie!"

My head was giving a fair imitation of a spinning-top and I let Robert come uncomfortably close. But then I managed to poke home the last four colours to clinch the game. The old man peered at Robert from under his shaggy eyebrows and wagged his head:

"You haven't been beaten like that for a while."

Robert beamed:

"I did enjoy that. We must play again, but—"

"—the ladies," I finished for him, taking his hint. "Another time then."

We went back to the sitting room. We passed Murdie, asnore in one of the armchairs. We filed by in a marked silence. The old Lord bade us good night in the hall.

The rest of the evening passed in pleasant gossip around the fire: but I contributed only little vacuoles of vapidity, my mind on the old man's remarks. Still, I absorbed goodwill and whisky enough to make a prospect of pleasant dreams as we all climbed bedwards.

Before I slept I thought again on the bait that had been cast my way. Tempting: very tempting. But I knew the penalty for swallowing such a shiny lure: you got gold-dust in the gonads, emasculating as any janissary's knife: and ended up your life as an ornamental fish singing silent tunes in a glass bowl.

I would write to him in a day or two: let the old boy down in a civil way.

But any bullion that got into my balls I would earn by myself.

269

Next morning I woke to a cup of tea, fragrant as jasmine. An elderly guy in a grey cotton jacket was helping himself to my suit and shoes.

I sat up in bed: laced the scented infusion with lemon: tried a sip. Then I sighed for a vanished contentment. My tea bags would never seem the same again.

"What kind of morning is it?"

"Better, sir. The sky is clear. Your bath is running. I'll take these. I'll have them ready in a few minutes."

We chatted for a moment. He turned out to be Susie's brother. Between them they ran the house to an old-fashioned way of the Lord's liking, with help from a resident cook and chauffeur cum all else and a daily parade of cleaning staff from the town.

"When is breakfast?"

"Whenever you are ready, sir. Mr. Ross and Master John, they're off to the city already. Lord Willie won't be up until later. But the ladies should be downstairs in twenty minutes."

I had done an unusual thing for me: I had bummed a morning off. As it would be my only overnight visit in the place, I had decided to make the most of it. Now, as I sipped my Cathay extract and thought of the temptations piling up, I hardened that decision. Time I was the hell out of this tender trap: away from these two women who loomed larger in my life than they had any right: out of reach of the old man's gin-traps set with glitterbait.

This leisured breakfast would be a good opportunity to kill two birds with one stone: a rock swathed in soft silks, to be sure: but none the less lethal.

I shaved by a magnifying mirror that made my beard look like black corn-stubble and showed the scar across my jaw like the first plough furrow for next year's crop. Then I had a splash in a tub that would have doubled for a dolphinarium.

My shirt had dripped from the night before and was dry and crisp. My trousers felt warm from the iron. My shoes had been buffed to the sheen of lacquer.

I strolled downstairs feeling very keen indeed. This money stuff was more magic than I had ever imagined.

Breakfast was wholemeal porridge, Tarbert kippers, and eggs and bacon from a keep-hot trolley in a glass-roofed morning-room-cum-porch. Early sunshine shone on this abode of

271

the rich. It gave a cheerful light by which you could work your way through enough morning editions to stock a John Menzies stall. You took one and propped it on a little bandstand affair in front of you. That left your hands free to butter toast and pick bones from your teeth.

Nella and her mother arrived in time to share coffee and toast and thick-cut marmalade with me.

Mummy was looking younger: restored. I took a professional satisfaction from that. But it was the girl who held my attention. Her make-up was no more than the wet rose-bloom left from a hot flannel and Cuticura soap: but the du Barry could have taken lessons in attraction from her.

Her interest was as frank and eager as a four-year-old with a lucky-bag to open. She plunged right in:

"I didn't dare ask last night. But now Daddy and Grandpa aren't here . . ."

She dismissed these elders and betters with a scoff: assumed that her mother would take her side:

". . . you can tell me—us—now. What about Grandpa's offer? Are you going to take it?"

I had to laugh. She could have modelled for the Easter Bunny: nose quivering, eyes bright and inquisitive.

Her mother went all adult on her: showed her affront:

"Nella! You mustn't . . ."

"Why not? You want to know as well."

"Yes. Well of course I'm interested. But not . . . You're so rude."

The girl opened her mouth to go on: but had it stopped.

"No! If you won't behave, go and take the letters to the post."

The girl looked at me:

"You're not offended, are you?"

"No! Heavens, no."

"I won't be long. Would you like to go for a walk when I get back? With the dogs?"

"Yes. I'd like that. I was hoping you'd show me about the place."

"Oh, sooper!"

She clapped her hands:

"Then I can ask you all to myself when there's no-one else about. See!"

She stuck her tongue out at her mother. Her enthusiasm swamped us both. She disappeared down the drive in a Land-Rover, bucking and rattling like she was in an autocross.

Mummy and I had some coffee in peace and swapped sticky newspaper. Then she put cup and paper down.

"Thank you for coming. I do appreciate it."

"My pleasure. I have enjoyed all of this . . ."

I gestured at the house:

". . . . and meeting your father. We haven't done much doctoring though. Perhaps I could ask you now?—"

She nodded.

"—You have no tummy symptoms of any kind? Pain? Indigestion?"

She shook her head. "No."

"And no fainting bouts? No sudden attacks of exhaustion that just flatten you?"

"No."

"Your scar is sound? No leaking? No red inflamed bits?"

"No."

"You really are as well as you look?"

"Yes. Better every day. Almost back to normal."

"Then I pronounce you cured."

"You're quite satisfied then?"

"Physically, yes, but . . . what about what you did to yourself?"

I remembered my promise to Charles: and I was still conscious of my own wish to write a final paragraph in her case sheet.

She wouldn't have it. She held up a finger: admonitory:

"We agreed. That's over."

She was right. It was time it was all over: time for a two barrel finish to this first bird: a puff of feathers and no pain.

"Then I've done all I can for you. I don't think you need any more of doctors. A good thing too. You want to keep away from that lot."

There. It was done: even well done.

"Ah!—"

Was there disappointment: just a hint?

No matter. I had said goodbye now.

"—But you will visit us again, won't you? Father did enjoy talking to you. He likes a fresh audience for his stories. But, more, he liked you."

I said:

"Thank you. I'd enjoy that. The feeling is mutual. And he's a fascinating old man."

I heard myself answer with a consternation near to dismay. A blow-back, by God. And me that kept his shot-gun clean and slightly oiled at all times. I needed to use a pull-through: on my head.

Still, a quick recce of the damage showed no more than the red face of a powder burn: or could it be embarrassment at my own humanity, frail and faulty in face of the attractions of this family?

There were no deadly wounds. All I had agreed to was to chat with an old man some time.

But I would need to look to the state of my resolution. The place for me was out of that house.

The Pixie arrived back in a swirl of dust and gravel.

"Dee! Don! Come here you idle dogs. Come this moment!"

I got the same kind of summons.

"Better do what baby sister tells me."

"Better not let her hear you say that."

"No."

We smiled at each other in our mutual fondness for this baggage.

"I'll see you before I go?"

"Of course."

I got my coat, all purpose as usual: went out in the winter morning to see the Firth ablaze with lemon fire from the still low sun.

I strolled over the lawns of this moneyed stronghold. I admired the policies planted with finest tax relief and the house built from blocks of shrewd investment. I wandered the woods of perquisite with two superior gun dogs trailing my heels and the nubile young heiress to all of this hanging on my arm and laughing at my every word like I was Rikki Fulton at the King's panto.

I was allowed to admire the realty for a bit: but then she was at it again:

"Now! I'll simply bust if you don't tell me."

I don't think it had ever crossed her mind that I would turn it down: not in the end. Her life was full of people who made the right decisions: the ones that would secure connections, underline position, plug into the power system. And since this offer was guaranteed by her grandpa, you would have to be some kind of a nut to stay loose from it.

"It's no deal, kid."

Her face changed: and then again. Puzzlement gave way to frank disbelief: like I'd climbed out of a UFO.

"You mean you're going to turn it down? But why? Grandpa says you would be just as well off with his offer. That you don't need to go to America."

Hurt took over then.

It was a shame. She had no idea what was going on. But I knew. You see, she was offering herself as an extra dowry. The offer was unknowing. She was as ingenuous as a maid in a nursery rhyme. But the message was as clear and simple as any couplet from Mother Goose. All I had to do was reach out and grab. I would get the pot of gold and her as well.

To turn it all down must mean something more: something hidden. She knew I wasn't soft in the head: couldn't imagine I would turn down a sock that clinked.

So, there could only be something wrong with her: something far awry, in a way she could not fathom.

I could see her grapple with the notions of what ought to be attractive in her experience of life: some schoolgirl ideas on looks and sex appeal followed by a brief apprenticeship in the bold, brash attitudes of the sixties. Having run through that, for the first time in her life she took an adult look at herself as a woman and what she had to give a man.

I had a strong notion to pick her up and kiss

it better. It was just as well my head was machined at the neck with a brass thread. I gave it a half-turn tighter. I wanted no repetition of my earlier lapse. This kid had to be let down: gentle: but good and final.

"Nella. It's a long, hard story. I won't bore you with the details. But I've had one hell of a struggle to get where I am. Now it's about to pay off. End of a long campaign. One I had to fight alone. I simply cannot change now. I owe it to myself. No-one, no thing, will I allow to alter that—"

Her face fell in at my finality. The pretty rose of her morning features was frosted.

A pity to blight that first bud so: but the second flowering would be the better, stronger for it.

We walked back to the house, silent:

"I'll get my bag now. Say goodbye to your mother."

"Have you a busy afternoon?"

She said it in a small voice: from a small face: chastened: still searching for understanding.

"Um. Pretty routine. Listen. Do something for me—"

She watched me with serious eyes.

"—Don't tell your grandpa about this

279

conversation. I left him thinking that the matter was still open last night because I didn't want to seem ungrateful. I'll either drop him a note, or perhaps tell him if I come down here again. Your mother asked if I would—"

That gave her no joy at all.

"But I did want to be honest with you."

I smiled and kissed her lips: just a touch. They were dry this time.

Growing up was a hard business.

5

I DROVE back to the city giving a fair impression of a dodgem driver. I got hooted and bawled at: my backside felt sore from the V-signs.

But the advanced motorist in me had handed in his red triangle badge. My mind was on other things.

When I got to the hospital, matters improved none. Even Roddie couldn't raise me with his moan about all he had been left to do that morning.

I said "Um!" in agreement: anything for quiet so I could think straight.

I had said "No" to a ticket of any kind—cheap day return or one way Pullman—but for all I had refused a trip to the fabled towers of Lordland: had turned down a flight through the ether of necromancy, second, third, and fourth thoughts would keep crowding the corridors of my mind.

All I need do was say the magic charm.

I wrangled over just what the hell I found so hard to take. This happened the world over: folks found oil in the alfalfa field: were claimed by wealthy uncles who had gone to Australia wearing convict suits. They said whoopee and got on with the good news.

Maybe I needed a change of shirt. This hairweave I favoured was bringing me out in heat bumps.

I had fancied myself as incisive: get it right in the head, then act: no messing. But that week there was a ditheration in all of my doings: a fractioning of the will.

That went on until the following Tuesday.

And that brought me down to the stony ground of reality again: to the giftless grind of a worn-out state monopoly.

Tuesdays I got to do my party piece: my clever thing: my trick with the main line plumbing.

Early in my career I had recognised that if you really wanted to get in among the shiny shekels, you had to be able to cut: to put your knife where your mouth was. I fixed myself up with a fellowship, sat back, and waited for fame and fortune. But one day I was up to my kiss curl in the torrent of work that was called training experience when I learned another truth. Like all great conversions, it appeared in a revelation of monumental simplicity.

I was seated one day at an organ: an apparatus of defaecation: the rear end of a lady. She had a dyed-in-the-wool, large bowel obstruction with vomiting and distention.

So I got to do a slick resection: a fancy division of adhesions?

I'll tell you what I got.

I got to dig out several pounds of inspissated turd that had stopped her backside like a wodge of clay. And the precise surgical tool I used to perform this delicate operation? The wrong end of a soup spoon from the kitchen.

I was sitting there like some green-gowned Abu Ben Adam, busy about my scatological task, when I was visited by the Surgeon-Angel of the Lord. And like that Bedouin boy, I said: put me down as one who has had enough of this: and who wants a sack of silver into the bargain.

And lo! it was revealed.

It was not enough to be your average Slash Harry: you had to do something special.

But what?

I took several visits to the library in the following week. I sat down with pencil and

283

paper: tried to work out the odds like a stockbroker valuing a share.

I looked up disease predictions and projections: new research projects: expanding fields. I scoured the journals for trials: hunted for trends in the future of surgery.

I soon realized that modern medicine, by its very effectiveness, was creating a whole new problem: there wasn't much left to die of, except living too well or too long.

If you wanted to see polio or diphtheria, you had to look in a book. The big, airy sanitaria that had been filled with tuberculosis cases, now housed an army of geriatrics. It was reckoned that in ten years smallpox would be a laboratory curiosity.

Even the big C was being turned into a killer of a lesser kind. The five-year survival rate was growing by the day. It might be slow: a bit erratic: but it was on its way.

New treatments were tried every month. In the backrooms, the boys with the Nobel prizes were working at vaccines and anti-metabolites. One day, someone would break through.

I would cheer with the world: but in the breaking, it could put an army of surgeons on short time.

Where did that leave me: a general surgeon with no fancy training: too late to start on the ultra-specialist trails of brain, or heart, or chest.

Then it stuck into my mind like a thumb in the eye.

What was the opposite proposition? What was becoming worse because of lives lived longer and better?

There was my answer: my special speciality: arteries!

They were ageing by the minute in a population getting older not only by the year but by the decade: and hell bent on living longer.

They were larded in fat: furred by atheroma. You couldn't even thread them with 00 cat-gut let alone the man-sized finger they should have taken. They were friable and frail, liable to balloon into an aneurysm: or clog and close, to kill a limb with gangrene.

And where was the best life-style known to man? Who were the most health-conscious citizens? Who had the money to pay for this chance of a longer life?

You got it!

And I would be right there to mend those

clapped-out vessels: to patch them: to tailor new channels: to buttress their thin walls: to cut them out and start fresh with implants of human vein: of ox and sheep and pig arteries: of nylon, rubber, Dacron: of any damn thing that the researchers came up with.

Just gimme the pipe, Jack: I'll get on with the plumbing.

But they would have lived too long already?—should move over for the unborn?

That was the problem for the moralists: mine would be to get my name spelled right on the cheque.

I had to learn first.

That takes me back to Tuesdays: that was when I learned. And that had not been easy.

To be good, you had to practise and practise and practise. But specialized units had been slow to come on stream in our tartan domain.

I had to migrate south: nibble on London buttercups for a year: pick up what I could at the Hammersmith at a one-day-a-week release scheme. I got to go to Munich for a month: then a real break—a six-month stint at a veterans' hospital outside of Vermont.

By then Maisie's letters had become a bit desperate. I sent home what money I could: but I knew she needed more than cash: needed me to be around.

I was due a Senior Registrar post by that time: so I hunted the Caledonian circuit for a job with vascular prospects. The vacancy with Charles came up. At the interview he asked about my experience in this field. Then he said:

"You might fit in very well with us. I have an iron in that fire. There is a need for someone in the hospital to take the peripheral vessel stuff under one wing. The present casual way gives no one person enough experience—"

Although it was a coming thing, it was still a small part of overall surgery. Only a few cases would get into the hands of any one consultant in a general unit. It was a bit of a dare to have a go at one. The patient dared too: oblivious in more ways than one.

"Norrie McFadzean—chap on our consultant team—has done more than most. He's keen to have a go. But he needs second string help."

So that was me set? A word in the right place? Things smoothly into action?

I should speak Gaelic.

This meant there was a whole new empire to be won in the Northern General: the whole Northern Group even. If a guy got his hooks in good and deep and early, he might stake his claim to stuff from Stobhill or Vale of Leven: even out to Falkirk and Stirling.

That could mean a cloak of coloured silks for someone: a garment of power and patronage: no figment of a tricksy tailor's fantasy.

But who should get it? Who was worth it: acceptable: might return a like accommodation at a later date?

Charles had to wheel and deal: to box clever: to canvass for Norrie with a box of big carrots and a very small stick.

Norrie wasn't so bad. He was a mild guy: would take a hint: could be persuaded. But more important, he was from the proper mould.

Me? I was different, with my broad a's and the hundredweight of granite on my shoulder. As the S.R. in post I could be viewed as a future contender if I became a consultant. And, though I was nothing like a crown prince—more a wrong side of the blanket by-blow—for some reason Charles favoured me.

He stuck to his guns and to me. In time he carried the day: in theory that is.

But then it had to go down the line.

We had to win clinic time: theatre time: nursing staff and technicians: beds and instruments. We had to get blood in the bank: make sure the lab could handle the extra lipid studies: and, what led to the final balls-up, fiddle an anaesthetist from the conjurer's hat.

Every single item and detail had to be fought for piecemeal: and I mean raise the voice, snarl across the table fight.

Not that I didn't understand. It was the old Health Service story. It had all to come from the same pint-pot: what we got, someone else had to give up.

Then when we were only halfway through, we lost firepower: Norrie took a coronary.

It was a regulation affair: two chest leads: no arrhythmia: no shock: normotensive. But it took Norrie off the park for three months in body: and he never did rejoin the fight in any mental sense.

I got to act as an unpaid, *sous-lieutenant* at the endless meetings.

We finally won through to one theatre a

week: Tuesday afternoons, starting at two: won all the back-up services until there was only an anaesthetist to fix.

Johnnie Finnie was the gas-bag: but he was no balloon. He was succinct and unambiguous.

We had a bar-side meeting the night before the official one, so we both knew each other's position: no punches pulled.

I bought him a drink. He started right in: levelled a finger at me: said steadily, so I should make no mistakes:

"You can buy me drinks all night. But you'll get no more change out of me than I'm going to give you right now. Which is bloody little. So save your money. You know the situation as well as I do, Neil. There are four of us. Consultants. That's all. By the time we get our holidays and do a postgraduate week, we're down to three for most of the time. And we cover the whole damn issue. General surgery. Chests. E.N.T. Gynae. Everything—"

He shook his head in marvel as he recounted. His voice got harder:

"—Now I've begged. Pleaded. Threatened. And all we got was left to do the work. To get on with it somehow—"

I shook my head at these truths.

"—No extra money. Not a word of thanks. Not even a bloody Christmas card from the Minister of Health. Just taken for granted—"

I thought they should make a song out of that last phrase: a swansong that would end the NHS one day.

"—Time was we took risks just to get through the stuff. Used trainees. Bright, shiny new. Never out of the box. Right in at the deep end. And with no proper consultant cover. But since that woman died on the table last year—"

A junior had got the tracheal tube into her gullet instead. She was sick: got the vomit in her lungs: asphyxiated herself. And the only consultant in the place had trouble of his own: couldn't leave his patient.

The fiscal had played hell. The case had been settled out of court: handsomely. It was that bad.

He said no more: diluted his bile with some more strong drink. Then he went on more quietly:

"—I know the sweat that Charles had to set this up. And I know that you and Norrie are keen to have a go. I want to help—"

He waved me quiet:

"—wait until you hear what I have to say first—"

The way he looked at me, I knew there was something funny coming. I didn't know how funny:

"—My boys will call the tune for time. And they finish at six."

"What in the love of God is that supposed to mean? You can't run a theatre like that."

"You're going to have to."

"Johnnie! be reasonable. No-one can give a guarantee like that."

He said nothing: looked at me. There wasn't a hell of a lot of reason in a lot that went on round about.

"You'll just have to work fast. And if my boy thinks you can't get in and out of the last case by six, he won't start. My orders. He must be clear for emergency call after that."

I shrugged: acceptance of less than best was a feature of modern British medicine. I would learn to be quick: good training.

So, Tuesdays got down to two cases at a go: maybe only one. Norrie was back at work by the time we were set up: but he was quite happy to let me do most of the stuff. Like my general work, this suited me well: but unlike it, the experience was slow in coming.

We ran over the limit a few times, but only by twenty minutes or half an hour: and nothing went wrong. I got to think of Johnnie's anger that night as a bit of steam-letting. He couldn't be that serious.

And I persevered. I had had another brush up in Chicago: that was when I met Arnie Caine.

In time I got where I wanted.

However, that particular Tuesday I got nothing I wanted: and a whole lot I didn't: and I sure as hell put the arm on the gas boys.

It might not have been so bad if the patient had been a sad bag: or if I could have found something in her to dislike. But she was special in all of her nicenesses: looks, manners, nature. She was a frank, open girl, devoted to her family of two—but in a sensible way that showed nothing of doting. She was a one man gal: married to a plater in Yarrow's.

And what had she done to be stricken?

While attending to these wholesome matters, she had got a gene out of place. That gave her more problems than any of the wild livers of the world.

The syndrome had been spotted a few years back by a Japanese with a name like Fujiyama: I never did learn to pronounce it.

I had looked up the translations of all known cases in the *Index Medicus*. It was a world-wide rarity. After the operation Norrie and I could earn a little kudos by adding our mite to the books of words.

But what anybody wrote didn't matter a bone-button to that girl. She was silting up. Her pulses were, literally, disappearing one by one. She was consigned to an end of rotting limbs or a blighted brain, according to which vessels went first.

In fact her bottom end was most affected. Her first complaint had been her man's: her feet were cold in bed at night. Then she went on to have cramp after walking a distance.

This meant that her main problems were in the big feeders to the legs. The contrast studies bore this out: showed the tell-tale narrowing just where the aorta divides into two. But there was more.

Her congenital conundrum had sown plates of fat and mush in the main abdominal branches as well. Her renal arteries, and the main vessels to the liver and gut would be as full of muck as the Forth and Clyde canal within a few months: a year at most. If we wanted to do anything at all, we would have to do the lot: new Dacron conduits put in as side-grafts for the abdominal links: then clamp the bottom end of the aorta and stitch in a prosthesis like a pair of long-johns, feeding the legs through to join the femoral vessels in the thigh.

They asked me what would happen if it wasn't fixed. They held hands as I told them. I noticed that they hadn't looked at one another: the nearness, the presence was enough.

"If we don't get to this soon, you'll lose your legs. If we do it now, you'll be playing hockey in a month."

What I didn't say was that the dough that had got into her system, mixed by her helical mix-up, would win in time. A few years was all she had to enjoy her children: love her man.

At two o'clock Norrie said: "Let's go!"

We had worked it out that it could be done within this silly damn time-limit: well, more or less. It was close, finicky work: and we were both still learning the tricks. But if we spelled each other: took vessel about, we could keep up the pace.

That was what we started out to do. At half past two I wished we hadn't bothered.

Norrie gave a kind of grunt.

I looked at him. The bit of his face visible between cap and mask was pallid: pouring with sweat. He was leaning his weight on the table.

"I don't feel good, Neilly. Can you come round my side and take over?"

"You got chest pain?"

Since he had had one infarct and got off with it, the next one was liable to finish the job. He knew it. We all knew it.

"A bit tight. That's all."

That was enough.

"Get him to medical side. Now!"

"No. I'll lie down. Be OK."

"Get him on a trolley and the hell out of here!"

I used a voice from my days past. One nurse even let out a yelp. And there was no more arguing. He got wheeled out, a lot of green gowns fussing around him.

I had someone phone Dougie Miller to come and hold retractors: reorganized the team: got on. But it was slower on my own: and the more because I wanted to do my very best for the girl: get it all right the first and only time.

I was utterly intent on the job in hand. It took me quite by surprise to get some advice from the character at the gassy end of things.

Usually we got to work with Barney Flynn, a refugee from the Dublin debt collectors. That day we had a young artiste of the aerosol: a young lion with his D.A. and the first part of his anaesthetics fellowship under his belt at twenty-four: and with a temperament he thought appropriate.

All afternoon he had been nattering on about his six-o'clock deadline: but in a *sotto-voce* mutter that stayed under the nuisance line: just.

This time he spoke up:

"You'll have to stop there. Five o'clock. I can't take the responsibility. Join the top ends and do the femoral canals later."

I was just about to start on the long-johns. You have to burrow from the abdomen down into the femoral canals: and join some other vessels on the way. His solution was that I should use a pair of jockey shorts: put the rest in later.

His tone went down my spine like chalk on a blackboard. I paid him no attention, except to be surprised at the time. No wonder I was thirsty. I called a halt: decreed a five-minute break and some orange squash up a straw under my mask.

"—No I don't mean just a break. You'll have to stop. If you don't I'll phone Dr. Finnie."

I sucked at the sweet, coloured stuff that a nurse held close to my mouth and looked at him. I waved away the cardboard cup. I looked to see if my hands were safely swathed in a towel. I moved away from the magic circle: off to a little cool spot in a corner: out of the light of the arc. I motioned him to come near enough to hear my lowered voice. It was for him alone:

"Son! I don't give a set of bum-boy's piles whether you phone Johnnie Finnie or the Shah of Persia. That's your problem. Solve it any way you want. But if I get one more cheep out of you until I'm finished, when I am finished, I'll break your fucking jaw."

He squeaked with outrage.

As I went back to work I could see him head for the wall-phone: hear him gobble into it like a Christmas turkey who's realized what the butcher is up to.

But by that time I was busy again.

There was one more small interruption.

Just after six, Johnnie Finnie came in.

This gas-arse took him aside and filled his ear like the Good-Year dirigible. Johnnie said little in reply: but pushed through the knot around the table to see what we were at.

We spared each other a look. Mine was indifferent: but I could see his was grim, even under his mask.

"I'll see you later."

It was a promise.

It all finished up surprisingly well: at least technically. How long her genetic curse would take to louse up the rest of her system I didn't know: but for a while her feet would be warm in bed. And the end of that day, for us, was half past seven.

I had been fagged out a few times in my years among the leeches. I had known frustration that would have had Freud rewrite his thesis.

They happened together that night to a degree that pushed me near some kind of limit.

The implications of the whole shoddy afternoon had gutted me: a polar bear rug for anyone to walk on: the lights and liver leached out by shame.

In the changing room I sat down and closed my eyes. I made no attempt to move. Maybe if I waited what had happened would all go away.

But no.

I heard Chloroform Charlie go yackety-yack on the phone again. He was reporting the score at close of play.

After a bit I shucked my uniform: had a shower. Usually the water needles sharpened me up. That night I felt I was made of lint.

I had on my shirt and was tying my tie by the mirror image when Johnnie Finnie walked in.

He came up to me, slow and grave: spoke to my reflection with his own:

"Neil. You've had it. I've had to ditch a theatre ticket and my wife to handle a fry-up that arrived in casualty and couldn't wait. A whole-leg, third-degree burn—"

I nodded. The wrong way round world was interesting. Maybe Alice needed a doc?

"Donnie Marshall was already out at an abdomen that had to be opened in a hurry. All because you had our young friend here tied up—"

Eustace Unctuous tried on an I-told-you-so look. It turned into a smug leer:

"—my days for that sort of thing are past, Neil. And well you know what I mean—"

I did too. Everybody's days for that sort of thing were over. It was called goodwill in its day. But it hadn't been enough for the Great British Public.

The boy-wonder chipped in:

"I told him—"

He stopped at what he read on both of our backs. Johnnie went on:

"—I'm telling you now. And it will be on the Super's desk in writing in the morning. The department cannot handle your Tuesday theatre without extra staff. As of now, it's off limits for gassing."

I turned round: put my pants on in a right way round world.

"Thanks, Johnnie—"

I didn't go into explanations: I wasn't sure what they were in fact. But I did know they added up to one thing that night: I no longer cared.

I said:

"—It's all too late, anyhow—"

He had expected a fight: was left looking uncertain.

"—only do one thing for me. Get that bloody tick out of my hair."

I nodded at the ether expert. Johnnie turned to him:

"You're wanted in receiving hall."

He left in a huff. Johnnie turned back to me:

"You OK?"

"No sweat," I reassured him. "You get back to your wife."

I was left in the changing room alone.

The feeling of shame lingered. By working in the Service I gave it countenance. We all did.

To think I had been tempted to stay: a plaything for an old Lord's pet in a job without honour.

Well, now I knew.

Before I left, I phoned medical side about Norrie. He was doing fine. As I talked to the resident I noticed a scrawl on the chinagraph above the wall-set: "Mr. Aitken to phone Surgical Three."

I thought of pretending I hadn't seen it: but see a Presbyterian conscience!

I clicked the handset: dialled the number. Flower came on:

" 'Lo, Pansy. D'you want me for something?"

"Yes. There's an anxious relative to see you."

"Tell him I'm not here."

"It's a her. And you're to come round. No nonsense. Been here since six o'clock."

I did an Edgar Buchanan: but I went. See ward sisters!

Six o'clock. Two hours on a hospital seat. It must be some worry.

I met Pansy in the ward corridor:

"Where is she?"

"In my room."

I made a face at her. She was unmoved:

"You'll like this one."

That sounded unlikely: but she was right. It was the Pixie Sixer.

She was asleep in an armchair. She had on a tee-shirt that said "I love Scott Walker" and was squeezed into a pair of jeans that threatened to bring on gangrene of the bum.

For a moment, her face was in repose. How could anyone be so young?

But it all went wrong as she woke and saw me. She became serious as a funeral.

303

Surprise won through my bleakness:

"For the Lord's sake! The last person on earth I expected. What—?"

My mind leapt to her mother:

"—Is something wrong?"

"No. Yes. No. That is nothing. About Mummy anyhow."

Her grammar was showing again.

She stood up: stuck out a hand for me to take. It was not to shake: more a gesture of formal regard: not sure what kind of friends we were.

I turned it palm up: kissed her wrist. We were very special pals: but just that.

"It's good to see you."

Her eyes were on me: grave: watchful:

"Yes. And you—"

I kept my tone neutral: but it was true. She gave a fresh-air feel to the place:

"—I hear you've been here since six? Have you eaten?"

"I phoned first. They said you would be finished by then. I wanted to catch you with this—"

She pointed to a parcel at the side of her chair:

"—They kept on saying that you couldn't

be much longer. So I held on. I'd made up my mind to see you anyhow."

"You must be famished. Tell you what. I'm about to buy myself a steak the size of a policeman's boot. Join me?"

Baby sister had left the nursery. I wasn't too sure who this young woman was.

"Yes. I would enjoy that."

But before she would have loooved it: and clapped her hands.

She handed over the parcel two-handed: it was heavy for her. I said:

"Can I open it?"

"Of course."

I undid the wrapping paper. Inside there were three suit lengths: a Glenurquhart, a thornproof in heather mixture, and a clerical grey in a fine bird's eye worsted. It would have taken two months' pay to buy that lot: and that wouldn't count a single stitch in the making.

The money was dolly mixtures to Old Willie. Buy a cloth mill if he felt like it. The thing was they had recognized me as a person: recognized my problems: a one suit man off to impress clientele who could change clothes three times a day for a week.

She went on:

"You should take them to this tailor—"

She handed me a card: an address in West Nile Street:

"—He does uniforms for the ships' officers. He'll make them up for you."

"Kid. You've caught me right on the button. I don't know what to say. Set me up for the Easter Parade, this will. Fifth Avenue had better watch out."

"Yes. I—Grandpa—we all thought that."

A Family decision, no less.

I got up:

"Give me a couple of minutes. Then we'll go and eat—"

I looked down at her get-up:

"—maybe not The 101 tonight, huh?"

It took me ninety seconds to stash the dry goods and shrug on my coat. But when I got back her hands had been washed in Sister's basin and her make-up had been repainted.

This missie showed more good points every time I met her.

We beat it for Friaoli's. That was a trattoria in Townhead where the pasta did all right by the palate. Besides I had done a little knife work on the eldest brother of the family who acted as head waiter. He had been grateful to the tune of a quick table and bit off the bill ever since.

It was a place that had booths with sliding doors along the back wall. You got to shut the world out if you wanted. This seemed a night for such privacy so solemn did her face stay.

I got the bigga halloa from my friend. Nella was my leetle cheecka. Forty years in the country and he still spoke like Leo Carillo in the Cisco Kid.

We sat at the bar. I asked if we could have one of the booths. I got some Dewar's set up in a glass: for Nella something she fancied that had sugar round the rim and a cherry in it.

Until we were near enough to rub knees under the table and make our thoughts in low voices, I kept it all on a safe plane.

"How are things at Toward Craig?"

"We're all well. You know we're doing up Peninver?"

"Yes. I heard you were moving back."

"I've to have the top flat—you remember—?"

I nodded:

"—to myself. A separate door. A new stair-way. Mummy and me—we're having great fun with architects and designers."

"That'll be handy for Johnnie."

I meant to tease: but the remark made her look down: silent. She wet her finger: dabbed it at the sugar: then sucked it off.

"I've not seen him for some days—"

A small silence rang in the babble and clatter. It echoed between us like a rehearsal on an empty stage waiting for the next lines: a declamation of some kind. I put my elbow on the bar top: looked at her. I wasn't the only one with problems that Tuesday.

A booth became empty then. We were ushered into it. We chose our food. I ordered a bottle of Frascati. Then I shut the door. That felt better. Such sayings and emotions as trembled in the air would be the better for short-range broadcasting.

"Nella. What's it all about?"

She looked at me. Her eyes were big. Not a sheep in sight, mind you: nothing lorn nor lost nor wistful.

I should have known what was coming. Hell! Of course I knew. The signals had been too strong: too insistent. You couldn't put a thing like that off forever. It had to be given a hearing. Her dignity demanded that.

What had been unconscious at Toward Craig that morning had slipped down into the forebrain: she now knew what she was thinking.

"I've told Johnnie I can't see him for a while—"

I waited like you do in the woods. Shy animals appear in time.

"—I know you don't care about me. Not in a big way, that is. And I know you've been putting me off. But—can't a girl even get to try—?"

I said nothing: gathered thoughts: put words in the scales to make sure of their value. It was no time for triteness.

The silence provoked her:

"—You are a big bastard. You might help me. You know what I'm trying to say."

I couldn't help my smile. She was a beaut. She deserved the honesty she was looking for.

"Listen, Nella. And I want you to hear what I'm saying in your heart as well as your head. Last week at your home—as you said—I let you down. For what you said tonight was written all over your face then. But I didn't duck out just because I didn't want to hurt you. Although there is that too. You know perfectly well that I'm fond of you—"

She was concentrating hard. From all she had heard or read love should be simple: but I was giving her a dissertation on its difficulties.

"—I told you too about my personal reasons. My career. And I lived through something this afternoon that confirmed the worst, if I ever need confirmation. But there's more. And you should know about this. You're worth that—"

I looked across the table at this nineteen-year-old chit. I took my shell off: exposed the nerve ends:

"—I am—always have been—afraid of love. I don't trust it. I don't trust me. I don't trust you. Or anyone. It's a game you get hurt in—"

She had imagined romance. It was right at her age: hand-holding: endearments. Instead she was getting a skein of my twisted sentiments.

But the eyes showed no disappointment: no dismay. They searched for understanding.

"—I can't start anything that would run that risk just now. Not for you. Not for me. I'm not up to it. I might react out of pity. Or self-pity. Or self-indulgence. Or just to relieve boredom. It wouldn't be fair to either one of us—"

The starters came. We broke shrimp shells as I went on:

"If we had met sooner it might have been different. Or later. Or we might write. Perhaps you could come out to the States for a holiday. Something. I don't know what. But not just now. I'm getting on that plane solus. Body and soul all my own—"

A little more then it would be over. Surely then I would be rid of this aristocratic lot forever:

"—I'm sorry. And that isn't an apology—it's real regret—that we can't give it a try. I think you're a real original uncut diamond. I'd love to make you shine and sparkle. But I will not take the chance it means."

The eyes went cobalt then: just like her mother when she felt deeply. But this was more. The blue washed on to her cheeks in streaks of mascara and eye-shadow.

The steak that came then was done to a turn: but I found it tough. She pushed some lasagne about her plate. The conversation turned just as savourless as we got back to the mundane things of life.

"How is your grandfather?"

She blew her nose and took my cue that it was time for less hurtful matters.

"He's well. He's looking forward to seeing you again. He got your letter."

"He wasn't offended?"

"Quite the opposite. Laughed in fact. Said you were a thrawn young bugger. Just like himself."

"I'm flattered."

"He's having a birthday party soon. Will you come to it?"

"Yes. I'd like that."

"Good. I'll send you a formal invitation."

We said "No" to the ice-cream: opted for coffee.

"—and have you any Armagnac? What was that stuff your mother had?"

"Clos des Ducs."

They didn't have that. But what they did have came close: dry as a squirrel's nuts in December. I had them leave the bottle.

"Cheers, kid? Luck to us both?"

"Oh. Yes. Yes. Luck to us both."

It was heartfelt.

What with the preprandials and the wine and a few noggins of the spirit, she began to find life easier. If there weren't many roses in bloom at least the briar pricks were blunted.

We had left her car at the hospital. She could fetch it next day. I drove her home.

She was slightly squiffy: still a bit wet about the eyes.

"I haven't—"

She swallowed: pride is such a mouthful to get over:

"—made a fool of myself?"

I reached for her over the gear and brake levers.

I stopped short of eating her. Then I yanked at her door lock: spilled her out into the night:

"Fair warning for you, kid. You might begin to wonder if I'm queer. Or impotent. Or just too old. Well I'm not. Not one of them. My balls are all where they should be. Right in the middle. If you come near me again, you'll need every colour of belt known in Judo to keep me off. And I'll still leave without you. Understand?"

She wiped all around her mouth with the back of her hand: tentative: bruised.

"Yes. Yes. I understand."

Such harsh genital declarations were strange to her: but she got the idea.

I did my space-craft act again: the one with

the carbon emission power source: and zoomed home to sleep off the whole affair.

But I wasn't to get to bed then.

As I turned into Passoud's street, I found it blocked by a police car and a crowd of spectators. I climbed out and sidled round the back of the mob craning: taking in clues.

Rahmin was in the middle of it all: talking to the police: waving his arms. I spotted Jen near the steps. She had a coat over her shoulders, clasped to her neck in the cold night, sheltering Rahmin's oldest girl in its folds.

"Jen. What the hell is going on?"

"Neil. I'm glad to see you. It was that bunch of tearaways. The ones that were in the basement opposite. You remember—?"

I nodded.

"They came back last night. They were larking about with a can of paraffin. Setting off fires and then peeing on them to put them out. Drinking lager to keep up the supply. And God knows what they take to keep up the badness. Anyhow, Rahmin spoke to them. They cheeked him back. So he sent for the police."

I groaned for such a foolish thing to do.

"Christ! He never did. They'll crucify him for that—"

They would too. He should cut his losses—take his profit more like—and head back for the Ganges or the Ghats or wherever.

"—What happened then?"

"They cleared off. But later, when he went to his shop—they must have been watching— they had a go at the windows here."

I looked up. There must have been a dozen panes in shatters.

"Then when he came running back, they put in his big shop window."

I nodded: true to form:

"—He chased them. Even caught one. The police have him now."

I winced for the trouble Rahmin had forged for himself. I eased through the throng to get beside him. He saw me. His mouth and eyes were turned down like the sad masque you see in theatres.

The police were finishing: snapping the bands back on the black notepads:

"Anything I can do?"

"And who are you?"

Not aggressive: but not a "sir" in earshot:

and very positive. They wanted to know.

"Doctor. Work in the Northern General. Live here. In digs. I know your face—"

I said that to one of the flat-hats: a chest like a Cadzow oak: a face like the ones on Mount Rushforth:

"—I've met you before."

So we had: the improbable coincidence of city life. We had met at a high-rise mugging not long before.

"Och, t'hell. It's you, doc."

We were comfortable now in shared memories of embattlement. Society wanted us: needed us, even. But it had a funny way of showing it sometimes.

"What's the score?"

"This object—"

He had one of the fourteen-year-old furiosos by the neck: massively casual in his contempt:

"—stove in the Paki's windows. He caught him. But he's no witnesses. We'll take him to the station. But it won't stick."

The white-faced whelp worked himself into a fury of revenge to come:

"Bloody Paki. Just let him wait. We'll give him something to call the polis for."

My tree-trunk friend looked at me: shook

his head. He wheeled the stunted desperado into the shelter of the car and his own massive frame. He fetched out his trusty thumpen-stick and gave it to Boy Bravo to sniff:

"See, son. If you aren't quiet this minute, I'll give the doc a job. Right?"

He opened one of the car doors and rammed him into it: like stuffing paper in a wet shoe:

"Now, son. If you want to really please me, just try to run away!"

He beamed with his own certainty. We went back to Rahmin: but he had had the same doleful news about the attempt at any prosecution:

"Aye do not understand you alle. Why arre you nott doing something about these terrible people? They arre breaking the lawe. All the time they arre doing it. And you do nothing."

He looked at us all in mournful anger.

I tried to get him to see reason: the reason that had been bred into me after thirty-something years surviving this great wreck of a city:

"Rahmin! There's not a lot you can do. These kids are a fact of life. You just have to say Ho! Hum! and get on with it. But don't get your dhoti at half-mast like this. That's just what they want—"

He was almost crying: I thought it was rage.

"—They won't forget you for this. Or for catching one of them—"

There was good advice: straight from an old Sauchiehall sodger. The police nodded approvingly. That was the old time religion: amen. I finished the sermon:

"—Keep out of it. Keep away from them. Don't let them get the eye on you. There's your wife and kids as well."

I had to step back from the blaze in his face. Rage: bright burning anger: but not at them: at me.

"Aye am ashamed for you alle. But Aye am ashamed for you mostly, Neille Aitken. You arre like this alle the time. Nott caring. Giving upp. You have no right to be talking to me. Let me be."

He pushed past me: through the crowd: huddled his family before him into the close.

The police shrugged: just like the docs:

"He'll learn the hard way."

I nodded. He would.

The flat-caps got back into their cars: went on to the next of the night's mayhems: the little Pakistani forgotten already: a nothing happening in their lives.

The crowd dispersed. But Jen stood by the railing waiting for me.

I gave her a look as I went up to her:

"Don't you start."

"I never said a word."

6

FOR the next week I was busy arranging my camel train to the colonies: visa: money: my bits and bobs to sell or give away. I even made a will. In a month or two I might have something worth leaving.

In the hospital only Charles and Herbie knew that my move was to be permanent. So far as anyone else knew I had taken four weeks' leave and was off on a holiday-cum-refresher-course.

My letter of resignation: posted the minute I got my feet on Kennedy airport: stamped with federal insignia, would say more than any rude speeches.

I didn't see much of Charles after he got back from hunting an Azores tan. He had looked brown and fit, but he had seemed tied up with some administrative affair at the Regional Hospital Board. He kept dodging off to meetings there.

One day he sent for me. I went to his room.

"Sit down, Neil."

"Thank you, Charles."

He had stayed Charles since his return: since my slip of the tongue that morning: at least when we were alone.

"Haven't seen you much since you got back."

"No, Neil. I've been busy. I want to talk to you about that. But first I should tell you I was at Toward Craig last night. Saw Helen Ross. She's looking well. They're all very pleased with you. Though I hear you turned down an offer from old Willie."

"Yes. I couldn't do that."

He nodded: but it was a gesture of neutrality:

"I hear you're going to his birthday party."

"Yes. Shall I see you there?"

"Indeed so. I've been once or twice in the past. Sumptuous do. You'll enjoy it. But I wanted to talk to you about something else."

"Yes, Charles. By the way, I hope your wife has recovered now."

"We both enjoyed our break. In fact the whole thing helped us make up our minds about something—"

I looked at him. He was smiling at me in a thin way: not unfriendly: quizzical:

"—As you know, I've been thinking of getting out for some time. Retiring early—"

I shook my head in commiseration. At one time, the only way you could have got rid of men like him early was to wire them to a Mills bomb. Who would want to leave the best job in the world? But all over the shop you met this new disease: guys quitting early to grow heathers or play the nineteenth hole or die of inanition: anything but stay on.

"—I've had enough. I intend to resign at the end of June."

My words came out without thought:

"I am sorry. I shall miss you."

The look he gave me made me glad I had spoken. He went on:

"I've been seeing about my pension and some other things. My successor for instance—"

"Ah!"

I knew now what the off-centre look was about. Sly? He could have been born in Kirkcaldy.

"I know that Lord Willie offered to help if and when this came up. And I know you turned that down as well—"

He cut across my explanations:

"—He understands. I understand. You don't want help. Do it on your own. Still, I would like you to apply for my post. For two reasons. First I would like to think of you carrying on for me here. Second, while I respect your wish not to have the old Lord put his oar in on your behalf, it will be just plain damn foolish if you don't let me speak for you while I can. That is a precedent as old as the hills."

There was a convention that gave precedence to a chief's wishes for his own job when he retired. It was a virtual guarantee.

"—Besides I would *like* to do that for you before I go."

I flushed:

"I would count that a privilege."

"Good. The advert will be in the *Journal* on Friday. Now, you've told me so often that you would like to tell them what to do with their consultant appointment. Here's your chance. But my bet is that you would be surprised by your own feelings once you were appointed. You know it's an old saw in life that you can never tell how you will react in any situation until it actually happens."

I had to agree with that: but I had to leave him in no doubts. I looked at him very straight to counter any rebuff in the words:

"I appreciate what you are doing. And I will apply. As you wish. But I must tell you

323

that my mind is made up. I go to the States in June."

He smiled: satisfied.

"You're not there yet, Neil. And when you're my age, you'll realize there is nothing—not one damn thing—certain in this world, until it has happened. Besides, I haven't finished—"

I looked at him in surprise: I had surely made my feelings plain.

"I heard about Tuesday's episode. But there's a little silver lining. When I was at the R.H.B. I heard a little bruit about this whole vascular business—"

I thought it wanted yelled from the housetops: but I let him go on:

"—It has to be funded. The money is promised. A unit solely for that purpose. The whole kit and caboodle. It'll take a year or two of course. Plans. Buildings. But if you get your consultant job now, your chances of ending up number one are very good. Especially since Norrie has been ill. Man on the spot and all that—"

He gave me the same straight look I had given him:

"You'll get all the facilities you could ever want. And no favours of any kind. No more money of course. Not the kind you'd make in America. But I could imagine a satisfying life—"

I almost put my head in my hands. See helpful people. I wished to Christ they would leave me alone.

"Charles, I'm in hock to the bank of my future for my sanity over these past few years. The promissory note was that I had to get the hell out of here. I must repay that, or I'll owe myself forever. I've gouged, clawed, kicked and scratched to get where I'm going. There has been nothing noble about it. No vision of any greater good except mine. There is nothing, no-one, going to stop me. If I quit now I would vanish in a cloud of frustrated atoms."

He said nothing: nodded again.

But there was still a quirk to his lips as if he didn't believe the half of it.

I was in the female ward the morning after my interview. I was giving it no thought. Why should I? I had applied to please Charles: not to promote me.

I was arguing a small toss with a couple of students when Charles appeared in the doorway. He was looking pleased with himself. He came towards us:

"Congratulations. I've just come from a meeting of the R.H.B. You are to have your well-deserved promotion. You start the day I retire."

I remembered that was the day I had to start at Arnie's too: I was having an Ides of June.

Of all things I had ever thought I might feel, gratification was the last: but it spread over my face in a soft grin.

The attendant nurse gave me a kiss: the two students looked impressed.

Charles insisted that we visit the drawer in which he cached his sherry:

"It just so happens I put in a few fresh bottles this morning."

He had to open three of them before everyone who dropped in had a toastful.

Consultants from every hidey-hole in the hospital turned up to say "well done". And all the time Charles gave me this sly look.

When the bottoms-upping had finished he stretched his arms in a luxury of objectivity. How would I react?

He said:

"Well?"

I knew what he meant.

He had been right in his prediction: in the dire truth of that guess he had made. I had not believed it possible: yet there it lay, as jagged and lumpy, as unassailably real as an iceberg slipped into the summer shipping lanes.

But I shook my head at him:

"I have to admit it's gratifying. And unexpected. But the answer is still 'No'."

My Scotch mind was fixed on the magnetic fraction of a million dollars that was my new bearings. I would not be deflected.

"Well, I've done what I could."

I could see he was resigned. He was too old to be disappointed.

It was all over the shop by lunchtime. Hospitals are terrible places for gossip, be the new good or bad. I had more congratulations from registrars in the mess, technicians, maids, secretaries: and all as if they meant it. I had not realized I had so many well wishers: friends.

This fact touched a soft spot. Charles's prophecy began to glow like a beacon I didn't want to see. It beckoned, I knew well, back to muddied, shallow waters: and I was all set for the big blue sea.

I got little time to dwell on this though, for that afternoon all of my forward motion stopped like I had run keel-deep into a sandbank.

There was one good wish I never did get.

My face was still in a silly mould, liable to grin for no particular reason, when Pansy came up to me.

"Your mother, Neil, on the phone. There's something wrong."

Pansy knew about Jock. She patted my arm. I guessed from that.

I took off the protective covering: the white coat that made me invulnerable to the sorrows of others, with some fear. For all of the certainty that he had been getting worse by the day, and that his life must soon end, now that the time had come I wondered how I would react. I went to him at once, insecure in my layman's mufti. And at his bedside the shafts of reality were unerring. They struck home without deflection.

I would never speak to my soldier daddy again.

By the time I got to him he was in a coma. His respiration had become intermittent in the eponymous pattern that precedes such a way of death. In this uneven, hopeless fight he was making a last atonement: he now sweetened the air with the fruity scent of ketosis as his acids and bases flew awry in electrolytic dissolution: while his kidneys, by then completely failed, damned back the sour filtrate that had plagued our days for so long.

At my first sight of him the bairn in me would not be denied. I said without volition: "Oh, Daddy!"

As I put out a hand to him, my own tears fell on it. I was surprised by how hot they felt.

After that I was able to put some kind of a face on things.

Maisie didn't want to speak much. We used the spare, workaday phrases needed to keep ourselves fed and the house running in low gear.

For the most part she sat, hands clasped in her lap, waiting for her marriage to end and her widowhood to begin.

Although the long silences between us should have been meet in the solemn circumstances, I was not comfortable in them. I could give her no help when she needed it. I wanted her breast for my own sorrow.

Maisie endured with her man to the very

end. But I found myself lacking in her fortitude. I only wanted it to be over.

I was brought to face my further failings, by the others who came about the house.

Gilbert Gallagher brought his parents all the way from their new home to pay a last visit:

"Neil! I'm right sorry."

And it was clear he was.

Neighbours from this area, new faces to me, knocked at the door:

"If you need a message—"

"If we can help—"

Friends from the old days of tramcars and Brasso rags to shine the knockers and handles on the close doors, walked from Clydebank:

"I heard he was failing. Came by to pay my respects."

With such commonplaces, they gave dignity to Jock's days on earth.

But see me: all I could remember was the black futility of his life.

And if that was bad, the calm matter-of-factness of Maisie's brothers: my Reid uncles: Willie, Joss and Tommy: these marvellous big men of oil and engines, who had had endless patience with wee Neillie who wanted a daddy that walked, brought me up short an inch from my own reflection and showed me further the sham I was.

Like me there was nothing they could do. But unlike me they brought a deep sense of occasion: an innate understanding that the death happening before our eyes was the end of a life that had meant something: and so all of our lives: every life that was ever lived.

Me? I could see only the cliff at the far edge of the world and sense the abyss of nowhere into which all of us must fall.

What gave them such certitude? Why was I tinctured with such doubt: such bitter lack of point?

The answer came when his last breath had passed.

It was unnoticed by us all for a few minutes.

It was Maisie who realized that the pause in his breathing had lengthened to eternity:

"I think he's away."

She might have said he had gone for a walk.

Uncle Willie Reid was sitting near him. He turned to peer close:

"I believe he is."

He rose and made respectful way for me and my expert knowledge: but he had no need of me to tell him: none of them had.

The years of their lives had taught disciplines I had abandoned in my struggle to get out from among them: had brought acceptance of truths that no amount of fancy education or assumed sophistication could change.

I need never feel guilt at the thought of deserting men like these. They could do fine without the likes of me: better in fact.

They stood together on the other side of the bed. Tommy had his arm around Maisie:

"He had a sore time, Maisie. But it's sad to see him go. We were all real close."

There was that ultimate strength: they were not afraid to love.

Where I wriggled to avoid the barb of this tender spear: to spare myself the tearing wound when it was wrenched out, they welcomed it for its present joy.

Somehow I must mend this weakness: learn to bear such lances.

We laid him out: removed the pillows: stripped the blankets: left him covered by a sheet.

"That man at the Store parlour is awful good. He made a real job of Alec Strang. Awful nice he made him look. Give him a phone."

So Jock had a Co-operative Society funeral on a day when the rain soughed in from the Atlantic.

With seemly gravity, the mourners—punters and peasants all—removed hats and bonnets and downed umbrellas to stand bareheaded.

When the minister got to his final prayer, his words meant little. Instead of listening I opened my eyes and looked over the bowed heads, hunched against the rain.

I could see Dumbarton Rock as old as the dinosaurs: then the skeleton of the new bridge at Erskine, manifest of man's possibilities.

For the second time in a few days the old lesson sank in. All we people of the Clyde valley: all we sojourners along its firth: all we West coasters who spent our lives under grey skies and in drooking rain: all of us humans shared the same experience.

Whatever it meant, whatever lay beyond the grave, we were going there together. There was no way I could opt out or claim exclusive rights. I would suffer or be happy: be bored or content: know hatred, jealous or gladness in the only company there was. I might not like the human race too much, but there wasn't another one in view that I could join.

If only I could pay my membership in full.

If only I could lose my fear of the great and strange emotion of love.

No women had attended. They stayed home to lay a spread of ham sandwiches and whisky.

When we men got back, the conversation started off studiedly solemn; but Maisie would have none of it. She presided over the occasion like she was opening a bazaar. She soon had a rabble going with jaw-jaw by the gallon and balloons of frank laughter.

By God, but life was for the living. And Maisie wasn't going to dwell on that death stuff. It might be catching.

On an impulse I got near enough to pay her a compliment:

"You're a big doll."

She considered that declaration. In the circumstances, and after two whiskies for herself, she allowed it:

"If you say so."

There was progress for you: and the softening effect of death.

Next day we bundled his clothes ready for the rag-man and cleared his warlike life from the walls. I went for a paint roller and a can of emulsion. In a couple of hours I had covered the rectangles left by the photographs, dismantled the bed, and humped the furniture into a dozen new arrangements, until Maisie was satisfied.

I left her sitting in her widow's weeds, discreet as a bed of wall-flower in April: and did I sense a hint of happiness?

That would be unfair to Maisie: but the freshness, the promise of freedom from the bed-mill of Jock's chronic illness would not be denied.

I got back to the Passoud palace with a sense of release. This was compounded by a message from the Pixie.

On the coming Saturday was the party for Grandpa's birthday. There was to be a decorous entertainment for the elderly like me: and a disco for those who could manage. If I did not feel too low after the funeral, would I please come. Besides they did want to congratulate the new consultant.

A party?

Hell, that was just what I needed.

I would go to Toward Craig and show

Murdie Ross how it should be swallowed. I would teach the teenage tyros a thing or two about rock, if that was still the fashion.

And I would find Nella.

I would seek her out. I needed someone's breast for comfort: it didn't much matter whose.

And her?

She would just have to take her chance.

I drove down the estuary road that night in a rage to indulge Jock's death. I would profess such love as need be for the sake of its slaking. I would swear the commitment needed for draining a cup. The well I would leave for someone else.

A shit's trick?

It was a hard world: and I had warned her.

When I arrived at Toward Craig the car park was crowded: a birthday jamboree no less. This was a *son et lumière* production with coloured lights strung up in the garden while a megawatt beat group sent vibrations clear away to Lamlash from a marquee where the stomping was at.

I got out my overnight bag, a flat case with a rented dinner jacket, and a parcel that I had

336

for old Willie. Susie's brother let me in. There were to be several house guests that night. I had lost my former room: but he took me up a narrow back stair to a slit-like cell that had once housed a tweenie:

"Come down as soon as you're ready, sir. Lord Willie was asking if you had arrived."

I eased myself into the dinner suit: stuck the parcel I had for the old man under my arm: went down to join the haggis-fest.

All of the double doors were open so that the guests could circulate through the public rooms and out into the garden. There was a cornucopian buffet in the dining room, with a bar that would have kept the cold out at a four-day bonspiel. Susie and her brother were in practised command of a covey of girls in uniform pinnies, who were toting trays of canapés and glasses. I saw Charles and his lady: gave them a wave.

Murdie was at the bar. He caught sight of me and gestured. I joined him.

He was supervising Ross's law of inverse proportions:

"Splash of brandy all filled up with champers? Bad f' ya! Gives ya gas! But splash of bubbly all filled up wi' brandy? Dat's da ting! Da sugar and bitters ya can stick in yar eye!"

He poured the two driest champagne cocktails in the *Guinness Book of Records*. I handled mine like a petrol bomb:

"Thanks, Murdie."

"Gettin' outta this soon."

He waved at the rooms visible through the doors:

"Back to my own house. Nearly finished. Next month. Not allowed to see it yet. Big s'prise. State opening an' that."

He put half of his drink down at a gulp. I shuddered and changed my plans to best him at his hobby. Murdie had slipped such slender leash as had held him. He was now leading the pack: and well clear of recall. No silver whistle would bring him to heel that night.

I emptied my glass, but put it down out of harm's way:

"Thanks, Murdie. I must go and pay my respects. Over there."

I had spotted the old Lord in the sitting room: his daughter and granddaughter on either arm, with Sir Robert facing them.

"I'll join you later for another."

But I lied in my craven teeth.

I escaped and headed for that close kinship. Helen saw me coming: spoke to the others. They turned to greet me. Charm: personality: charisma—call it what you will—hovered around them like a charge of loose electricity looking for an arc lamp to spark.

I realized I was close to the unknown state of love with this whole damn Family: but I was going to concentrate on the one member and make a job of it: at least until June.

I searched her eyes: had my dismissal of her charms spoiled my chances?

No. I knew I need make no promises I couldn't keep. All I wanted was there for the taking.

She displayed her grandpa like he was a three-year-old allowed up late in his velvet suit for a special occasion:

"Isn't he sooper?"

She didn't exaggerate. He was in great form. I said:

"Good evening, sir. She's right, you know. You look like an advert for somebody's long-life pills. Good evening, Helen. Robert."

I was drawn into that warm enclave: the rest of the room cut out. I went on:

"Please accept this with my best wishes."

It was a print of an etching by Muirhead

Bone. I had noticed it by chance in a junk shop near Partick Cross. It was a dry-point of an Upper Clyde vista, near the Cart inflow: ships, docks, masts. In the foreground was a double gantry crane astride a yard basin. Picked out in the lattice steel-work of the cross-beam was one word: Taggart: to be read from miles away.

That had seemed to say it all.

He unwrapped it and stared at it in silence. Then shook his head, remembering how it had been.

The Pixie gave a squeal of pleasure: Helen murmured "Oh, how perfect," and Robert set his glasses straight to smile at me.

Once again deep emotion thickened the Ayrshire in old Willie's speech: forced a stilted statement of his feelings:

"You could have given me nothing better, lad. I shall hang it where I can see it from my bed. Good of you to think so kindly of me with your own troubles and all."

Then, putting such old matters behind him:

"And I hear we have to congratulate you."

There were handshakes and kisses. I was almost airborne on a cloud of their charged adulation. I thought it was time to earth this high voltage transaction before I got burned up:

"I'm not going to take up my appointment. I am still going to America. My arrangements are made for the end of June."

I spoke to him: but I looked straight at Nella as I said it: all implications clear: no change in the ground rules. Now was the time for her to retire to the blue room if the going was too much.

But no: she was staying the course.

"I'm sorry to hear that. We all are. But you'll know best."

I was a big boy. I had made up my own mind.

His theme changed. This was a party: and he hadn't too many left under his belt:

"But since you aren't, come and take me round my guests."

He kept hold of Nella on one side. We were to escort him on a parade of honour. We set off on a stately promenade.

He smiled and chatted through these ranks—the Scots Battalion of the first hundred thousand—with easy panache: comfortable in a lifetime of shared memories.

The reminiscences meant nothing to me: even Nella was left groping for meanings and associations from years too far away for her. She left him leaning on my arm: detached herself and came to my other side. We formed a flying wing of our own. My perceptions of her began to take on extrasensory harmonics.

Two things became clear.

The first was that she was worried about Murdie. His appearances side-stage were increasingly noisy. She said "I wonder when we could get him upstairs. The trouble is if he gets the idea that you're trying to keep him quiet, he drinks all the more."

"The thing is to catch him just before he falls down, is that it?"

"That's right."

"Don't worry. He's about ready now. We'll keep an eye on him. I'll help. All very discreet."

For a moment I had slipped back into big brother: all seduction lines forgotten. But Novello couldn't have written me a better sentence.

I turned to look at her in reassurance: but stayed to stare, shocked by my second finding.

I knew this kid had a thing about me: sure enough to count on turning it to my own use.

But the look she returned me was naked in its avowal: indecent in its exposure: open to any hurt. There was no shred of self-defence: no kind of artifice.

I was loved: with every immaturity her youth could offer.

In face of my own selfish offering I might have felt shame: but I couldn't afford that. Besides just then Murdie took the spot-light away from me and my conscience.

Nella said:

"Oh, God! Look at Daddy."

For once the teenage nonchalance she posed was ruffled. The remark was as savage as any four-lettered malison in a tenement back court.

She disengaged from her trysting with me: went to coax and cajole him into some sort of privacy. I took the other flank.

Murdie had already loosened his collar and tie. His present struggle was to get his arms out of his jacket. In his mind he was set to do something funny: something to amuse the company. But between concept and execution there was a gap of maudlin incoordination a bottle of brandy wide: not to mention the bubbles.

We half-tugged, half-wheedled him

upstairs. He pulled and tugged at his clothes and chuckled in drunken glee at the wheeze he was about to pull. We got him into his bedroom.

Once inside he got his eye on his bed. You could see his mind change. All he wanted to do then was reach that comfortable landing pad, which he did face down with only a foot to spare. We rolled him square on. I got to the business of opening his shirt buttons: unzipping his pants.

"Can you get a towel? Some cold water?"

She fetched them from the loo that ran en suite and leant over him: sponging and bathing and caring despite herself.

Or because of herself? Because of the woman growing out of the minx by the very minute?

She left the basin by his head: pulled the quilt over him. She went into the bathroom to renew her make-up: to comb her hair back into straight, short order.

In the mirror she gave me a smile: derided her own infatuation:

"Hardly the stuff of passion?"

There were tears along her lower lids.

Shame at her father? Afraid for the love she

had exposed so recklessly? Hurt by me: and not for the first time?

Whatever: I had to try to help.

I held out my hands to her. She gave hers in return.

"My dear—"

That combination of simple words was difficult for me: like pronouncing Russian for the first time.

Her translation was faultless. She stood on her tiptoes: tried to put her arms around my neck. Only when I stood her on the bath stool was it comfortable.

She buried her face in my neck and sighed: a whole Venetian bridge.

"That doesn't sound too happy?"

She thought for a moment:

"Modified rapture, I think it was."

Gilbert and Sullivan for the upper classes.

"Well done. And will that be enough?"

"Yes. Yes. I'm worth that, aren't I?"

"I've no doubt that you're worth a damn sight more, but—"

She nodded. And I knew it was a bargain as binding as any of the old Lord's contracts.

Then we tried the first kiss of the shorter edition of love we were to write.

At first it was a cream-puff caress: the

merest setting of sights: delicate. It was enough to trigger a reaction like a twelve bore going off at the back of my head.

Her promise? Anyone's promise?

I neither knew nor cared.

I felt rather than heard her grunt of surprise and pain: felt salt blood on my tongue. She hadn't been in this league of ball game before: but if that's what it took, that's what she must give.

"This must be—what word shall I use—nice. Proper. To be remembered. Where can we meet? How?"

I was used to rear-seats and bachelor flats. That would never do.

"I don't know. This place is crawling with people. Will be all night—"

Then she had it:

"—I know. Peninver. My flat is liveable. Mummy's going to London for a couple of weeks to choose some things. And to visit my Aunt in Hindhead. Murdie's going too—"

There was something appropriate in that: to have our caprice in the place we had met.

"—they leave on Friday night. I'll see them off. Then meet you at the Shell?"

"Fine. Great. Sooper—"

That was a good word: said just what I wanted.

"—I have to work Friday night. But I'll be there with bells and ribbons and dancing shoes. We'll set up our bower before I start."

When we went downstairs we gave Helen a sign that all was well. Then we rejoined the party.

And, d'you know, I had a ball.

I said my goodbyes at Toward Craig the next morning.

I did not want to meet Nella again in that house. Whatever was to be between us, I wanted to be as frank and as fresh as possible: no strings apart from ones I could loosen on her lingerie.

Peninver, so far as I could gather, was to be refurbished from the very stones and timber out: a new vehicle for the lives to be lived there.

That ought to give us the proper setting.

We agreed that it should be whole-hearted, if short-lived. We would give this brief affray every chance of success: happiness even.

Into our two weeks we would cram all the caring we could muster: a crash course of affection: take what we could from our liaison, the span of an April shower: then quit. And if we each carried some remembrance of a sort of love into life, she would be that much richer and I that much more certain when my main chance came along.

But despite this commonsense approach: despite the matter-of-fact disposition of this short-haul event, as the time came near, I was aware of a mounting emotion. It was not one I had identified before with such an occasion: or that I had known for a long, long time.

Definition escaped me until that Friday in theatre. Fay McArthur said:

"Singing again, Neillie! My, your promotion hass cheered you up. You were always sso grim before."

Then I realized: I was happy: plain, smiling-at-the-world happy. This feeling glowed and smouldered inside me, and broke out in smiles on a world I had glowered at before.

It came to a head the night I was packing a bag in Passoud's palace, ready to start my two weeks' awooing. In fact I was clearing out altogether: giving up my room.

348

I had a minor problem. I went to talk to Jen about it.

"Jen, I ordered a trunk for my books and box of bones and such. I'm having it shipped by sea. It was supposed to be delivered today, but it hasn't arrived. I've stuffed my things in a couple of tea chests. Can I leave them with you until the trunk arrives? I'll come back and pack as soon as it turns up."

"Sure, Neil. Put them in that corner. I'll cover them with a rug."

I hauled the boxes through: then got ready to leave. I went back to her:

"Good night, Jen."

"You seem very pleased with yourself. Off on the skite?"

She indicated the weekend bag. I couldn't help the smirk.

"Well, be nice to her. Women have a hard time in this world."

"I promise, Jen. Maybe I'll bring her to meet you when I come back for my things."

I wondered how they would rate each other: this older woman I admired so much: and the younger one I might have got to admire, had I been around a bit longer.

"Goodbye just now, lover."

Our kiss was full and fond.

In the hallway I said goodbye to the Lesser Asiatic Alliance of Garscube and gave Shulie a box of Turkish delight: Rahmin I cuddled like a Teddy bear: Ranji, his wife, I pecked at with respect.

"You arre nott cross with me for speaking to you soe? I was greatlee upsett that night."

"No. No. You were right. I deserved it. It's all ten years too late for me now. But I do not doubt I rated everything you said."

He tucked his head into one shoulder like a snowbound Robin saying thank you for the crumbs.

"—Did you ever hear from those buccaneers again?"

"Noe. They have nott come near againe. Nott seen skin nor haire. You see. You have to stand up to themme. To alle of life. They will nott trouble me againe. You wille see."

"Good on you, sport. I'll be back with a trunk for some stuff that Jen has in her room. I'll keep my door key until then."

I got slices of moonlight all around to show me out as I left.

I had sold my car. I thought of taking a taxi: but they were as rare as chameleons in the wastes of Maryhill by that time. I would walk to the subway at St. George's Cross.

At the close entrance I paused: took a deep breath of night air: and made quite sure that Rahmin's ragamuffins had pissed off. I would hate to be left with just my case handle for luggage and my honeymoon haberdashery scattered from here to Hillhead.

But no: there was peace: not a whisper of suspicion. And I was an expert. I could hear a single decibel of that kind of danger at five thousand paces.

They were clean gone.

It was then I mounted my *summun bonum*.

Normally the sight of the Friday foot watch as they passed in pub parade depressed the hell out of me: the joggling Johnnies who strap hung with me to St. Enoch's would have moved me to nothing but a careful watch on my wallet.

That night I caught myself beaming at every single act of the Clydeway Follies with a benign inanity.

When I climbed the steps to Argyle Street, I saw on the old Bulletin clock that I was early: it had just gone ten.

Nella was to put her parents on the ten-thirty sleeper.

Instead of taking the short cut, the lane to Boots' corner, I indulged myself. I quartered, for a final time, at an easy saunter, the rectilines of Buchanan Street, St. Vincent Street and back down Renfield Street to the Station: the very centre and essence of home-town.

The world had finished its work for the weekend. Now he hung his woman on his arm and squired her to Friday night joytime in this city of Presbyterian fun: everywhere shut by half past ten: last bus home at eleven.

They had had to work at it: but, by God, they were having a good time or know the reason why.

But if the gaiety had qualities of grimness in its execution and of determination in its achievement, there was no doubting the chemistry of the mixture. It was exothermic: like my own feelings that night. Together the citizens of that town and me warmed the May night by several degrees.

As I went to stand by the Shell, to watch the untidy, half-circle crowd that waited around the London barrier, I began to feel like the time I got sweeties and a balloon at my first Sunday school Christmas party. I let it all rip: held nothing back: grinned like any young country gallant.

Santa Claus ruled: OK?

And when I spotted her cap of white hair, bobbing along six inches below the regulation five foot six Brigton brigade: saw her look of joy, I found a response eager and willing to match it. I barged and lunged my way to her until we could clutch at one another. I echoed her gasp of need and desire. Man must have his soul-mate and she was mine: at least for a couple of weeks.

"Neil! Neil! It's wonderful to see you. I've been longing for this time."

"So have I, kid. So have I."

"Have you? Truly?"

"Yes. Oh yes."

"Tell me more. Lots more. I lap that sort of thing up."

"I promise. Every day. Got your car?"

"No. It was easier by taxi. With their luggage and all. Shall we catch one back to the house?"

"Not tonight. You're coming down to my level."

We went down the steel steps to the Ca'doro bus stop: green and yellow transport would suit our anonymity: and my mood. We caught a south-side number: got off at Prince Consort Drive: walked up to the house.

We went in the big, front gates. She whispered:

"Watch! It squeals."

There was no-one near: any possible visitors warned off. But a pantomime conspirators' caution gripped us. We dodged down the drive with snorting, suppressed giggles. She opened the door with a series of keys.

I could see the new outside stairway at the side of the house:

"That gives on to the top-floor corridor at one end. Can you remember?—"

I nodded.

"—When it's finished it will make me quite private. But there has to be a fireproof door and it won't be ready until Mummy gets back. So there are no workmen. Nobody. Just us."

Inside the house was all so different from my last visit. The house was warm now. The smell of mould had gone. There was the slight astringent bite of fresh paint. New carpet had been laid. Furniture was stacked in corners. Bare ends of electric flex dangled from the ceiling. Our way was lit by a jury rig of two or three dim bulbs. You could feel the big house responding to a change of mood. It had lost its air of shame.

But if downstairs was incomplete, upstairs, as she had promised, was finished: to a perfection that surprised me.

I had imagined a splash of poster paints: Habitat furnishings: the garish gew-gaws of youth and rebellion. Instead the attic had been spread with a plain light carpet: decorated with matching Sanderson fabrics and wallcovering: dotted with some minor bits of Victoriana, to give an up-dated sense of period. The only concession to her youth was a posse of dolls arranged in artful confusion on a chair and a wall full of Scott Walker memorabilia in the kitchen. Her bed-sit was the one-time Nanny's room, now lush and handsome.

I crooked my arm about her neck to keep her prisoner as we inspected it, the scene of our coming together.

"It's all gorgeous—"

I gestured at the room. It was too.

A litter of big, floor bolsters did duty for all permutations of sitting, or lounging or lying you could imagine. I picked her up and threw her on one. It whoofed with the bruised cry of a hundred ducks' feathers.

"—I know this is going to be a happy time. Listen. I don't have too long. I'll unpack. How are you on food-making?"

"Must you leave me?"

"Now don't go all female. I did explain."

"I know. You made a promise."

"That's right. I'll be back for the biggest breakfast you can cook at the back of 7 a.m. Then I won't leave go of you until Monday morning. With a promise of evening performances thereafter. Even twice a night if you think you can stand it. But I owe tonight. And I must pay it."

Morrie Bishop had a hellish job. He was the co-ordinator in Benny McIndoe's E.T.S.: driver, doctors, cars, in the right place at the right time. But one or the other was always breaking down: or up: or out in a rash: or the traffic laws, leaving Morrie skint for a replacement with five minutes to find one. Morrie had been good to me: looked after my interests: fitted sessions into my hospital time-table: put extra work my way when I needed the money. In return I had sold him my soul on Fridays since I could remember when.

Every night carried its handicaps for Morrie: but Fridays were real sods. Nobody wanted to work then. That was the night of the large gins: the time the wives wanted taken out. That was when I put up for him:

"Until I get the boat for Broadway you can count on me for Fridays. Late night or early morning shift. You choose. Just let me know."

So Morrie sent me a list weeks in advance: and I hadn't let him down once. I had kept my word: appeared in time: been sober. I had promised him this last session weeks before. I would not renege:

"Some seduction."

"I'll make up for it. I'll tuck you up in bed at midnight when I leave. Be back before you're awake."

"I don't want to lose the—our—"

"—closeness?"

She nodded:

"Something like that. You feel it too?"

"Yes I do. It feels delicate. Precious. Like you, I don't want to spoil it. But it's only for a few hours. Then I'll be back."

"Why don't I come with you?"

I looked at her like you spot the crossword clue after hours of staring at it:

"Now why didn't I think of that before? Are you serious? Would you like to?"

"Oh! Yes! Please!"

It was genuine. It would fulfil a wish, a need, for her to be of some help in this world, even for a few hours. Insulated by the Family folding money that quilted her days on earth, she was starved of true-world stimulus. And, for all it was a small gesture in her comfortable life. I respected it.

Besides, it would give me company. Morrie didn't have a driver for me. He had phoned me at the Northern the day before:

"Can you drive yourself, Neil? I had George booked, but he's got an abscess on a tooth. Not up to driving for a day or so."

"Morrie. I bloody hate you."

I did too. It wasn't just the navigating, it was the loneliness: no-one to sound off at: to rub against, for all of those early hours.

Well, here was instant chum: already mixed in the cup: and very much to my taste.

"We'll do that. More, I think you might get paid for it. One problem, though. I can't leave you sitting in the car alone, outside a call. I'll think of something."

I did my dialling while she did things with cans and pans. By quarter to twelve we were fed, and ready: waiting outside the front gate. Ronnie Stuart's car drove up:

" 'Lo, Neil. You taking over?"

"That's it, Ronnie. This is my co-pilot."

He looked at Nella with no surprise. Six night hours at that caper and nothing—but nothing—under the moon and stars surprises you.

We squashed in the back: drove to Renfrew Street. Ronnie and his driver signed off. I said to Nella:

"You sit in the front, kid. I'll be back in a minute."

I sprinted upstairs to get my call sheets, street directory and maps: to pick up a bag and to arrange a little transformation I had dreamed up.

The telephone girls had been nurses at one time. That way they could weigh the weird messages they took: give some sort of professional priority to the docs in the cars.

Bel Hamilton was on that night. I knew that she always wore her blue belted raincoat and her porkpie hat from her days on district. She used to think it gave her some sort of immunity from roustabouts and rapists: although lately she hadn't been so sure.

"Special favour, Bel? Borrow your coat and hat?"

"Sure. If you want. What in the name d'you need that for?"

"Tell you later."

Morrie came out of his office:

"Who's this driver you've got, Neil?"

"A friend."

He came downstairs with me to inspect the replacement:

"God, Neil. Will it be safe? A woman?"

"Watch. Come out, Nella. Try this on—"

With the collar buttoned up, the hat squashed down, and the black apron shoes from her schooldays laced up, no-one was going to ask for her nursing certificate: not at that hour of the night.

"—All you need do is hold my bag. Give me out things if I ask for them. Take the pulse and temperature if I say. Can you do that?"

She nodded:

"—Thermometer in that pocket. Stethoscope in that drawer. That box has a thing called an auriscope in it. OK?"

I turned to Morrie:

"Union rates?"

"Couldn't do less."

As we drove off, she squeezed my arm:

"Oooh! This is exciting."

Exciting! I winced: but not so she could see.

Exciting! God give me strength for the last toll I would have to pay for my career west of the Carolinas.

It started as she imagined it would: a jazz:

"Medic A.Q. Come in, Medic A.Q.—"

I showed her the send/receive switch:

"You write the name and address. Look up the map. Come on. Earn your corn."

She squealed and weaved all over the road: but she got it done right and took us to the first call.

The cause of the noise was a wife of fifty-something, seven years deep in the sherry cask, with menopausal depression. She was doing a floorshow on the landing that would have set a Soho stripper on her mettle. She had an audience of dispirited neighbours out of their beds for the third night running. You could see they weren't going to vote her entertainer of the year.

"Something terrible, so it is. Something should be done."

They lowered at us: indignant to the last

nightshirt. Where the hell had we been? Loafing?

The husband was hovering inside the door: a pathetic man who looked at his carpet slippers:

"Will she come inside for you?"

"Do nothing for me."

There was a long story behind that. He looked at me then: and I knew who was the real patient. I went back to the landing:

"Show's over, folks. She'll be all right now. Nurse and I will take over."

The kid was there before me: trying:

"Come on back in. Nothing to hurt you. You can trust me. Trust me."

Trust: good stuff that.

I went into the bedroom. The discarded clothes lay scattered. I opened my bag and filled a syringe with a double ration of promazine, then hid it behind a clock with one hand: ticking minutes off in hourless circles. Nella coaxed our girl into the bedroom.

I went to the door: said to the husband:

"You make some tea. Nurse and me, we haven't had a cup all night."

I shut the door. Nella was indignant: "I gave you an enormous tea. I'm full to here."

"I know. But it gives him something to do. Something else to think about."

I snuck up behind Nutty Norah: put an arm lock on her: threw her face down on the bed.

I thought Nella would crown me with the wardrobe:

"But you can't do that. I was getting her to believe me—"

"I've just done it. Now sit on her head."

"Sit—! I will not."

"Listen. The real patient is in there—"

I jerked my head towards the clatter of a kettle:

"The quicker we can quieten her, the more good it'll do him. He's at the end of his tether in this world. She's quite happy in the one she's made for herself."

My pupil nurse hadn't thought about that:
"What do I do?"

"Turn her head to the side so she can breathe. Put a pillow over her ear. Sit on it."

There's a lot of laws about not forcing treatment on patients: technical assault. But if the guy dunking the Darjeeling next door didn't get some kind of help in a hurry, we'd get his head to pull out of the oven.

Nella took my word for it: with a scowl. We

got Wriggling Wilma still long enough for me to get the whole hundred jolts into her system: mainline. It worked like a pile driver. In five minutes she was in a nightie under the sheets: peaceful as a dove.

Her husband knocked:

"Tea's masked."

"Good. I'm ready for it. Come in and see."

He opened the door: looked at the still form. Nella was brushing her hair tangle out to lie neatly over her shoulders and her pillow.

"She seems younger—"

She did too: the lines and puffiness of her debauchery in fortified wine smoothed and eased.

We went to have the tea. As a sacrament to this kind of confession it has communion wine whipped into a vinegar bottle. He told us all about it.

His wife should have been in Woodilee. He knew that. But she wouldn't go near the doctor. Besides it was such a disgrace. She wouldn't go to the shops either. Or keep her turn at the stairs. He did all of that.

The housewife's apron that she had tied around him should have made him more pathetic. But—

"—She was my girl. The only one ever. Been my wife for forty years. A good mother. A fine woman. Until this happened—"

He had borne with it all patiently: hoping for betterment: hoping that the girl in the sun-bonnet and the flowered dress would come again. In the telling he didn't lose stature: he gained it.

"—I haven't the heart to put her away."

In his carpet slippers: his darned cardigan: his neck without collar and tie, he was still her knight: parfait and gentil in Garrowhill.

My pocket bleeper sounded:

"We have to go now. But I want you to do something for me—"

I stressed the inversion of the usual medical transaction:

"—Two things, in fact. First, here's a couple of pills. You haven't slept for three nights. On top of months of worry. Take these. You'll have a good night. Tomorrow things will seem better. Second, in the morning I'll leave a note for your own doctor to ask a specialist to come here. There's all sorts of treatment possible. She may not have to go inside. I'm not promising magic, but this is a hell of a state you've got yourself into. Can't go on. Can it?"

He looked at me. He knew I knew:

"—It will help nothing if you leave her."

Relief and release poured down his face:

"No. No. It wouldn't help. But it's been so hard to bear—"

He came to the door with us:

"—Thanks. Thanks, awful. And you too, nurse. You were both so kind with her. So gentle."

She looked at me. I winked: but without a trace of slyness. She could work that one out for herself.

Back in the car, I could see her fun thing had taken a serious turn.

"That poor man. Was he—? Had he really thought about suicide? Yes. I know he had."

She was shaken:

"He won't now. Not tonight."

"But what about later? If she doesn't get better—"

I cut across that line of chat:

"No buts, kid. We've done what we could. Now come on. Your job is to drive. Take messages. Get on with it."

She gave me a look that consigned our recent warmth to the ice-cap at Novaya Zemlya:

"This is Medic A.Q. Medic A.Q. Over—"

She was getting her involvement all right: more than she had bargained for.

Next we went to a block of flats: new wave corporation, circa 1965. We scrunched our way through the splinters of every pane of glass that had glazed the stair window. A bicycle tyre decorated a wall light that had been bent at right angles: the fitment shattered to give eternal darkness.

Plus ça change . . .

I knocked on the door after some study. Someone had put a foot through the lower panel: two of the upper glass squares had been replaced by cardboard: but I found one bit that would stand a chapping.

Stoun, Malky and Frezz had signed the free handspray work on the walls. It was reassuring to see that their ethnic art form had survived the translation of their culture: from eighteen-nineties tenement to five-year-old slum in easy lessons: techniques taught nightly.

Lydia Pink opened the door to us. She had a headful of curlers mounted in a beehive coiffure: a bright pink scarf was draped over it to stop the workers from swarming. The rest of her was mounted to match: dressing gown, lipstick, nail-varnish, furry tops

on satin slippers. Her face was full of fag:
"You took your time. 'S the old one. Canny draw a breath."

That was my girl. No dickering with the diplomatic dialectic: no hello, I'm glad to see you. Instant citizens' right and no messing.

The old one was laid in a bed along one wall of the living room. She was sitting erect in an awesome attempt to breathe: to relieve the blue-black congestion of her face.

A family party was going on under, over and around the patient.

The men had done terrible damage to a bottle of White Horse. They were drinking to its memory with some bottles of Wee Fowlers. A bottle had rolled under the bed. Someone lay flat fishing it out.

The ladies were on vodka and Barr's Irn Bru. A glass of this Romanoff refreshment was being passed over granny's head to someone who, from the look on her face, relished the idea.

The lot of them sat around the old lady, at every point you could box a compass, smoking Lydia Pink's fags. Granny's inspiratory efforts sucked in the fug: asphyxiating her by the minute.

I saw Nella's face blacken again: her mouth

open. But I warned her off with a frown as dark as her own. This was no ordinary party. This was a wake being held in advance: a celebration of their fear of death in general: a homage to what had been their mother figure.

This mixture of naked emotion and alcohol had made them as primed and unstable as a shipload of nitrate gone sweaty. One wrong word could detonate the lot. They would go off in animal reaction. Kick the cat if there happened to be one: and if there wasn't, anything else that moved. That included uppity docs who got above their station.

But I had the perfect therapy for them:

"Go and make some tea. Nurse and I are parched."

They filed into the kitchen, meek as Cinderella's mice. See me for a fairy godmother with the magic patter.

The old lady's hair was the lank, grey-black of long ill-health. Though she could breathe only with the intense effort of every accessory muscle she could bring to bear on her distress, her black eyes gleamed at us: a tiny nod showed she was glad we were there: a miniscule smile said what a hell of a life it was.

"Your bronchitis, is it?"

She nodded: gratified I was a clever Dick: saved her speech:

"Are you on tablets? For the wheeze? Heart ones? Water ones?"

She nodded: satisfied. I was in the know all right.

They were on the mantelpiece. I checked the dosages. Nella had gone to the window: wrenched it open.

"Good. Now sit in behind her. Help prop her up."

The orthopnoeic support of six pillows was not enough. The woman was sitting bolt upright to extract every last benefit from her struggle.

Nella got in behind her: cuddled her erect. The woman nodded again. Relieved of the effort to sit up she could concentrate all of her will on her respiratory muscles.

"Taking all these pills? Had them today?"

This time she merely closed her eyes in assent. Anything else was too much.

I got out the stethoscope. I didn't need it: but the ritual might give comfort. I listened to the coarse crackle of lungs bathed in moisture: the thin whine of bronchioles narrowed and thickened: the thrumpety, thrump, thrump, thrumpety of a fibrillating heart, trying to pump black blood into her face.

She had the lot: a living—only just—Muir's textbook of pathology.

I would risk a poppy-shot. It might knock off her respiratory centre: shut off her air supply good and proper: but that would be a favour.

I filled a syringe. Held it up so she could see:

"Listen. This is sleepy medicine. Marvellous stuff. Five pounds a throw in Hope Street."

She nodded: the smile less: the gasps bigger. I put it under her skin. If she was going to die I wanted to be long gone from that bunch of relatives when it happened.

I sat on her bed: held her hand. Nella sat dead still, sensing the need for calm.

She nodded again: it was working. She had a huge repertory of nods: each one telling a different story. She had had long practice.

As she went under she nodded at the bottles, the cans, the smoke clearing slowly:

"Don't mind—Don't mind them—They're upset about me."

She took six pants to a phrase.

"I know."

The nursing assistant chipped in:
"Surely they should stop smoking. She's choking in all of this."
The old lady shrugged:
"I don't mind."
What the hell. This way she had company at her end.
We eased her back on to the pillows. She began to drift into sleep. I summoned the mourners-in-life; got them to bring the tea. We sat and sipped it until the old lady was well away.
They were quiet: awed by the difference. I carried strong ju-jus. Now was the time for the serious stuff:
"You all realize how ill she is. She may come out of this sleep. She may not. If it isn't this time, it'll be the next. Or the one after. But soon—"
One of the men: a son by the black of his eyes, began to cry.
"—I'm going to radio for an ambulance to bring some oxygen. If you smoke in the same room, you'll go up like a box of squibs."
They doused their cigarettes on the instant.
In the car Nella blew out a long, slow breath: the longest of her teenage life. I asked:
"You all right?"

"I'm all right. But you—"

"What did I do?"

"—you are the biggest, most conniving bastard I could dream up. I could never trust a word you said."

"I never said you could."

"No. You never did, did you?"

What a lot of bitterness there was in this growing up.

"You're doing well, girl. I've been at this for years. It takes practice."

I spoke gently. She liked not the road I was on:

"Medic A.Q. Come in . . ."

It's the insistence, you see: the endless demand, with barely a breath to sort out your own emotions.

She reached for the microphone: clicked on the dash light: fished for pad and pencil.

Involved? She was up over her ears despite her amateur status.

But that was the end of the excitement she had imagined: the Ben Casey stuff.

For the next dozen calls—from that time until the dawning—we had to deal with a dozen cases of functional illness: a bag of assorted nuts that neither I nor anyone else with a medical degree was going to crack.

I sat Nella in the corner of strange rooms and showed her pages from an unwritten encyclopaedia of acute illness: the afflictions of the inglorious: the miseries of those who had missed out.

There was a time in my career when I thought the same as her: and with fair reason. After all, the whole medical curriculum was geared to sorting out organic disease: things you could cut out with a knife: or cure with a syringeful of side-chain analogues: or save with a canister of oxygen and a positive pressure respirator.

The professors consigned this other stuff to the shrug department: not a medical problem. For a solution try the Samaritans, the Salvation Army, or the suicide tray in the mortuary.

But my nights in the calamity bus had taught me different.

I learned that such disease carried crises as sudden as endotoxic shock: as pole-axing as peritonitis.

Insight into your own inadequacy could strike as deadly as any infarct: and as sudden. Realization that the iron rations dealt by fate were going to be the staple diet of the rest of life could happen in the wee small hours: and be as catastrophic as terminal cancer.

If a phone call at half-past something in the dark brought someone to register your complaint: to give you a pill or a potion as an earnest that somebody gave a damn about something in your life, who was to blame them.

But you had to dig for the real illness: like with sad Sadie.

Time and again you found shame and embarrassment: guilt and self-doubt: defeat and impotence buried under the symptoms.

The trick was to winkle out the truth.

After a couple of years at this frolic I became expert at this new game. And I came to respect the family docs. They knew this terrain and their patients like a Highland shepherd knows his hills and his sheep.

Somewhere about four o'clock I said: "Some fun, huh!"

She shook her head. Disbelief and dismay had compounded to still her chatter: to numb her comprehension: to dull her bright optimism.

Yet there was more to it:

"Neil, I feel so depressed."

She didn't understand that.

I squeezed her hand. I should have known it would get to her. She had that kind of intuition.

For, you see, there was something else: something more: an X-factor. It had taken me a long time to put my finger on it.

Anyone who did those stints got a whole new view of the circus: a top of the tent-pole view of all three rings at once: more than any single family doc could take in.

On such Friday nights you got to work your way through every back court from Burnside to Bowling: to climb every corporation stair from Castlemilk to Carntyne: to top every tower block from Tradeston to Easterhouse.

I found I was watching not only more human nature than you could shake a stick at: but, also, the piecemeal destruction of the city.

In every airt and corner I travelled, the big sandstone buildings that had made a town-scape, unique in the land: the world, even, were being destroyed. I was made to witness the decimation—not of a city—but of a way of life: a whole culture.

I never knew the Empire. It was a whiff of

nostalgia in the history books by the time I got to it. I wouldn't know a colonial if I met him in my bath.

But this had been the second city of that fabled time: the workshop of that globe-cast conglomeration of colours and creeds.

And what a city!

Oh, it was a place that had banged and rattled: that had more than its share of booze and beltings: blood and bootings. But you knew you were alive in it. You could feel you were a corpuscle of its life: squeezed along its arteries of commerce: regulated by the secretions of its trade: pumped through its big, iron heart: laid out for oxygen in its smoky lungs.

But it had made engines that gave a new word to the lexicons for excellence. And it created ships that earned a new synonym for elegance: Clydebuilt.

That had bred a self-respect in its people: take on the fates, the world, the future.

My life had been spent among folk who knew this above all else: who had taught me by an innate precept and example, bred into them for decades.

The entire metropolitan enterprise had been kept afloat by pride and guts.

But now? For what?

Wrecked and wasted: bulldozed and burned, the background of generations, the stamping ground of a culture, was being annihilated by the hour.

All of the struggling: all of that slog, had gone for nothing. The whole Clydeside civitas had been decanted into endless, amorphous, council-house schemery: a certain death for the life it had known. And the great industrial engine of coal and steel that had sustained it had left only an Ozymandian rubble of rusted iron.

And it had gone without a whimper: without knowing it had happened.

This deluge of unfathomable illness that had trebled and quadrupled in the past few years: that swamped the family docs by day: this flood of undiagnosable malady that drove the deputies daft by night, was more than any expression of loneliness or poverty.

It was an animal keening for this greater loss: felt in the bones as sure and final as any fatal toxin.

It had affected me, too.

God help me, this was my hometown. I wanted to wander round its back streets, love its tumble-down old shack streets: but every time I turned my back they put the bloody blasters in.

Even one night of it had affected this kid beside me.

About five o'clock I swapped her into the passenger seat. She didn't sleep: but she got her eyes closed in a sort of chin against the chest dazement, as we parked under one of the piers they were building for the new motorway bridge and the squawk box kept quiet for an hour.

The last call was back to medicine as revealed to the suckers. It came in about 6.30. I could almost feel the relief in the girl beside me.

"Medic A.Q. Come in A.Q. Child with earache . . ."

We climbed three sets of stone stairs to a single end built into the roof before the days of planning and fire regulations. The close was clean: the walls new painted and marked only by the scrapes of daily usage.

"This seems different. Better."

"Bought houses."

"What d'you mean?"

"These were owned as investments by heritable trusts, insurance companies, some of the churches. It became uneconomical to repair them. They'll be demolished soon. In the meantine they sell them for a few hundred quid. Glad to get out with something."

"And the people in them?"

"It's a start. Either that or go on the corporation list. Or live with mother-in-law."

I knocked on the door. We were ushered in. It would have knocked your eye out.

The guy was young: maybe twenty-five: the muscular throat and arms of a joiner: a craftsman. And, by God, he had joined and crafted at his roof-top room to make it the penthouse of the year.

Our visit coincided with the new baby's first feed of the day: Nella was in seven transports of rapture. She went to join the milk and talcum set.

I turned to dad and the patient:

"Sorry to bother you this early, doc. But he's been up all night. Pulling at his ear. This last couple of hours have been bad. Screaming. Banging his head."

The son of the house would have put the Pears' bubble boy out of business. He sat up in the settee bed. The scarlet cheeks: the runny nose: the insignificant sobs told it all.

His right tympanic membrane looked like a blood orange.

"He's got a sort of boil in his ear. Painful. But we should be able to get it settled quickly. He needs an injection though."

That made him howl the more.

For all his angel looks I knew he would struggle like a pit pony.

"Nurse. I'll need both you and dad to hold him."

They got him laid over dad's knee: ready for the jab.

I waved a big 20 mil. syringe in front of his eyes: and the biggest needle I could find. I put some sterile water in it: laid it six inches in front of his nose, so he couldn't miss it.

Nella looked as if she wanted to shove a garden syringe up any orifice she could find in me. Dad licked his lips a touch. The boy was mesmerized. He moaned in anticipation of this big jag, his ear relegated to a minor discomfort: saving his screams and his fear for this agony to come.

"That's the big injection, son. The one that's going to hurt. But first a little prick to freeze the skin."

I slipped a million units of penicillin into his bum while he was still mesmerized:

"That's it. All finished—"

I whipped him upright on his daddy's knee. The three of them looked at the big syringe: still loaded. I took the needle off it: squirted the water in the air: gave it to him, a present to drive his parents dotty when he felt better and could get to the sink to mess about.

"—I cheated."

The father crowed: a caw-caw-caw of delight that he had been taken in too. The patient ran to his mother. His whimper became tremolo as relief brought laughter through his tears.

The nurse's mouth was a small, soundless oh of disbelief. She had forgotten how rotten I could be.

"Get this prescription. See he gets it faithfully every four hours. See your own doc tomorrow. Check that his ear is improving."

"Great, doc. You'll have some tea. You and nurse."

The pair of us had fluid levels in our eyes by then. But, what the hell. It was the end of an era for both of us: several years for me: a lifetime for Nella by the look on her face.

There was a fire going roarie-o up the range canopy. He shoved it back. Heat flooded into the room.

We drew in chairs: clasped our mugs: chalices of goodwill: swilled the stuff down as if it was a rare treat.

"You've got your house beautiful. Must have taken a lot of work."

Pride wrestled with contempt: but he had to allow he had made the effort:

"Aye—"

Then disgust won:

"—but we'll not be here much longer. Imagine a man and his family having to live in this. In this day and age—"

There was the other awful truth: the other jaw of the paradox. The only place for a building this old and done was the breakers' barrow.

"—but I'm going to no corporation scheme. I'm away to a New Town. Glenrothes. Next month. Been biding my time for the right job to come up—"

He winked over at his family:

"—be all right then."

Nella got in the driving seat again: but she sat, hands in her lap, young shoulders in a slump.

"Don't take it so hard, kid. You can't change the world single-handed."

"You can try to help."

I looked at her face. That night that had started as a lark, had changed her life:

"And you—"

I was in for more stick:

"—I don't understand. How can you leave them? All of that. Just for money."

I roared. I really put my head back and had a belly laugh.

But you can't laugh forever. And when I stopped, her eyes were still on me: grave, confused: but, as always, trying to understand: seeking a truth.

I shook my head at her:

"That's easy. I can't stand any more."

"There seems to be an awful lot you can't stand."

That very thought had just crossed my mind.

7

I CARRIED Nella upstairs, half-asleep on
my shoulder. I turned the shower to hot
and put her under it: clothes and all.

I went into the kitchen. I took off the mac,
opened the window and threw the coat into
the back yard of my new tomorrows.

I hunted in the cupboards: found a bottle of
Queen Anne, lemons, sugar and mugs. I
boiled some water in the kettle. Then I
carried these all into the bathroom: put them
in easy reach of the shower: climbed in beside
her.

We pulled off our stale clothes. We soaped
the smell from our skin and hair: a pot-pourri
of our own rank sweat, petroleum exhaust,
antiseptic, and the ineffable, unmistakable
taint of decay from the dying city. We toasted
the thought of it from our minds with
mouthfuls of sweet-sour Toddy.

I dried us both with a big, furry towel. We
slept naked, our flanks asprawl, our legs
entwined: out like someone had put the three-
phase cable to our lives.

The next thing I knew she was pulling hairs out of my chest, complaining that she hadn't been seduced yet and when was I going to do something about it.

"I thought you'd gone off me."

She considered that:

"No. Nooo. Not really. No—"

It wasn't the most positive statement I had ever heard.

"You're not what I thought you were. Different. Kinder in some ways. Harder in others. But I can see how. Why?"

"That's more hopeful. I thought you might ask me to find other digs."

"No. Not until I've had your way with me. Like now?"

"Sex? On an empty stomach? You've a lot to learn, kid."

"Do I come second to food?"

I laughed at her: at the kid that kept peeking out. And laughter seemed a good ingredient for a love-in that was one-sided.

She made an extravagant claim that she could devil kidneys and bacon. She would do that diabolic thing after I gave her tea.

"Yass'm."

I made with the Macleans and the moustache mower: than carried the Melrose mash in to her on a tray. In between sips I explored the territory about her neck and ears. Then she rose to her hell-bent duties, while I went to make us gay with a little Gordon's.

On such occasions I had been known to use a brace of still Dutch courages, but that day we wanted none of the sensations blurred: no issues clouded. So I used fair quantities of quinine water but the merest modicum of gin: enough to free the mind from the mould of the expected.

Then we sat at the breakfast bar making a righteous attack on her devil's work. There was music from—guess who? Scott Walker. After we had washed the dishes, we arranged a soft-landing pad on the big floor cushions: started our orbit around the lesser sun of desire. For a start it was friendly: even fond. For next, I discovered that, for her, it was a special occasion. I hadn't expected that.

We were at the end of the swinging decade: the sexual revolution was now an *ancien régime*: the daring of ten years back was today's normality. And it had seemed clear from his proprietary air that Johnnie had established rooster rights.

But there was the hint of tautness: the slight clench of anxiety.

I put a finger under her chin: turned her to me:

"Is this—? Am I the first?"

She went red: not the scarlet of admission: but the gorgeous, rosy blush of virginity:

"Well, I'm damned—"

I said it softly: with reluctance:

"—I ought to feel a dirty dog."

"Do you?"

"No. In fact it makes me feel bloody marvellous—"

And I did. I felt a surge of rotten, male, breast-beating pride:

"—I'm glad it is to be me."

I have never counted myself a professional on the strings of appassionata. I was more an enthusiastic amateur. Like Queen's Park in their day, give anyone in the league a game for their money.

But that Saturday I informed my loins of all the patience and care I could command.

I had my reward in a deepening of the unusual experience of her first, grateful kiss: sweetness. Reception distilled this into a flowered perception: so delicate, that each memory was disbelieved until refreshed:

clover heads sucked on a hot June day.

"I hope you've laid in lots of food."

"We can get more tomorrow. Or Monday."

I shook my head:

"Nope. Nobody's going nowhere. Not for a week. All they'll find is our skellingtons."

She sighed: happy at the prospect of starving for love.

On Monday morning I phoned the ward: spoke to Pansy:

"Flower. This is Neil Aitken. Will you tell Ronnie that I have this awful 'flu? I don't think I shall be in all week. Ask him if he'll cope."

And sucks to him, the bastard. He owed me for many's the time.

"You sound all right to me."

"What? Not a word of sympathy. If you knew the prognosis in my case. Nothing but complications."

There was truth in my prophecy: complications I did not foresee.

Beneath my hands: loose in her ungirdled gown and sitting apart: sensed in the scent of her essences, she grew in womanliness. The whole mechanism of her youth: all her breathing, beating and moving came together in a while that was so much greater than the sum of these vital parts: a whole that threatened to overwhelm me.

She asked:

"Have you—? I know you have. Before. But do I please you?"

I was hard put not to make a declaration that I—we—would both regret. But I could be this honest:

"Yes. But it was never, ever, anything like this. I promise."

She took some content from that: and I kept the rest of my troublesome declarations to myself.

We did go out occasionally: strolls in the darkening: a race through the dawn dew in Maxwell Park. But we made no serious attempts at provisioning: milk, butter, a few perishables for the occasion, was all.

By the following Saturday we had worked our way through the bulk provender: had emptied the fridge: were down to the weevilly biscuits at the bottom of the barrel.

"Neil. I must do a proper shop. Come and carry the parcels."

I shook my head: pulled on my green bathrobe: put on another Scott Walker tape. You get used to anything in time.

"Hurry home."

"Ooh. You're just a—"

"—big bastard?"

"So long as you know."

"You're not leaving much room for doubt."

She came to me: put her head in the middle of my chest:

"Let's not fight. Even in fun. There's so little time."

That shaft of perception lit up the other, bitter side of our agreed term of affection. The world had been lost for a week: and well lost: and for a week to come. But finding it again was going to be a sore business.

"If you bring home mutton pies, I'll take you out tonight. We'll do something special—"

I leered at her:

"—I'll be waiting."

"I don't know much—anything—about this kind of interlude, but I think you must be perverted."

"Priapic is the word."

"Is that bad?"

"No. I've enjoyed every minute of it."

She wasn't long. I heard the door close

391

downstairs: the confident clatter of someone who had used it for years.

I judged time enough to let her reach the upper corridor. I called down then:

"Your Mummy did bring you up well. Are you always so quick? I've got your lunchtime drink ready."

Midday gin and tonics had become a feature of our castaway lives. I primed it ready with ice and a twist of peel: turned to the kitchen door as it opened: handed it to—her mother.

"Christ!" I said. Then:

"It's a gin and tonic. If you want. You look as if you should sit down."

I said it warily. I wasn't too sure how fond Mums reacted to scenes like this. Did I get an axe in the back of the head?

Colour suffused her cheeks: then drained away, leaving her white. She took the drink: sat down heavily on a stool at the eating counter.

"You're back early. We didn't expect you yet. Not for a week."

The expressions that had been chasing over her face settled into dismay: unhappy: weary.

"I knew there was something wrong. That's why I came back. Something different about her when we spoke on the phone. Something suppressed."

I knew what she meant. Nella had been sitting on my lap when she made the calls.

"I thought she might be moping about Johnnie. She's broken with him. But of course—"

She looked at me in full dawning:

"—you'll know about that—"

I nodded.

"—I never guessed—"

You could see the implications striking home: little facets of vision coalescing into a full picture.

I was uneasy. My own selfish ends were tied in a knot to scourge me now:

"—She—I—we all trusted you."

"Helen. I have no excuses. No regrets. This was—"

I searched for a word to describe the unusual: the unique in my life:

"—necessary almost. Like sleep. To both of us. For different reasons."

She sat back. Dismay abdicated. Resignation took over. She loosened her coat, reached for the drink and sipped it.

"Mothers get dewy-eyed about the thought

of this. Even when it's legal. Women have to take so much on trust—"

That word again.

"—If it blows up in their faces it's so much worse than for men. Have you been able to do this with caring?"

"That has been easy. It also makes it much more difficult."

"Yes. I believe that. I suppose—legal or not—I'm glad it was you—"

I blinked.

"—You would be honest. It isn't always easy to be honest. With yourself. With the other person. In this sort of situation—"

She seemed to want to talk. Then came a pay off that I never expected: that I had given up thinking about.

"—You were always curious what happened. My night of the pills—"

The words came in an odd, mechanical way: as if she had repeated the script over and over:

"I have never been a full woman. I have had two husbands. The only men. And I have borne two children. But I have never known what it's all about. I've never known—horrid word—orgasm. My first husband was a boy-hero—"

I had seen photographs of him: ethereal pictures, as if taken through muslin.

"—a poet, whose poetry came from his emotions. Never his intellect. I mustn't seem to sneer. I was the same. He was a sweet boy—"

She paused: then filled in some background:

"—It's difficult for people like you—of your time I mean—to understand the romantic cliché of the thirties. It was a game played on our generation. As if the world couldn't stand the truth. A final attempt to believe in—to manufacture innocence. When the war came it was glamorized even more—"

She relived that great stimulus of her young womanhood for a moment: but then came back to the bitter aftertaste of her own experience.

"We had managed some fumblings—a few moments of what we imagined was rapture—to prepare us. The true intimacy of marriage came as a shock—particularly to him. He wanted to get the panting bit over with and then to be soulful about what had happened. I got left at the gate—and I wasn't even sure what I should be waiting for—"

I stood as still as I knew how. The story got no better:

"—Oh. I got excited from time to time. And I was so awash with romantic notions myself, that I didn't recognize my own frustrations. Then I got pregnant, which shifted my emotional target. Covered up the problem. Focused all on the babe. The more so when Alan, my husband, was killed. I poured it all out on my boy. All my bets were on him. But underneath my emotions were conniving—"

She looked at me. A smile softened the bleakness for a moment. Remembering she forgave us:

"—When Murdie came on the scene he seemed just what I wanted. Needed. You know what he's like. Big. Hearty. Male. But I hadn't reckoned on Murdie's drinking. He wasn't an alcoholic when I married him, although he had been drinking for a long time. But when I knew him at first, he could stop. I found out that under his exterior he was—of all things—insecure. Shy. One of his problems—although I didn't find out until later—was a fear of not performing. As our wedding got near this became worse. On the day he drank more than he should. Just to help him over his nerves and to be sociable. Later, he drank a little more to help him over me—"

She went on without rancour:

"—I drank a bit too. I was going to be a wanton for that night at least. I was going to make up for lost time. In the passing I would give him all the confidence he needed—"

Her tone stayed matter of fact: a dispassionate view of many years with a problem of no solution.

"—But randyness isn't my style. Despite the alcohol I had to try hard. Too hard. As he did. Between us we failed. Miserably. He couldn't—what's the phrase—get it up. I couldn't believe it. He was so mortified. And I was so ashamed—"

I looked at my lemon peel. Helen had had to suck some sour truths in her time.

"—It never came right after that. Not once. Oh, he could manage. Look at Nella. But for me it was all over—"

Her voice had a drained sound about it: such revelations exhausted the soul:

"—He began to drink more. And the more I couldn't stand him. He would pester me until I gave in, just for peace."

She considered that:

"—It's an odd relationship, marriage. The most complex there is. I never hated Murdie. I don't now. I'm sorry for him. For me. For us. He sensed that. It only made him more cross. That day—or rather the night before—"

After all these weeks the circuit was about to close: the current to flow: the display to show on the screen.

"—He came to me. Wouldn't be put off. Again I let him try. Over the years I've found it the easiest thing to do. He ground and ground and ground. It seems like hours—"

I grunted: closed my eyes. I couldn't look at her:

"—When finally he knew that he wasn't going to manage, he reared up between my legs and gave me the most awful slapping."

I thought of his big, beefy paws: of her slender, chicken bones.

"—I covered my face with my hands, but he hit me all over the head and ears. I was sick and dizzy for hours after. Poor chap. He doesn't remember. He would be even more ashamed. And he has enough to bear—"

A complex relationship indeed:

"—I felt so degraded. So useless. Women of my age do, you know—"

398

I remembered Abie's little lecture.

"—The pills seemed an obvious way out."

We looked at each other during a long silence. In time her bleakness lessened:

"And now?"

"I've come to terms with it. This—"

She waved her arms at our love nest:

"—brought it all back. Fear for her. You can understand?"

"Of course I can. And what you are doing now. And saying. It's all very generous."

"No. It's an attempt to be honest. With my own disasters as signposts. I would give anything to have a memory as happy as I think you will have made this for her. For I'm sure you care."

She was making an anthem of that last phrase:

I flushed:

"It has been easy to do that, Helen."

"I'm glad of that. I won't interfere in any way. It isn't my business. I mean only to give a blessing. And to hope for happiness for Nella. For you both—"

She finished the drink: stood up: made ready to leave.

"Despite all I've just said, like all mothers I wish marriage for my daughter. Is she going with you to the States? With that as a possibility if nothing more."

"No. It isn't in the contract."

I cited that like a High Court defence.

"Ah!"

She had had experience of Taggart contracts before.

"I can't take the risk."

"What risk?"

"I've had a hint that a job—one I badly want, but thought I could never get—might come my way. In this country. Lots of prestige. But—"

"Well?"

You could see her with her grandchildren in a villa in Bearsden:

"—There isn't too big a salary. I would never be quite sure why I had done it."

She jerked her head back: as to ride a punch. Her voice dropped to a whisper:

"Neil. Neil. Can't you do better than that? She's worth more from you."

"Can't be done. I must be my own man. Must be sure of it."

She took it all in. I meant what I said. I was stuck with my hang-up: worse by far than anything she had dangling in her cobwebby cellar:

"Poor Nella. To think I envied her a moment ago. And you, Neil. You're not only poor. You're bankrupt. Not an emotional asset between here and hell."

I nodded:

"It's safer that way."

She was shocked into silence.

The door downstairs crashed to again:

"Cooeee!"

She gathered her things: handed me the glass:

"God help the pair of you. Don't say I was here. I'll slip into the schoolroom. Make a noise. Keep her busy."

But she took the time to salute me: lip to lip: as if to confer the need of love? Certainly the gesture led straight to my heartland. Just as well I had trained it in defence.

I had fresh ice and lemon in the glass before Nella puffed to the top of the stairs: arms around, nose atop, a hug of brown paper bags and parcels:

"You are a pig. You might've come down to help me—"

She ended in a yelp. I gathered her to me, groceries and all: growled in her ear like a daddy-bear. But I stared at Scott Walker on the wall without a glimmer of recognition.

401

These manoeuvres seemed to take her mind off things. Only I heard the schoolroom door whisper open: the stockinged feet. Although moments later she said:

"Wasn't that the downstairs door?"

"Rubbish, girl. Tell me. How many pies did you bring?"

Around tea time Nella asked:

"What's my special treat to be?"

"There's only one thing to do on a Saturday."

I broke into my renowned Suzie-Q: remains of the big band scene of my boy days:

"Come dancing with me?"

"A disco? Sooper!"

"Nah!" I scorned.

I caught her to me: gave out with a twangy-twangy bit of a Bolero tango. To my surprise she did a few instinctive steps.

"I didn't think young women knew that sort of dancing. Not nowadays."

"I don't. Not truly. But Mummy insisted I learned. I had some formal lessons. For social occasions. Good fun. But I don't get much chance to practise. And you?"

"I live next door to this widow. Jen.

Ballroom dancing used to be her life. When her man was alive. I squired her sometimes. If she was lonely. She taught me the fancy bits. Not that I'll ever get on *Come Dancing*. But enough so I don't get my ankles in a fankle."

"Sooper fun. Where shall we go?"

I tapped my bent honk:

"Only one place for a night as special as this. The Plaza."

Dance halls were dying the death by the dozen at that time, but one Glasgow institution stayed the course: the Plaza: a palais de danse from away-back times. It had a fountain: a strict tempo band: and an air of middle-class gentility that had been bred in the days of afternoon tea at Miss Cranston's.

"Ooh. Soooper—"

It was the longest sooop I had heard yet. I wondered if it would be the last. I couldn't go on with our next, planned week in face of Helen's visit. She had made a huge effort to be understanding: give her blessing. But it would be too cool by half to go on as if nothing had happened.

But how and when did I tell her? And what reason to give? I couldn't split on Mummy.

"—I've always wanted to go there."

Whatever I told her would have to be later. I couldn't burst that shiny balloon: not just then.

I put on the dressiest of my new suits. She found ankle strap shoes with heels the height of a fractured fibula.

Before we left I phoned Jen:

" 'Lo, lover. Has my trunk arrived?"

"Yes. It came a few days ago, Neil."

"Great. Listen. I'm going dancing. I'll stop by on my way home. About eleven. Can I bring my girl to see you?"

I glanced at Nella. My unconscious phrase had blown her balloon even bigger.

"I'd like that, Neil. I'll have the kettle on."

Resplendent in our rapture rags we went to do slide turns on the slipperene at St. Andrew's Cross.

We pirouetted and did point turns like Victor Sylvester never saw. I laughed until my face ached and my eyes went pink. If it was to be the last event, it was a joyous way to end it. Nella seemed to feel the same. Her eyes glistened in varicolour as the tinted spotlights shone on a saltwash of happiness.

After a few rounds in practice we danced as one: and as one we danced every bar they played until they came to "Auld Lang Syne".

The floor emptied, leaving us hand in hand.

"I'm so glad we have tonight. After this. And a whole other week—"

Was this the time? But no. What the hell. I would do the decent thing tomorrow.

"—I've never felt so close to anyone in all my life."

I said nothing. You could talk yourself into something you would regret.

Outside we hailed a taxi. It took us through the May-blue evening. At Passoud's I paid the guy: gave him a quid on top:

"Come back for us. Midnight. Fare all the way back to Pollokshields."

"Right. I'll give you a toot."

"Come and meet Jen."

I let us into the hall. Ranji came to meet us. She smiled shyly at Nella:

"Aye amm so pleased to meet you. You have come to take awaye our Neille. He is needing a woman to have good care of himme—"

Careless talk could cost a man his freedom. I censored that line of conversation:

"Where is Rahmin?"

"He wille be home soon. He is atte the shopp. He wille be glad nott to have missed you."

I nodded: happy I could bid him a formal farewell. There had just happened to be a kiosk at the ballroom. I pulled a packet of Nestlé's croquettes from my pockets: handed them to Ranji:

"See Shulie gets them tomorrow."

I ushered Nella along to meet Jen. It was a success on the instant. You could see. The rapport rang like a crystal bowl:

"So you're Neil's lass. I'm so happy to meet you. He's needing to get settled down."

See propaganda. The women in this house could have won a war without using a bullet. I said loudly to cover up the innuendo:

"Jen. You've done us proud."

She had too: her best crochet work as a table mat: her wedding china: plates of fine sandwiches and sweet biscuits.

I sat down. My hamstrings ached a little from the recent eurhythmics. I was pleasantly tired: thirsty: hungry. I let the pair of them serve me hand and foot. Then I sat back and watched the night come down behind these two women who meant so much to me. It was just as well I didn't feel like talking. The pair of them went at it like a clippies' convention.

It came time to get my trunk packed: time to take the kid home: time to tell her that this particular midnight had a spell all of its own. It must be our last. I was still wondering how, when an answer came: unexpected.

It took the noise a few seconds to convey its message into my dream state: encoded in the staccato rhythm of running feet. There was nothing of ordinary hurry: to catch a bus: be home by midnight. There was only one thing that drove feet into the pavement like that: piston-pounding in an effort to reach some kind of safety: any kind of sanctuary. That was fear.

And there was only one reason for the explosive effort to stop: to change to the slithering, dodging, dance-steps of a despairing defence: only one cause for the ragged, mortal cry.

I levered myself out of my chair, my arms pumping. I jabbed a finger at Jen:

"Hang out of the window. Scream bloody murder!"

For bloody murder it might be.

At Nella:

"999. Get the force out."

I didn't even bother to look out of the window. I knew Rahmin's larrikins were playing a return fixture: to win the cup outright.

I raced through the house: yelling:

"Ranji. Ranji. Blow your whistle out of the window. Blow the bloody pea out of it."

Rahmin made her wear one round her neck if she was out at night. It hung from a hook in the hall.

I was downstairs: out in the road: steaming straight for the gaggle around the straw man, limp and limbcast, on the ground, when I realized where I was going. And just what in Christ's name would I do when I got there?

It was years since I had been in a fracas worth the name. I was seven pounds into a paunch. My work was all sit and stand with no more effort than would blink an eye or cut a suture. The most exercise I got was pulling the sheet over my head when I hit the flock biscuit.

The women were doing their stuff: making a huge noise: raw with terror. In my day a few seconds of that sort of hoo-ha would have made even the Billy Boys beat it. I added some more. I shouted as I ran:

"Yoyoyoyoyoyoy!"

Anything to distract them: stop them: make them run.

But this bunch of bangers went right on kicking out his brains: scoring spot goals with

408

his spleen. They finished their Pakistani football practice: then turned to me. It didn't matter who I was: just so long as they got to maim someone else.

"Jesus!" I said to myself: but it was a token prayer. There wasn't a chariot of the Lord for miles around. What I had started I would have to finish on my own.

There were six of them: one girl: the deadliest of them all. They had been playing three a side with Rahmin. They kept this formation. I made for the female: nearest on the right: committed her with my eyes.

At three yards I changed charge: went slightly outside her: going away. She could read it only as feart: at the last moment. She shifted her weight. Her hands started to claw where my face was going to be: except I was back on course by then, with her wrong-footed.

I had to keep going. I couldn't stay to tangle. That way Neillie would get to be the Frido ball.

I ran the girl down. I slid the heel of my thin dance shoe down the front of her shin. She must have lost a foot of skin. The ego in her Zombie would not be denied. She howled as I went over her.

Number two simply went down in the crush. I couldn't get to a vital spot: damage him without stopping. That was bad. He would be on his feet in a second.

Boy three put his hands up in instinct: to fend off his falling friend. The pinkie of his left hand stuck out. I caught it and kept going: until all of my two hundred odd pounds bore on his metacarpo-phalangeal joint: the one where the finger meets the palm. It dislocated with a snap I could feel all the way to my shoulder. His indifference dissolved into a present agony. He said "Hoo-hoo, Hoo-hoo" like an owl that had been sat on a hot-plate.

That was two down. There were four to go.

I was puffing like the pug engine on the Llanberis railway: and not another idea in my head: except to draw them off. I kept going across the street to the close of the disused building that had been their nest.

They left Rahmin: came after me. I had bellows to mend and the entrance was three steps up. But I made it in a oner.

Fear breeds athletes second to none. Me and my shadow merged into the black opening.

I clamped my teeth: forced myself to big,

silent breaths. My heart tripped down two gears in air-starved protest, but silence was an ally.

I sidled back, deep into the shadow. The close entrance before me was lit by the last gasp of the day and the street lamps. I peered out. Ranji and Jen had stopped their racket. I saw them come out of the entrance with Nella: run to Rahmin.

There was neither sight nor sound of a patrol car, but these lads were quick on the job: four and a half minutes maximum to a call that near the city centre.

I had four minutes to go.

Figures, sharp against the street lights, threatened the entrance.

"We going in after him?"

"Too true. But he's a great big bastard."

Nobody loved me.

"You pair. Round the back. Give a whistle. We'll go in both ends. Hurry. The polis will be here."

I worked back to the inshot where the stair went up. My back would be safe there.

The whistle sounded, and was that the faintest wail from a siren?

I put my left shoulder against the corner of

the wall: hung my right fist back like Discobolus winding up.

They came with a soft shoe rush. The pair behind me groped and kicked into the shadows. The pair in front came side by side: arms linked: catchall.

I got the character nearest to me on the button. I brought my fist round flat: a one hundred and eighty degree arc. I smashed his coeliac plexus against his vertebrae: paralysed his autonomic outflow. He said "Whoop": but it would be his last breath for a while.

The three others came on me: ravening. I expected a steel hornet-sting in the belly: but none came.

I got into my corner: secure of my back. I took some clouts about the arms and shoulders: some kicks about the legs and groin. But the absolute darkness was on my side. They missed any vital bit.

Then I heard the wahoo of the police car: saw the headlights sweep across the blackness.

Until then I had been thinking defensive and scared as all hell: but here were the mounties. I would indulge me in a little grudge work now.

" 'S the polis. Come on. We'll get this big

bastard again. I'll mind his face for later."

I lunged after their scattering footfalls: grabbed into the darkness. I got one by the neck: the other by a handful of shirt. Then I wrestled the pair of them out of the close: main force and running. I fell them down the steps with me on top. I reared up and skelped their skulls off the pavement with the back of my hand.

"Jesus, doc. Leave something for us to do." It was the same patrolman as last time.

"There's another one in there."

I was panting like an asthmatic walrus.

"Right. I'll sort that out. You had better see to your friend. He's got a bottle in him."

"A bottle?"

"Tizer," he said patiently.

I went to the source of this conundrum and pushed through the crowd. It had gathered by then. Jen was there: holding Ranji: comforting her. Some of the children were standing, heads back, howling like locked-out puppies. Nella was doing her best with them.

Rahmin was barely conscious. They had given him a real canvassing with their sporty shoes. If they had been leather shod he would have been dead already from the foot flogging.

413

As it was, he was working on that problem in another way: the neck of a bottle stood proud of his belly: the cork in place: the name clear on the label. Tizer the Appetizer: and the taste that night was for blood:

"Can you bring a light to bear?"

The other patrolman moved the car: put the lights to beam on the damage.

I undid the cotton shirt; touched with feather fingers; tilted it gently this way and that, to give me measure of the weapon.

The bottle had been shattered: a time-honoured dodge. You knocked the bottom off and cut doughnut rings from the other guy's face. But this bottle had sheared off longways, leaving a glass sword point on a hilt of neck. This had been plunged home twice: then a third time to leave it *in situ malevolentis*. He should have been as shocked as hell: but his little wog heart was all warrior.

An ambulance arrived: the lads piled out with the stretcher. I pointed to the soft-drink stiletto:

"Easy with him. We don't want that digging into things."

It was better left in place until he was opened up.

I turned to Jen and Nella:

"I'll go with him. You get the kids in bed. Arrange some sort of child-minder. Bring Ranji to the hospital."

Jen asked:

"Where will he be taken?"

For a second I stared at her. My work-shy trip on the stratocirrus had washed such pragmatics out of my mind:

"We'll take him to the Northern. Of course—"

But there was nothing on course anywhere in my mind. The habit of decisions, made fast and without doubt over the years, seemed to have slipped out of gear. Then time-tables and work-schedules flooded back: gave me bearings.

"—Dammit. My own unit is on call until midnight. We should just make that."

"Then you can look after him, Neil. That's marvellous."

"No. Not me. Not tonight. I'll have been written out of the schedule. I've been off this week."

Roddie would be about: would have to. He couldn't pull rank on the other consultants. And even he wouldn't get sloshed on a receiving night: not at the busy end of it.

But Jen would have it:

"Yes. But you'll be there with him. If anything goes wrong."

She meant well: but it made me frown. My week of release had done me no good at all. I felt I never wanted to try again.

But Ranji agreed. She said only:

"Oh, Neille—"

It was clear that her Tote accumulator had a run up on me.

Nella gave me a look that showed she fancied my silks as well.

But see racing certs?

This feeling of disassociation: of wanting only to spectate, persisted as I followed the trolley in through the swing doors. I saw the casualty department: this stockyard of human travail, with the shock of fresh sight.

I felt my forces fail.

They could stop the polar spin any time: park the globe in some cosmic layby. I wasn't ready for these vortical coercions again: not yet.

The gung-ho, get up and get at it humbug I had professed to the world and myself for years was torn to shreds of sheer funk.

My dance among the Maypole ribbons had unmanned me: taken me to bits and found a main-spring wanting. I had had enough of man's inhumanity: to himself: to the world around him: to me.

Even Herbie's face—disbelieving at my appearance: at my bruises—then full of welcome for me back in my rightful place—could not restore me.

"Neil. Thought you were ill. What are you doing here? And what's this you've brought?"

"Something unusual. Is there a cubicle empty?"

"Yes. Over here."

We wheeled Rahmin in. I opened the blanket heaped loosely over him.

Herbie called on the deity used by us pallid creatures: "Dear God—"

Neither understanding nor answer was granted to anyone in that cubby-hole. Then to staff nurse:

"—saline drip. Cross matching. Next in theatre—"

He looked at me:

"His condition seems fair. All things considered—"

I nodded. What was inside that lacerated

belly was a lucky-bag of spoliation: but whatever had been sliced open hadn't let his soul out: not yet.

The midnight bell rang: the shift changed then.

"—You just made it in time to be among friends."

I was to regret the fast time made by our driver. A four-minute delay would have saved me a lot of grief: and just possibly my little friend's life.

"Who's on tonight?"

"Roddie. Dougie Miller. Me."

"Roddie's all right then?"

"He has not been pleased by your absence. But he has turned up on time for his clinics and theatres. And apparently dry. He's been around since lunch."

A feeling of relief washed over me. For once I would be glad to shelter behind him.

Rahmin could be roused: but with difficulty. He was concentrating on living at the vegetable level: conserving all of his powers. I bent to his ear:

"Don't try to speak. Or open your eyes. This is Neil. You're all right now. In hospital. Soon have you fixed—"

He furrowed his forehead a fraction: he had heard. I squeezed his shoulder.

I said to Herbie:

"—I'm going upstairs. Only to watch. His wife and friends will be in soon. They're all friends of mine. I'd like to be able to keep them posted."

He nodded:

"Right, Neil. I'll get him upstairs. Soon as his drip is going. Will you tell Fay to slot him into the list?"

I went upstairs to the changing room.

It looked like a left-over day at the laundry. There were cotton trousers and tunics: bloodied gowns: towels sopping from the shower: caps: masks. They hung from doors: spilled from lockers: draped over seats. The debris left from dealing with the day's disputes with fate lay in a litter that would have flummoxed Mary Poppins.

I was back all right: but still glad I was stripping for the reserves.

I went over to the observation window: waved at Fay.

"Thought you were off?"

"I am. Was. Better now. Listen. There's an acute case to come next. Abdominal wound. Weapon in place. Tell Roddie will you?"

"He's not here just now. Dr. Miller is doing this case. An acute appendix. He's done the last two."

I considered that remark. Like very cold ice-cream, I wasn't sure of the flavour.

"Any idea where he is?"

"Went for tea, I think. We've been at it steady."

"Yes. That'll be it."

I turned away: shrugged at myself. Of course. Roddie would have vetted those cases. Decided they were OK for a junior. Left Dougie to it. I shook my head at my suspicions. No-one would be nut enough to get on to the noggins on a major session. I went into the loo suite: looked at my face in the mirror. It was not too bad.

I had indigo smudges under each eye: a shade more purple than a sleepless night. My lips weren't fat: more like I'd been necking with the nozzle of a vacuum cleaner. And the scrape along my jaw was no worse than I might have done with a razor.

I filled a basin with cold water: held my breath: dipped my face and scalp until I needed air. I did that several times. Then I wound a towel round my head: patted myself dry.

My shoulders and upper arms ached. My shins and thighs felt stiff. I consoled myself: compared to the case coming up on the theatre cart I was a king.

I had turned to leave: had smacked the swing door open, when I heard a sound from one of the loos.

I had paid no attention to them: had not realized that one was occupied.

There was a row of three end on to the far wall. This made a narrow corridor giving access to all three doors. The far away loo was in the corner: isolated: shadowed.

The sound had come from this one: a furtive, stealthy clink. But it rang as loud as the bell of St. Clements: and sang a song to my suspicious mind. This was no rhyme of oranges and lemons: it was of best French grapes.

I let the door bang to as if I had left. I threw my towel in front of me on the floor: stepped silent on its carpet into the cubicle next door: put my foot on the john: levered myself up.

Maybe I was going to give some innocent, constipated sufferer a dose of instant relief from sheer fright.

But no. My eyes met Roddie's, turned up-

421

wards to the ceiling as he slugged at a flat half-bottle.

Outrage and guilt had a workout on his face: caught with every pair of pants down. The liquor slopped from the bottle: ran over his face: splashed on to his greens.

"What—! How dare you. This is monstrous. I'll—"

I dropped out of sight: walked into the changing room. I pulled a fresh theatre strip from the cupboard: started to change. Dougie Miller came in: stripped off his sterile outers: massaged glove powder into his eyes and face.

"'Lo, Neil. What a funny time to come back. What's this thing you've got lined up for us?"

Donnie Marshall came hard on his white heels:

"Neil. What have you done to your face—"

Roddie spoiled his lines. He appeared from the lav: backstage left. Outrage had won the field. He went for me with a battle cry of squeaky rage:

"I've had enough of you. You think you're so shit hot. Can't teach you anything. So bloody high and mighty. Well for the rest of your time here you'll remember I'm the consultant. I'm the one who says what goes.

By Christ! And you'll do what I tell you."

Roddie suffered from his middle-class upbringing. His profanity had always a prudish quality: brought out of the box for occasional show. Despite this his sheer venom was impressive.

The other pair were cloven to an instant silence: embarrassed. The bottle was nestled safe out of sight: under his blouse: held in place by a casual hand: known only to him and me.

It was a good ploy: his word against mine: carry it off with a high hand. I wouldn't dare lay a finger on him.

Nor did I.

I simply stared at him: a sudden, savage move. Threw my hands up: a green-sheeted afrit. Yelled "Haaah": a Samurai about to strike.

It was enough. His hands flew to protect his pot belly: his slack face. The bottle dropped to the terrazzo floor: smashed to slivereens sparkling in the spirit wash. His professional sin spread out in redolent waves.

"If you put one foot inside that theatre until this next case is over, I'll see you get invited to a command performance of the G.M.C.—"

I jerked my thumb at the two involuntary witnesses:

"—and they'll be there to sell programmes of all that went on."

I had never at any time felt anger towards Roddie: not a true contempt: more a dispassionate interest so that I would never get to be like him.

But that night I forged an anger for him: cold: black: hard as iron. Not for his weakness: but for the spot he had put me in: the glare of a theatre arc with not a shadow in which I could hide.

I wasn't ready to cope yet. I needed more time in the pressure chamber: to work up the poundage needed.

But I was the only raffle that Rahmin had a ticket for.

I shook my head at Roddie in disgust: but whether at him or me I wasn't sure.

I turned my back on him: pushed the other pair in front of me: went in to scrub.

I swabbed the belly: towelled it: wrapped the incongruous, irruptive artefact in sterile gauze:

"Hold that. Don't wave it about."

"Lightfingers Miller. That's me."

I went through a paramedian incision: looking for the trouble this frangible barb had caused. It had caused plenty.

There was shit and blood slopping about like a slaughterman's holiday.

I was worried about the top wound. It seemed to go in and up: a shade left of centre. The stomach, the liver, the spleen are all at risk: even up through the diaphragm into the heart.

We cleared out the sludge with a sucker. I defined the structures at hazard. In a few minutes I was feeling happier.

"His liver is undamaged, apart from that little nick." I pointed to it.

"His spleen?"

"Seems all right."

That was a surprise. Neither the stab nor the kicking contest had torn it.

That was also good. Suturing spleen is like embroidering a sponge cake. If there's a lot of other haemorrhage you don't have time. You have to ditch it into the pail.

I leaned down: squinted up at the diaphragm. There was a minor laceration to the front of the dome: two cents' worth: no bleeding: a little fresh ooze, but not worth grieving over.

I left that area: went to poke around: peer at the other two wounds.

"I think all we have is a lot of slits in the gut. Faecal spillage. Moderate bleeding. But no major vessels."

We swabbed and sponged like Jack Tars at the bilges of a lineship. I stitched the bowel shut where it gaped. Dougie got in among the mesenteric bleeders with artery clamps: and by the grave of whatever soapstone gods Rahmin's ancestors had worshipped, his big vessel had got off without major damage.

In time I isolated the point of this glass skewer. The blade was about five inches long: the penetrating edge shaped like a chisel. This had splintered to a chamfered edge. It was stuck into the disc of cartilage that lay between the fourth and fifth lumbar vertebrae: slightly to one side: missing every important structure by a strand of spider-silk.

I pulled it clear: clunked it into a kidney dish that Fay held out for me. I looked at its squat, truncated shape. Something troubled me: a message from the deep cavern of memory and instinct that had served me so well in the past. But it was unclear: indistinct.

I asked for fresh gown and gloves, to cut down soiling. I looked at Donnie Marshall.

"How are things at the talking end?"

He didn't answer at once: pursed his lips against his mask:

"Puzzling."

"Any ideas?"

"His pressure is low."

He said it tentatively. I tried to encourage a positive approach:

"Seems reasonable. His abdomen was like the left-overs of a midnight feast in the Dracula dorm."

"I know. But it's still going down. So's his pulse pressure. The drip ought to be making a difference by this time."

It was going in at a healthy rate: the red drops running in at a fast trot:

"Turn it up for a minute."

He increased the rate until it formed a thin, scarlet jet. After a bit he took the pressure reading again.

He shook his head. He looked unhappy:

"Something's up."

"I knew it. I just bloody knew it."

My mind had been sending messages from

that far oracle: but it was still in riddle-me-ree: giving no solution.

What was wrong! Where?

I went to work again: fast. I hunted around the abdomen: no fresh bleeding: verified the major vessels, the vulnerable organs a second time: no missed trauma. I defined the pathways of the three stab wounds from below up. The first two had all damage mended: all sutures holding: all ties firm.

The third track was more difficult to be sure of. The area is more confined. But there was no major haemorrhage: the stomach, spleen and liver all as I had found at the first foray.

"Better get a move on, Neil."

And Donnie wasn't the guy to get his camisole about his knees: not without good reason.

The only thing I hadn't checked again was the piddling wound I had seen in the diaphragm. If the blade of that glass dagger had been longer it might have gone on: up through the dome: into the heart. But I had considered that.

The blade was too short. Besides, such a wound would have caused bleeding like the fountain in Kelvingrove Park.

There was only an ooze: the merest token of blood: a cypher of the small unimportant wound it was.

Sometimes in surgery your fingers will tell you things your eyes can't see. I stood on my toes: slid my hand underneath the ribs: ran my forefinger gently along the line of the lesion. For all of my care I felt the glove part: then my own flesh as I found the fine cutting edge of the rest of the blade.

I spoke to Donnie. Not from any perception I had then: but from this knowledge I had had within me it seemed forever. My finger only confirmed the disaster:

"He's got a tamponade. That's what's wrong. He's got a bit of glass in his heart."

The most important thing you can ever learn as any kind of a doc is that there is no rule that can't be broken: no system without a quirk: no discipline but can go haywire under your very hands.

The yesses, the definites, become buts and imponderables even as you work.

God alone knows what kind of resultant had built up within Rahmin's chest. I can only take the autopsy findings: stir in a quart of guesswork: give you some kind of an answer.

The heart lives its frenetic life in a fibrous bag: the pericardium. It is tough: durable: won't burst under pressure. At its bottom end it is moored to the upper surface of the diaphragm by a fibrous ligament.

The spike of glass had gone through at this very point, three inches into the corpus cordis: then broken off, its base wedged among the fibres of the muscular dome.

By every rule he should have been dead.

He should have died on the instant: died of cardiogenic shock. He should have died within minutes of his wounding: died of haemorrhage, his blood spilling into his lung cavities, his abdomen, his pericardium.

But he didn't.

The heart has one natural function: to contract: to squeeze. Even as it impaled itself with determined regularity at every pulse beat it clasped the splinter fast, reducing the loss to an ooze. The precise point of entry stopped blood from entering the pleural spaces: the diaphragm opening was blocked by the base of the very instrument of destruction: the pericardial loss was no more than a dribble.

It was the last complication that had caused Donnie's worries and led me to such a fearsome answer. Usually fatal in moments, the slow development of pressure outside the heart had allowed a cockeyed balance of forces to develop: one that defied every law: one that had somehow maintained an equilibrium that allowed Rahmin his life.

Until then. Until I disturbed it.

Even as I spoke to Donnie, the glass loosened at my touch. The pressure of pent-up blood shot out the vitreous bung. And the first great gout of his death poured over my hand.

His pulse leapt: last gesture of defiance from a brave heart: went over the ton.

Half a cup of blood is pumped out of a ventricle at every beat. The glass point had gone in right at the septum. The wedge-shaped blade had gashed open both of these main chambers. So, he was losing a whole cupful at a stroke: thirty pints a minute.

Of course there aren't thirty pints: not in anybody: not in Man Mountain Dean nor the Gentle Giant. There are only ten pints at best. It goes round and round, you see.

And my pint-sized friend had already lost a couple of those.

We had replaced some with the drip: and it was still going in. But if I tell you it takes a minute to open the chest and get to this wriggling, squeezing thing: then you have to get your hands on it and stitch it closed—you can see the arithmetic for yourself.

I didn't even try. I let him die in this blood-bath of his own pumping.

"Jesus Christ!" whispered Dougie: shocked.

A silence came down. The nurses huddled close. An earnest of our own deaths reeked and wraithed at us from the whorling, congealing flux.

Donnie Marshall asked:

"What happened?"

I held out my hand. The glass shard lay there in malignant impartiality: it could have killed anyone.

"Ah. Well then—"

Donnie sounded relieved:

"—I mean you can't get off with that sort of thing, can you? Fart against thunder."

I could feel the cold, the fright evaporate at this evidence before their eyes: its inescapable verdict.

That particular game had had the fix in: no hope of even a draw: the goalie had been nobbled the night before the game. Even Neillie Aitken couldn't have saved the points.

Despite this I had to fight to control a great,

432

ague-like shivering that threatened me.

Donnie unhooked his machine: said to Fay:
"Better phone for the body box, Sister. I'll go and write my bit of the report. You'll do yours later, Neil?"

The surgeon and anaesthetist who officiate at the death have to declare it was all their own work.

Dougie sucked out this red, dead mess: once a few minutes before, such a vital fluid. I stitched the big incision into some sort of post-mortem propriety.

In the changing room Donnie was talking to Roddie: telling the tale of the incident. I went over to the table where he had just finished writing: took his place to write up my part of the report.

I looked at Roddie to give him his chance: his say: his revenge.

He said not one word. In his eyes I read two things only: compassion for me: and a pleading for some kind of understanding.

Despite everything we were brothers in a difficult job.

Roddie drank to help him get on with it: get him through his days. Where would I go for help? I had nothing: not even that solace: my goatskin cracked and empty.

I wrote the report: dressed: left the changing room. I went to the ward. Outside, sitting on the wooden bench, I met the three women: waiting.

"I'm sorry, Ranji. We did all we could."

It was like the script of a bad "B" film. I hid behind the anonymous we, like the bum I was.

"I'll send for my things, kid—"

Then to Jen:

"You'll see they both get home. I'll get the ward sister to give you a sedative for Ranji."

I dropped my eyes at her look. But I had no more to offer.

I went back to my mother.

All I wanted to do was live out my last few days in the self-misery I had generated: in the knowledge of this lack within myself: its crippling effect. More than ever I saw the following Monday's flight as a way to a new start.

The fiscal's report was a formality. At the case discussion it was decided that it would be worthwhile writing it up in the College journal: a professional memorial.

I was clearing my locker when Charles appeared. He sat down beside me:

"You're off then?"

"Yes."

"Resigned yet?"

I patted my pocket:

"It's ready."

"Yes. I wonder—"

He looked at me: grave.

I wondered if Roddie had, after all, gone complaining. But no. This was between us.

"—I'm not sure what to do. It would be kinder to let you go in a way. Yet, I think you ought to know. I think you will want to know."

I sat beside him: evidence of my coming dereliction scattered about me: old books, a crumpled shirt, hockey stick from a game with the nurses. Not much to show for three years of sweat.

"Yes. I want to know. Everything about myself is important just now. There are some answers I don't have. Maybe this will give me one."

"Yes. I can understand that. Well, here it is. You've been washed out of the vascular job—"

For a moment I didn't connect.

"—I tried to push it. No joy. If you don't resign, if you stay here, you can only have the number two slot. They want someone with more academic distinction to be top man. The man appointed will be young. Your own age. Unlikely that you would ever get it after that. Unless dead man's shoes—"

My look was as grave as the one he was giving me.

"—I said I thought it was rubbish. Mentioned your offer from the States. Although I only said you were considering it. Brilliant offer. But you know there's a bit of jealousy on that score—"

Some guys claimed that anyone worth his groats had gone abroad long since: the men left were the second raters. Sometimes it caused the eyes to turn green: the skin to go scaly.

"—I don't know what that makes you feel."

"I'm not sure either. I don't think it makes any difference. But you were right to tell me. I'll turn it over in my mind."

We shook hands formally.

I pondered the news. But all it made me do was pack my things the faster.

What the hell! What did I care?

But when I left the hospital for the last

436

time, for all my fine, assured future, I knew what I thought.

In some way, still not clear to me, it confirmed that I had failed: but not in any competitive sense. The job wasn't that important.

I had failed myself.

When I arrived at Prestwick for my escape flight, the big building was echoing from early morning disuse. In the corner at the International Departures door, a huddle of relatives said goodbye: the tears and hugs told of harsh lessons remembered through the generations, from the days of the Highland clearances.

I was spared all of that, though. I had forbidden Maisie to come.

"What would you do at Prestwick at that time in the morning, anyhow?"

She had agreed with a matter-of-fact alacrity that had soured me. She might have protested: just once: just for the look of the thing. But her guard was up to the very end:

"As you say. What would I do?"

I was hoist on my own logic.

"I'll send for you soon. For a visit. Then we'll see if you want to stay."

"Aye. That'll be fine."

Fine! There was enthusiasm for you: pleasure at a prospect.

I settled in my seat, glad to be at a window. I saw that I was to be carried away on thrust developed by Messrs. Pratt and Whitney. That seemed apt. To have left on Rolls-Royce engines would have seemed some kind of solecism: treachery even. This way I could ride to freedom without guilt.

The intercom clicked: then crackled as background to a you-all drawl:

"This is your cap'n speaking—"

He gave us the bit about the seat-belts and the life jackets. I admired the confident, Southern underplay of command. Perhaps I might allow myself a touch of the Confederate panache in a year or so.

The last of the cabin staff ran up the big ramp steps. The engines whined up to taxi speed. The cabin door was slewed shut: or at least it should have. But the chief steward could not get it fully home. There was a bit of heaving and pushing: then some confabulation between him and his girls. One lifted the hand-set of the internal phone and spoke.

The flight-deck door opened and the engineer joined them: he too spoke on the telephone.

Then:

"Ladies an gennlemen. We have a minor problem with the door lock—"

But they would have it fixed in no time flat:

"—in the meantime if you will kinely relax, Ah will shut down powah for a time. Ah beg youah kinely indulgence."

I had a preliminary look through the magazines I had bought: a stare about at my fellow passengers: then a look at the airline people, out of kilter and routine with this problem. The ramp was returned to the fuselage. A mechanic in overalls and carrying a blue, cantilevered toolbox ran up the steps. From where I sat I could see him spread out screwdrivers and spanners and start to work on the catch.

I glanced at the terminal buildings: then at the observation deck. A few people were standing by the rail, waiting to prolong their goodbyes in final waves and fluttered hankies.

I remember closing my eyes. Perhaps they would go away: two women. I even groaned aloud in a sort of supplication.

But neither gesture helped. When I looked

again they were still there. They stood a few feet apart, for they had never met: could not guess at a common interest in the plane about to leave. But I knew them both: the big-hipped woman with the burnished top-knot: the girl, small and with a cap of white hair cut in a pudding bowl fringe.

And their presence was the measure of this fearsome failure I suffered.

It seemed that the thin, cold atmosphere of my native Caledonia bred love of a hardy kind: spare: growing in unlikely soil: prickly as thistles if you went to pluck it.

But these women out there had their arms wide open to clasp it still: to savour the last of its rare flower, even as it hurt them. They had the guts I lacked.

That was what I needed. The kind that grew in lusher pastures would never do. I must match their courage.

I picked up my flight bag: made excuses and commotion: "I need to get off."

I could see there was going to be an official rigmarole. I cut it short:

"You see, I take fits. In the excitement of leaving this morning I forgot to take my medication. I now realize I've left the bottle

440

at home. If I don't get my tablets soon, I'll have a seizure."

The chief steward's eyes glazed in shock. Clonic spasms at 30,000 feet over the Atlantic he did not relish. His opposition was transformed into a fulsome eagerness to get me the hell off his plane as fast as I liked.

One of his girls was more sympathetic:

"Will you be all right? What will you do?"

I paused with a foot on the ramp. I chucked her under the chin:

"Honey. Don't you fret. All I need I can get right here at the airport."

And I walked down the steps to take my dose of this drug I could not do without: the bitter-sweet medicine of love.

THE END

This book is published under the
auspices of the
ULVERSCROFT FOUNDATION,
a registered charity whose primary object is
to assist those who experience difficulty in
reading print of normal size.

In response to approaches from the medical
world, the Foundation is also helping to pur-
chase this latest, most sophisticated medical
equipment desperately needed by major eye
hospitals for the diagnosis and treatment of
eye diseases.

If you would like to know more about the
ULVERSCROFT FOUNDATION,
and how you can help to further its work,
please write for details to:

THE ULVERSCROFT FOUNDATION,
The Green, Bradgate Road,
Anstey,
Leicestershire,
England